The Planetary Trilogy

Book 2:

Mars Run

MARS
RUN

Stanley Salmons

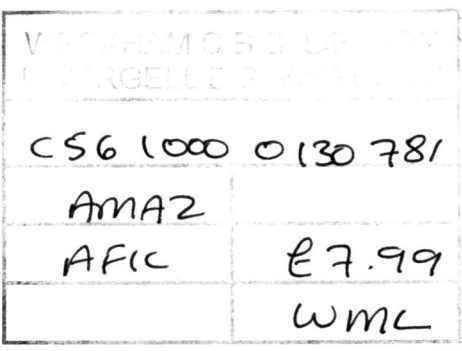

The right of Stanley Salmons to be identified as author of this work has been asserted by him in accordance with the Copyright, Designs and Patents Act 1988

ISBN: 1985567164

ISBN-13: 978-1985567160

Cover attributions: NASA Space Science Data Coordinated Archive (from Mars Digital Image Model Vol 14) and European Southern Observatory (ESO)

This novel is a work of fiction. Any resemblance between the characters and actual persons, living or dead, is entirely coincidental

Stanley Salmons was born in East London. He is internationally known for his work in the fields of biomedical engineering and muscle physiology, published in over two hundred scientific articles and twelve scientfic books. Although still contributing to the real world of research, he maintains a parallel existence as a fiction writer, in which he can draw from his broad scientific experience. He has published over forty short stories in various magazines and anthologies. This is his ninth novel.

For Paula, Graham, Daniel, and Debby
And for Lilian, who kindled my early interest in science

PROLOGUE

Nine modified C-class spacefreighters, armed and armoured, approach Mars. They make their orbital insertions independently so as not to attract interest. Shortly after the onset of Martian night a communication laser beams out from one of the ships and flickers to each of the others, passing a signal that nothing else can intercept. Moments later they rise into a higher orbit and close formation.

On the flight deck of the lead ship, Deputy Assistant Commissioner of Customs Henry Leighton sits in one of the two slightly elevated seats behind the pilot and copilot, overseeing their every move. He knows his proximity to the pilots makes them nervous and even resentful, but that means nothing to him. He's worked hard to set up this operation and he's going to direct it in person, not from behind a desk.

And what persistence it had taken! He'd used every argument in the book: the cost to society of illicit drugs; the need to set an example; the importance of showing that no one was beyond their reach...

Commissioner Nicholson had held up his hands as if someone had pointed a gun at him. 'It's out of the question, Leighton! The service couldn't possibly afford something on that scale!'

Daily meetings, more arguments.

'Does it have to be nine ships, Leighton? Couldn't we do it with one or two?'

'Commissioner, we could well encounter a hostile navy. Are you really prepared to risk the lives of your staff by under-resourcing the project?'

'No, of course not, but...'

'Politically, Commissioner, that could be a very costly mistake...'

Eventually the man had caved in. And now, at last, the operation is under way.

The pilot turns his head. 'We're at target altitude, sir. Cutting main engines.'

Leighton nods. 'Set course and bring closing speed down to fifty kilometres an hour. Then cut auxiliaries as well; I want silent running. Tell the others – by laser, of course.'

There's the trace of a sigh, a muttered 'Of course', and the Captain relays the message.

Leighton leans forward, peering into a sky thickly carpeted with stars. Somewhere out there is the orbiting drug factory. It moved after its position was first reported – but that was only to be expected. It was hard enough to pick up in its new location but something like that is too large to cloak and large enough to eclipse the star fields behind it. That's how the sky survey telescopes at Hawaii found the satellite, and that's how the torpedoes waiting in the launch tubes on Leighton's C-class will find it – if he chooses to use them. And he does choose to use them, although at this stage no one else is aware of that.

'How close are we now?' Leighton asks.

The Captain replies. 'About ninety kilometres, sir, assuming it's still at those coordinates.'

'It will be. Any sign of hostile ships?'

'We're not picking up anything on infra-red. If there are ships around they're not using their engines. Do you want a radar scan?'

'God, no, that'll tell them we're coming!'

Ten minutes pass, twenty, thirty... The pilot says, 'Sixty-five kilometres.'

'All right. Activate all weapon systems. We're going to board if they'll let us but if they make things difficult we'll use the torpedoes. I don't want a single casualty on our side. And tell the others to start the cameras rolling.'

That's crucial; he wants the whole incident recorded from every possible angle.

The Captain relays the message while the co-pilot flicks several switches on the control panel. Both faces are now weakly illuminated in red light from the warning lamps.

Ten more minutes go by. There's a heavy silence on the flight deck. The pilot moistens his lips. If the target does have an escort they are now well within accurate range even for non-guided weapons. He glances at the console.

'Fifty kilometres. I have a visual.'

Leighton cranes forward to look at one of the screens. There's an irregular blank in the star field. Just one. No hostile ships anywhere in view. A relief, but not a complete surprise.

'Zoom in.'

The picture enlarges and the outline of the satellite emerges. About thirty metres long: four modules, each one probably cylindrical. If it's the standard layout for an orbital factory there'll be a sleeping module, a living module, a lab module, and a module for storing the product; an airtight emergency door at each node will allow a module to be sealed off in the event of an accident. Syndicates aren't usually over-concerned about the lives of their rank and file employees, but synthetic chemists are harder to come by and this is a safer arrangement than cheaper monolithic structures. An array of antennae and solar panels extends to either side. There is no shine or reflection of any sort. Leighton's lips tighten. No wonder it was so hard to pick up; it's stealth coated.

'Target it.'

Fine white cross-wires appear, centred on the body of the satellite.

'Let's see if we can elicit a response. Use optical.'

The Captain flicks a switch and a pencil-thin green laser beam extends to the target. Leighton speaks into the mic on his lightweight headset.

'Satellite in Mars high orbit. You are being intercepted by a Customs fleet. Prepare to be boarded for inspection. Do you copy?'

No response.

'They may not be receiving optical, sir. Do you want to try the multifrequency channel?'

Leighton feels a stab of impatience. 'Yes, yes, all right.'

The pilot flicks more switches and Leighton repeats the message. Still nothing.

'Forty-five kilometres, sir.'

Without warning the silence on the flight deck is shattered by a siren, and a display flashes 'INCOMING, FIFTEEN SECONDS TO IMPACT' in red. Leighton's pulse races. He's seen no sign of syndicate ships so where is the hostile fire coming from? His fate is now entirely in the hands of the ship's defensive systems. For someone who likes to be in control that is not a comfortable sensation.

He watches the display ticking down the seconds to impact.

14... 13...

He knows about these systems but he's never seen them in action and he suspects the two in front of him haven't either. The software will be tracking the shells, predicting their path and at the same time extrapolating backwards to locate the source.

Four large red circles appear on the screen and shrink quickly as the accuracy of estimation sharpens.

12... 11...

The circles are small enough now to pinpoint the source. There are no hostile ships. Just four shell-throwers, two at each end of the satellite.

10... 9... 8...

Leighton is breathing fast. The predictive targeting ought to be good enough by now...

Beams from five megalasers mounted above the flight deck lance out, criss-crossing in front of them to intercept the approaching projectiles, whose trajectories now become visible as four streams of aerial explosions patterning the sky. The defensive system is good; nothing is getting through. Leighton's lips tighten in grim satisfaction. With half a mind on the filming, he lets the dazzling firework display continue for a suitable interval before giving the command.

'Launch torpedoes.'

The Captain and co-pilot look sharply round at him. The Captain says, 'Sir? What about personnel on board?'

Leighton's voice is hard. 'I said launch torpedoes.'

'Aye, aye, sir.' He nods at the co-pilot, who releases a safety catch and pulls the switch down. 'Tube One armed.'

'Not one: all four—now!'

The man swallows. He repeats the action three more times, then presses the red firing button.

1

Dan Larssen stirred, then opened his eyes. A thin early morning light had entered the room, grey and diffuse, and he rose into it like a swimmer surfacing from a dive. His mind cleared the vestiges of sleep. For the moment he just lay there, warm and comfortable, thinking. A tingle of excitement crept through him as he anticipated the day ahead, a day that would probably be as different to the one before as it would be to the next. Variety and challenge: that's what he loved about being a test pilot. He'd almost be happy to do it for nothing.

He turned his head to look at Neraya. She was still sleeping, her hair a dark splash on the pillow.

The woman he loved, a job he loved – for someone with his past it all seemed too good to be true. He'd been battling against one thing or another his whole life. There'd been moments of happiness, for sure, but they were fleeting, quick to escape from his grasp.

A faint feeling of unease disturbed his reverie. Would it be any different this time?

*

Dan's office at the Space Fleet Test Establishment was

small, which was fine because he didn't need a lot of space. The window had a restricted outlook – a long shed blocked his line of sight to the runway and the landscape beyond – but he had a clear view of the apron. Even through the multiple glazing he could hear engines starting up or winding down and if he glanced out he'd know just how far they'd progressed through the day's schedule.

His office was just a few doors from the Common Room and he went along to it now. The pilots always checked in here first thing in the morning to look at the duty rotas, and would often drop by between flights, helping themselves to coffee or a light snack from one of the autochefs. There were armchairs, low tables, and plenty of e-readers for flight manuals and current copies and back runs of aerospace journals. Large panes of electrogenerating glass occupied most of one of the long walls. The view here was unobstructed and extended right out to the runway, which ran from left to right, east to west. At the eastern end were the hangars, just visible from the window. On the far western horizon was the city of Armstrong, the tallest buildings climbing through the vapour haze from the skimmer traffic.

Three of Dan's colleagues had already arrived. Two were standing by the window, chatting and sipping coffee. The third, Andy Cogswell, was studying the electronic message boards with the rotas and recent notices. Andy had been at the Establishment for more than ten years now and he was the one who'd shown Dan the ropes when he'd taken up his appointment. Andy had a gentle, good-humoured manner, and they'd hit it off right away. He caught sight of Dan, smiled, and came over.

'Barry was looking for you, Dan. If I were you I'd go straight up there.'

'Right. Thanks, Andy.'

Dan took the stairs two at a time and went along the corridor to an office labelled 'Barry Curtis, Director of Earth Flight Testing'. He knocked on the door, opened it, then hesitated in the doorway as he saw that Barry had someone with him, but Barry gestured to one of the two chairs in front of his desk.

'Come in, Dan, join us.'

Barry's office was easily the most interesting and unusual Dan had encountered. Every available surface – desk, shelves, window sills – was occupied by a model aircraft or model spacecraft, the smaller ones all to the same scale. These were craft that had been tested either at the Establishment or off-Earth by members of their staff. Two model spacefreighters, made to a smaller scale because of their size, were hung from the ceiling. One was a C-class, its profile similar to that of an oil tanker but in reverse, with the superstructure, including the flight deck, at the front. The other, suspended at several points, was a giant triple-hull E-class of the type Dan had flown to Saturn and back. Even at 1/2000th scale this beautiful model measured nearly a metre from nose to tail, more than three times the length of the C-class. In spite of this comprehensive collection Barry somehow managed to keep a small area of his desk clear for his touchscreen and a nested tower of empty disposable coffee cups that became progressively taller and less stable during the course of the day.

Dan sat down and exchanged smiles and nods with Tim Almond, who was in the other chair. Like Andy, he was one of the more experienced pilots. A British guy, he'd joined the Establishment after many years flying, first multi-role combat craft in the RAF, then airliners long-haul out of London. He'd lost much of his hair by now, as had Andy. It seemed to go with the job, at least in the more senior people.

'Dan,' Barry said. 'We're currently testing a Silverpoint. You know it?'

'Never flown one. I've flown a Steelpoint, its little brother. Why are we testing the Silverpoint? It's been in passenger service for years.'

'This is a new version, the Silverpoint 700. They've extended the fuselage to increase passenger carrying capacity and enlarged the loading bay. To compensate for that they had to lengthen the wings, update the avionics, and fit more powerful engines. General Aviation sent us a pre-production model. They're anxious to avoid the lengthy procedure for getting a full Certificate of Airworthiness. They say it's similar enough to the previous model to get common certification. Tim's been putting it through its paces and he has some concerns. Tim?'

'It's cleared the bar for every test up to now, Dan. The transition's smooth and supersonic performance is good. But there's something sloppy about the low-speed handling. Happens on turns, doesn't recover quickly enough.'

Dan nodded. Tim would know exactly what roll rate to expect of this craft. If he said it was sluggish then it was, and there had be a good reason for it. 'You going to send it back to them?'

He sighed. 'You know these guys. Redesign and retooling is going to cost them. They'll say it'll fly fine in normal service. I'm not happy with that.'

'Nor am I,' Barry put in. 'If it's not handling properly there's a design flaw somewhere, and you never know when or where it'll surface. Even a badly distributed load could be disastrous. I don't want to be responsible for one of those things coming down with everyone on board. Right now I'm not convinced it's airworthy.'

'And there's nothing obvious in the telemetry?' Dan asked.

Barry shook his head. 'No. We've looked at telemetry data from all the sensors on board, but this effect must be too subtle to show up. Tell him what you had in mind, Tim.'

'I think it's a question of loading. I need to put it through a few steep turns so I can figure things out.'

'You want to push the envelope?' Dan asked.

'Not a lot, it'd be inside design limits. I just want to increase the load factor enough to give me a handle on what's happening with the controls. But I need someone there to take video and generally keep an eye on things. I said to Barry I thought you could fly chase in the Ninety.'

The B-90P was a tactical bomber which had been modified for photoreconnaissance work. It carried a battery of cameras, ideal for a task like this, which was why they kept one on base.

Barry turned to him. 'That all right with you, Dan?'

Dan nodded. 'Fine with me.'

'Okay. I'll get the tech team together to monitor the telemetry. You can go up in an hour.'

2

Dan climbed into the cockpit of the B-90P and settled himself behind the controls. The Ninety was designed for a two-man crew, a pilot and a mission commander, but since he'd be flying it on his own there was plenty of room. He hadn't flown the bomber version but he imagined it was very similar to this photoreconnaissance variant. The main difference would be the instrument panel, which had been modified to accommodate four screens; these could display either selected camera views or videocomms. He started up the auxiliary power unit to run systems and began the preflight checks.

He was pleased to be chosen for this. Flying chase was a skilled job of the kind Joe Lau often did. Joe was only a few years older than him, but he had several years more experience as a test pilot. Perhaps he was doing something else at the moment.

The much larger Silverpoint was on the apron over to his right. It sat slightly tilted back, a slim metallic pencil supported on spindly landing gear that looked barely strong enough to support the weight. The gear was only ever used for taxiing; take-off and landing on a passenger craft like that were always managed more smoothly on air cushions.

Tim's face appeared on one of the screens.

'How're you doing, Dan?'

'Ready when you are.'

'Okay. Starting main engines now.'

'Starting main engines.'

The B-90 trembled slightly as the engines turned over with a distant whine that gradually rose in pitch.

Tim's voice. 'Tower, are we clear for take-off?'

Barry's face appeared on the second screen. 'Affirmative. Separate take-offs. Form up at flight level 200 and go through the sequence we discussed.'

Ted and Dan each confirmed.

A few moments later the Silverpoint began to roll, heading for the runway. Dan waited long enough to allow a decent interval, then released the brakes and eased the throttles forward to follow.

He watched the Silverpoint turn to line up on the runway, heard the engines roar and noted the slight change in attitude and a puff of dust as Tim vectored some thrust to transfer the weight from wheels to air cushions; then he sent the craft surging onwards. Moments later the airliner was clearing the runway and soaring into the sky, the wheels already retracted. In another fifteen seconds Dan was pulling back on the control column and climbing after it.

They formed up, flying at three hundred knots and twenty thousand feet. It was lower than the Silverpoint's normal cruising altitude but the slightly higher air density would be better for exploring any anomalies in the airflow. Dan moved to station himself level with the wing of the larger aircraft.

Tim appeared on the videocomms screen. 'All right,

Dan?'

'Yes.' Tim's face disappeared as Dan activated the cameras and their displays. 'All set here.'

'Okay, commencing thirty degree turn to port. On my mark. Three... two... one... mark.'

The wings of the Silverpoint tipped towards him and Dan copied the manoeuvre precisely, holding close formation and turning inside the big liner. He was vaguely aware of the screens switching as some cameras lost the picture and others acquired contact. He paid them no attention; he was too busy balancing the throttles, rudder, elevators and ailerons to preserve level flight and to maintain station at the same time. They held the turn. Far below, the landscape rotated, a parched terrain patterned with green circles of irrigation, stretching to the angled horizon.

Tim's voice. 'All right, rolling out on a count of three. Three... two... one... mark.'

Dan rolled the B-90 smoothly out of the turn – and found himself on a collision course with the Silverpoint. Several things happened at once: his heart rate shot up, an alarm sounded in the cockpit and the head-up display flashed 'COLLISION WARNING!' His hands and feet had already responded instinctively and the craft banked sharply left, veering away from danger. He pulled out of the turn more slowly this time and saw that the Silverpoint had levelled off. It took a moment or two for his shrilling nerves to settle; then he took a deep breath and closed up again. He switched from cameras to videocomm.

Tim said, 'Dan, you okay there?'

'Yeah, sorry, I misjudged it. I thought you'd completed.'

'That's exactly what I'm talking about. You were

14

allowing for a normal course correction. The response is far too slow.'

'Tim, you experiencing any flutter?'

'Slight vibration, that's all. But I hear what you're saying. The wings could be twisting under load.'

'Right,' Dan said. 'That would affect the handling.'

'It didn't show up on the strain sensors.'

'Well, there's an answer to that. Push it harder.'

'How hard?'

'Load it to the design limit. See if it gets worse.'

There was a pause. Then Tim said, 'We should check with Barry. What do you think, Barry?'

Barry's face appeared on the screen below Tim's. 'With Dan still flying chase?'

'Yes.'

'I'm not entirely happy with that, Dan. That Silverpoint's behaving unpredictably. Flying close formation could be dangerous.'

'What do you say, Dan?' Tim asked.

'I've done more dangerous things.'

Barry sighed. 'Okay. I must say it would make my life easier to have some good solid evidence to put in front of their engineers. Up to 2.5g then. Not more.'

'Copy that. Ready, Dan?'

Dan quickly switched on the cameras and screens. 'Ready.'

'Sixty degree turn to port, on my mark. Three... two... one... mark.'

Again the Silverpoint tipped over, banking much more steeply this time, and Dan did the same, balancing the controls as before. He was pressed into his seat by the g-force, his body weight more than doubled.

Tim's voice. 'Lot of flutter. Controls are heavy...

putting in a lot of aileron…'

The turn continued, taking them around 180 degrees.

Tim's voice. 'Rolling out, three… two… one… mark.'

Dan rolled out of the turn carefully, his reflexes tuned to respond to any sudden change in the other craft. It came soon enough. Something caught his eye, there was a brief expletive from Tim, and the big craft was yawing and wandering into his path. For a moment it seemed to fill the windscreen and every audible and visual alarm in the B-90 went wild. He threw the craft over, down and away from certain disaster. When he straightened up, the Silverpoint seemed to be under control. His heart was pounding. He swallowed hard, settled himself into an icy calm, then climbed back and closed the distance, inspecting the other craft carefully.

'Tim, looks to me like you lost a trim tab, port wing.'

'Jesus, is that what it was?' Tim said. 'For a moment back there it became a real handful.'

Barry's voice was tense. 'Come in, now, you two. We've got what we wanted.'

'I'll escort you back, Tim. I don't trust that thing.'

He heard a laugh. 'Okay, here we go.'

Dan pulled away slightly; there was no need to maintain close formation any longer. The two craft set course for base.

*

They joined Barry in the Post-Flight Analysis Section. He electrodimmed the windows and they watched the telemetry records on the big wall screen.

Barry pointed to several traces moving across the screen, signals from strain sensors attached to the wing. 'Watch this part.'

Tim's commentary over the speakers:

'Sixty degree turn to port, on my mark. Three... two... one... mark.'

The traces drifted in one direction then several of them started to swing wildly above and below the line.

'Lot of flutter. Controls are heavy... putting in a lot of aileron...'

Tim's voice had risen in pitch. The trace on the screen oscillated up and down.

Barry slapped the table excitedly. 'There's your flutter, Tim, right there! For a moment I thought it was going divergent. Nearly gave me a heart attack.'

Tim shot him a rueful smile. 'You and me both.'

'No wonder the handling's sluggish,' Dan said. 'The wings are twisting under load. It's playing hell with the aerodynamics.'

'That was on the turn-in,' Tim said. 'What about the recovery?'

'It's the same,' Barry said. 'Maybe even worse in that direction.'

A technical officer brought in four three-centimetre squares of black plastic, the memory squares from the B-90's onboard computers.

'Thanks, Mike,' Barry said, and plugged the squares into the computer. 'Let's see when that tab came loose.' They played through the record, watching in silence, waiting, the screen split to display four cameras at a time. They watched the beginning of the banked turn. Then the reverse manoeuvre – and something fluttered briefly in the top right-hand screen.

Barry slapped the table again. 'Sonofabitch! Exactly when you started to roll out. The strain reversal must have been enough to shear the retaining pins on that trim tab.'

17

He rewound a short stretch, then selected that camera position to display on its own and played it again in slow motion. They saw the tab detach and fly off. He stopped the record there and noted the time.

He smiled at them both. 'Nice flying. I'll make a copy of all this. The idle buggers didn't do their simulations properly. Good work, both of you. Write it up for me, would you?'

Tim left the room and Dan was about to follow when Barry put a hand on his arm. 'Got a minute, Dan?'

Dan turned and they stood facing each other. Barry made a fidgety movement. Dan thought he looked slightly ill at ease. 'What is it, Barry?'

'You've been with us – what? – two months now?'

'Nearly that, yes.'

'You know how you got this job, don't you?'

'I guess someone put in a word for me.'

'Yeah, no less a personage than Dr John Trebus.'

Dan nodded. 'Trebus was pretty disgusted with the way I was treated after the Saturn run. I didn't want to work for SpaceFreight any more and he understood that. But he's a Director of Space Fleet as well as SpaceFreight. He said he'd recommend me for this job.'

'I have a lot of respect for Trebus. He's a powerful man and he could have put the arm on me, but he didn't. He just said he knew someone well worth considering for our vacancy, and he gave me your resumé. Left the final decision to me.'

'That's not untypical.'

'Well, I read about your Silver for flying when you were at the Academy and your other experience, but frankly it didn't say a whole lot to me. It takes more than that to make a successful test pilot. We had a vacancy to fill so I took you on,. But I got to admit it; I had my doubts about you.'

Dan frowned and tilted his head. 'Why are you telling me this?'

'Why? Because I wanted to tell you I was wrong, dead wrong. I've felt it for some time but the test today cinched it. You were almost on Tim's wingtip when that tab flew off. You captured the exact moment on camera, and we still have both of you safely back on the ground. I don't ask for more than that. I'd just like to say it properly. Welcome aboard, Dan.'

Dan took the extended hand and felt Barry's firm grip.

Barry said, 'Okay, now go and write me that report.'

3

Dan and Neraya often compared notes back in their apartment at the end of the day, which was a legitimate thing to do; the nature of her work at Strategic Planning meant she carried the same high-level security classification as he did. He had no intention of worrying her, so he left out the details whenever there'd been an element of risk in what he'd been doing. On this occasion he mentioned flying chase for Tim merely to tell her what Barry had said to him after the debriefing.

'He was pretty pleased about the flight,' he said, handing her a glass of juice and taking the seat next to her on the sofa. 'He admitted he had his doubts about me when he took me on.'

'Really?' she said. 'A trip to Saturn and back, single-handed, made no impression on him, then?'

'Not in the slightest. It takes more than that to make a successful test pilot. That's what he said.'

'The nerve!'

'Yes, well he didn't know all the ins and outs of that Saturn trip, did he? Anyway, he wanted to get it off his chest. He wanted to tell me he knew now he'd made the right decision.'

She arched a slender eyebrow. 'How good of him to say so.'

'Oh, it's unusual even to go that far at the Establishment. People never comment on other people's flying abilities. It's accepted that everyone there knows their job. That's fine with me. I'm not asking for praise. Just being treated with a modicum of respect makes a pleasant change.'

She smiled at him.

He changed the subject. 'Saw some friends in the gym today.'

'Oh, who?'

'Simon and Raffi. I went down for my usual work-out and found them in there. Just back from Serenity.'

She frowned. 'The Moon base? What were they doing there?'

'Orbital skills for a bunch of fresh graduates.'

'Bit expensive to use Test Pilots for that, isn't it? Why don't the Academy instructors handle it?'

'Maybe they're short staffed. It's in our contract, anyway. The Establishment keeps a bunch of very experienced pilots and I guess it's part of the deal with Space Fleet management. We're only really busy when there are new craft to test, so at other times we can be seconded to help with a bit of line flying or training or air accident investigation. Barry's asked me to deliver a passenger liner to New York next week. Should make a change.'

'How long were Simon and Raffi out at Serenity?' she asked.

'Three weeks. They won't be flying for a bit. First they'll have to recover some bone and muscle strength.'

'You've had your share of that.'

'Too right. I've had my fill of microgravity. I think they're jealous because I negotiated a full year without off-Earth duties.'

She placed her hand over his. 'I'm so glad you did that.' She looked at him. 'What happens when the year's up?'

'We'll have to see, won't we?'

She finished her juice and got to her feet. 'I'd better get the dinner on.'

*

Neraya went into the kitchen and started to prepare one of the many Lebanese dishes she'd learned from her mother. She and Dan could well afford to eat out or order meals in, but they seldom did. For her, cooking was an escape. Her work at Strategic Planning required prolonged and intense concentration and when she got back it was soothing and relaxing to go through the familiar routines. Not for her the robotic chefs, smart wallpaper and surround sound systems of other modern kitchens; she valued the simple, artisan pleasure of preparing food in a silence broken only by the gentle bubbling of the saucepans.

She paused for a moment, motionless, a lemon held to the chopping board, the knife poised, resting on its skin. With her eyes closed, the fragrances liberated by the warm spices transported her back to her childhood, first in Beirut, then in Paris. With it came a wave of happiness, then a familiar weight as she remembered yet again how much she'd lost.

'You okay, honey? Need any help?'

She looked up, brushed a tear from her eye and summoned a smile. 'Yes, fine, it's just the onions. You go and sit down.'

'Smells lovely,' he said, as he turned back to the sitting-room. Her eyes followed him for a moment.

He'll go and stand by the big window. He loves that commanding view over Armstrong, superb during the day but magical at night, when he can look down on the skimmers flashing like jewels through the illuminated flight lanes below.

Danny wasn't a lot of use in the kitchen, but that was all right. She enjoyed making meals for him, and he was good about doing the clearing up afterwards. It was part of their life together, and after the long months and years of separation she treasured every moment.

*

When they'd eaten, Dan cleared the things away as usual while Neraya sat down to watch the newstream on WorldNet. The first item made her sit forward.

'Customs has successfully carried out the interception of a satellite in orbit round Mars. There were reports that this satellite had been operating as a factory for the manufacture of illegal drugs, specifically Dramatoin – the drug known on the street as Blaze.'

She called out, 'Danny, quick! It's that orbiting drug factory.'

He appeared in the doorway. The presenter was saying:

'...intended to carry out an inspection, but they came under heavy fire and were obliged to retaliate, with devastating effect.'

The picture switched to a starry sky with dark shapes moving through it. Then laser beams sliced through the darkness and the screen lit up with four streams of explosions. The flashes illuminated a C-class freighter, which appeared to be leading a fleet of other ships and engaging the target on its own. The dazzling display went on for several seconds, then four blue-white stabs of flame shot out from the lead ship and the camera followed them as they diminished into the distance. For several more seconds the barrage of aerial explosions continued. Then the screen went white. When the light faded there was a brief glimpse of glowing fragments spiralling slowly through space.

An interview followed with a large, plethoric individual with a heavy mane of white hair – the Commissioner of Customs, Miles Nicholson.

'Mr Nicholson, this was a violent encounter. Do you think destroying the orbiting factory like that was justified?'

'Absolutely. Of course we would have preferred to take it over without loss of life, arrest those on board, and then either retrieve the entire satellite or destroy it. But the syndicate involved has a reputation for violence and, as you saw, we were met with armed resistance. We were obliged to defend our ships and our personnel with both offensive and defensive weapons.'

'It was a costly exercise.'

'True, but the cost to society of these deadly drugs of addiction is much, much higher. That's why I've supported this operation from the outset, and I'd do so again. What we've shown here is that there is no hiding place for these gangsters and their murderous rackets. We have the determination and we have the reach to pursue them to the ends of the solar system.'

Neraya clicked the picture off and looked round at Dan.

He gave her a sardonic smile. 'So, they managed it – at long last.'

'Spectacular operation.'

24

'I'm sure that was precisely the intention.'

'What do you mean?'

He wiped his hands on the towel he was holding and came into the sitting-room. 'As hostile actions go, I'd say that offensive fire they were up against was feeble stuff. Four shell-throwers? The Customs ship could have taken them all out with a few rounds from its own.'

'Maybe the satellite was equipped with countermeasures too.'

'Maybe, but that Customs ship didn't even try – did it? – just sent in the torpedoes. *Four* torpedoes! Jesus, one would have done the job very nicely.'

She sighed. 'Whoever was on board didn't have a prayer.'

'I'd be surprised if there was anyone at all on board.'

She looked at him. 'Really?'

'Look, I reported the coordinates of that factory more than two years ago. If they'd pounced on it right away it might have been different, but SpaceFreight's esteemed director Karl Stott declined to pass on my transmission so it didn't come out until my court martial. The syndicate had more than enough time to move manufacture elsewhere.'

Neraya nodded. 'Even if they didn't know about your original transmission they've had nearly three months since the court martial.'

'Precisely. No way was this a surprise attack.'

'Yet they encountered hostile fire.'

'Autotargetting shell-throwers. Just enough resistance to encourage Customs to destroy the thing. That way they wouldn't find out there was nothing on board worth inspecting.'

She pursed her lips. 'Do you think Customs knew that when they sent in the torpedoes?'

'Maybe, maybe not. But like that interviewer said, this was an expensive operation. If they boarded the satellite and found nothing, what would they have to show for it? Zilch. This way at least they get a big public relations boost for destroying an orbiting drug factory, even if they did know it was just an empty hull.'

'So where has production been moved to?'

He gestured with an open hand. 'Now that's the question they *should* be asking. If Customs had the answer to it I expect they wouldn't be treating us to displays of fake pyrotechnics.'

4

Everything is cloaked in mist. The street is barely visible, the roadway strewn with detritus, the gutters overflowing with rotting vegetables, dead animals, vomit, and excrement, everywhere the stench of decay and death. The only sound is the distant rush of skimmer traffic whisking overhead, level upon level, trailing the water vapour that settles through the air, creeping over every surface, penetrating every crevice here below. In all this heat and humidity it's hard to breathe, and every laboured breath brings with it odours so foul they rot the lungs.

A piercing scream splits the air, then dies away. More sounds: someone vomiting, an insistent jabbering that stops suddenly. Shadowy forms materialize and disappear like ghosts. A hooded figure looms out of the mist, its separate parts coalescing like water drops on a windowpane. It walks towards him, rubbing its upper arm. He tries to say something but his mouth will not form the words. His breathing becomes shallow and fast. All he can hear now is the thudding of his heart.

The vapour curls around his ankles. It begins to rise. It reaches his thighs, his chest, his neck. It is so viscous he can barely move.

The figure comes closer and raises its head. Under the hood the face is cadaverous, the eyes strangely vacant, the pupils like pinpoints. A bony, clawed finger extends towards him. It touches his chest. He feels the point of pressure grow harder and harder until suddenly it breaks through skin, muscle, and bone and plunges deep into his heart...

Dan woke with a start, eyes wide, mouth open, gasping. He rubbed the heel of one hand over the middle of his chest and it came away slippery with perspiration.

He drew a shuddering breath, then got out of bed carefully and went to the bathroom. He closed the door softly.

It must have been that Customs hit on the orbiting drug factory. Brought it all back: being thrown out of the Academy, doing whatever work came along. And then being hired by Mikhail Rostov...

'Mr Rostov, I don't want to seem ungrateful, but you're paying a good deal more than the going rate. Why's that?'

'Discretion. I pay for your discretion. This is a commercially sensitive operation. I don't want rival companies to know what we are doing. You fly your ship, you ask no questions, you give no answers, we get along fine.'

How could he have been so goddamned naïve?

He turned on the shower and stood under the drenching spray, washing the sweat away, trying to flush with it the weight of oppression that his recurring nightmares always left behind.

Once, at the lowest point in his life, he'd inhabited those streets under the flight lanes, seen the figures wandering aimlessly in the mist. How many of them had been destroyed by drugs he'd unwittingly transported for Rostov?

He dried off and returned to bed. Neraya stirred as he slid in beside her. She reached out and he took her in his arms, letting her warmth flow into him.

'Sorry honey, I didn't mean to wake you.'

'It's all right. Same nightmare?'

He rubbed his cheek gently against her silky hair and sighed. 'Yeah.'

'With all you went through on that trip I'm not surprised. It'll pass, Danny. Give it time. It will pass. You're safe with me now.'

He held her tightly. After a while he heard her steady breathing and knew she had gone back to sleep. For him sleep would not return as easily.

The details change but otherwise it's always the same: the half-alive figures, the pain, the suffering. She doesn't know – it's better that way. Let her think it's the Saturn run. That was the stuff of nightmares all right, only it doesn't come back to haunt me. Why not? I guess those things were resolved, that's why – I can draw a line under them. Not the Dramatoin, though. Two freighters, full of the stuff. No way can I draw a line under that. That's something I have to live with.

For me life's the best it's ever been. Somehow that only makes it worse. All those sad souls, all those shattered lives. Poor bastards, they're paying a heavy price for what I did. I wish to hell there was some way… but there isn't. So let them come to me in my nightmares. I can wake up from mine. There's no escape from theirs.

5

The Deputy Assistant Commissioner's Office was on the fourteenth floor of the Customs building in Armstrong's Central District. The window behind his desk faced northeast, and although the view was largely blocked by other high-rise buildings there was a gap, through which it was possible to see across the San Joaquin Valley and, on a clear day, out to the mountains of the Sierra Nevada. The room was large enough to accommodate not only the desk but also a table and chairs for small meetings and three armchairs for informal conversations with senior colleagues.

Henry Leighton rose to greet the four people who'd just arrived, gestured for them to take seats at the table, and sat down himself.

'All right, let's get started. What I'd like to do is reassess the position following the destruction of the floating drug factory in Mars orbit last month. It was a big operation and broadly speaking I believe it was helpful to give it media coverage. But that's a two-edged sword: we've raised expectations in government and among many concerned groups in the general population. What they want to see now is clear evidence that the distribution and use of Dramatoin has declined as a result of the action we've taken. The question is: do we have such evidence?'

He looked around the table. They were all watching him intently. No one spoke. He continued:

'We're pretty sure who was running this factory – almost certainly the syndicate formerly headed by the late Mikhael Rostov and now in the hands of Raoul Hernandez. We can assume that our strike came as no surprise to them. They'd had ample warning and they'd evidently responded to it, because their satellite had been moved to a different orbit in a different sector. It was hard to pick up, and they could have continued to use it. But it's possible they've moved part or all of their operation elsewhere. Have they done so and if they have, where is it now? This isn't a formal committee meeting. If you have anything to say, just say it. You may not have met each other before, so it would be a good idea if you introduce yourselves as we go along. Colonel Bell?'

Bell was next in seniority to Leighton. He had a tired look these days; his eyes were hooded, his complexion sallow, the neck fleshy and sagging, the small black moustache flecked with grey. It was protocol to invite the man, although on previous form Leighton wasn't expecting much of a contribution from him.

Bell glanced at the others. 'Steven Bell, Space Fleet Police Division.' He came back to Leighton. 'We'll know soon enough whether they've moved operations, won't we, Henry? I'm talking about your Customs interceptions in Earth orbit.'

Leighton shook his head. 'It's not feasible to make interceptions like that routinely. The only time we can do it is if we receive a reliable tip-off. We've concentrated on cargo arriving at the shuttle terminals on Earth. What we see is the tip of the iceberg – our successes haven't been enough to get a true picture of the volume of traffic. That's why I convened this meeting. We need to put together information from different sources.' His gaze settled on a woman similar in age and seniority to Colonel Bell. He knew her well and he'd learned not to be deceived by that motherly appearance. 'The Drug Enforcement Agency, for example. Claudia, I assume the DEA monitors street use?'

'Sure we do,' she said, adding for the benefit of the others at the table, 'Claudia Zobel, DEA. The Agency keeps a close eye on the number of new addicts in police custody, fresh admissions to the secure psychiatric hospitals, and so on. But that's also the tip of the iceberg. We have undercover agents working the streets and the clubs, but they never get close to source. It's a complex tree of distribution and our people are out on the twigs, not the major branches.'

'All the same, it's useful intelligence,' Leighton said. 'Could you feed those figures back to me?'

'I don't see why not. I'm assuming,' she said, with an artful smile, 'information will be passing in the opposite direction as well.'

Inter-agency politics, Leighton thought. 'Of course, you'll continue to have our full cooperation. Good. Now what about manufacture?'

Again it was Zobel who responded. 'Dramatoin's one of those chiral compounds which exists as an active and an inactive isomer. Making it is tricky. In full gravity you get a mixture, mostly inactive, pretty useless. Under zero gravity conditions you can synthesize the pure active form. The syndicates have always gone for orbiting factories for that reason.'

'We picked them up when they tried it in Earth orbit and Moon orbit.' The speaker was a young man wearing the regulation black Customs tunic with red epaulettes and trim.

'Introduce yourself, Kennedy,' Leighton said sharply.

He coloured up. 'Sorry, Special Agent Alec Kennedy. I'm an Intelligence Officer with Customs. Like I said, we caught them when they tried to do it in Earth and Moon orbit. That's why they moved to Mars orbit. Now we've hit them there, so what's next? They could go further afield. With a large enough spacefreighter to carry the cargo it could still be worth their while.'

Leighton nodded. 'That's a possibility. I've been talking to some people about more effective ways of monitoring space traffic. In the meantime it's vital to know if a new factory has been set up in Earth, Moon, or Mars orbit. Colonel Bell, this is police business. Could your people conduct a census of satellites, cross-checking with the licensing authority for anything large enough to be a drug factory?'

Bell blinked. After a pause he said, 'That would be a mammoth task.'

'But it's crucially important. You'll assign people to it?'

He grimaced. 'Very well.'

'We'll want to know, obviously, if that trawl picks anything up, so we can make an immediate inspection.'

Bell nodded. 'That's understood.'

'Excuse me, sir.' The speaker was a woman in her thirties. Like Kennedy, she was in Customs uniform. Her dark hair was tied back, emphasizing high cheek bones and a lean jaw. 'Captain Lauren Marks, Customs,' she said to the others before returning to Leighton. 'If you're concerned with orbiting factories I'm not sure why I'm here.'

Leighton gave her a grim smile. 'Because, Captain, they may not be in orbit. As Mrs Zobel said, the syndicate can make the pure form of Dramatoin if they synthesize it in zero gravity. But these people aren't all that concerned about purity – they cut it when it reaches its destination anyway. Transporting an impure product is less economical, but with large volumes and the current street price of Dramatoin they could easily cover the costs. Would you agree, Claudia?'

She nodded. 'Yes, I would. Gravity on our Moon is about one-sixth of normal; on Mars it's about one-third. Neither one would give them pure Dramatoin, but it would still be highly profitable.'

'The Moon's not feasible,' Kennedy said. 'Every inch is mapped and there's a lot of traffic. Any activity there would be picked up instantly.'

'What about Mars? Marks?'

Lauren Marks nodded. 'Much more difficult to police than the Moon. It's a larger area, of course – four times as large – and there's some very rough terrain. Tharsis City is big, but outside the colony there's nothing like as much activity as on the Moon. On the other hand they'd have to take into account the survey satellites. It would be hard to set up a factory there without being spotted.'

Leighton said, 'I want you take that under your wing. Survey the terrain, look for any unauthorized construction.'

'Very good, sir.'

Leighton turned his attention back to the Special Agent. 'Kennedy, I think we should review successful interceptions of Dramatoin between Mars and Earth. They may still be transporting it by the same routes.'

'There haven't been many interceptions, sir,' Kennedy

said. 'The State Prosecutor should be familiar with the major ones.'

'Good point. Have a word with him, would you? Any other comments or suggestions?' He paused to look at each face in turn. 'No? Very well. Any information such as we've discussed here to me personally please. Don't tell anyone else what you're doing or why, not even a hint. If we're going to stay one step ahead of these criminal gangs we've got to keep everything tight.'

He stood, and they all got to their feet.

'Thank you, ladies and gentlemen. Steven, Claudia, thanks for coming, I appreciate your cooperation. We have to move quickly on this so we'll review the situation again in—' he looked around, 'shall we say two weeks?'

The four exchanged glances. Colonel Bell shook his head. 'Be reasonable, Henry, there's no way we could do anything useful in two weeks.'

'Three weeks, then. Thank you all.'

6

James Quenby, the State Prosecutor, shook hands, then went behind his desk and sank heavily into a chair that was the size of a small sofa. He held out an open palm.

'Have a seat, young man.'

Special Agent Alec Kennedy felt a flash of resentment at the patronizing tone, but Quenby probably used it on everyone. He was a big man, known to cut a striking figure in court with his shock of white hair, bushy black eyebrows and senatorial manner. The office was spacious and plainly but comfortably furnished, the distinguishing feature being an extensive collection of beautifully bound law books extending from floor to ceiling on two walls. They were almost certainly there to impress; all the information would be available – and much easier to search – on local databases. A third wall was occupied by framed certificates and smart photos that cycled through pictures of the Prosecutor with various prominent people. The fourth wall was dominated by a window, although the view was not impressive. Most of the private law firms had offices here in the centre of Armstrong; even at this level Kennedy could see only the windows of the high-rises opposite. The skimmer lanes were far below them.

He took the chair indicated. 'Thank you for access to those files, Mr Quenby. They were very helpful.'

Quenby acknowledged this with a nod, a movement that rocked his hair.

'I must say,' Kennedy continued, 'there were fewer successful prosecutions than I'd expected.'

A shadow passed over the lawyer's face. 'You will be aware,' he said heavily, 'that everything brought to court was successfully prosecuted. There's not much of a defence for people arrested in possession of drugs. If that file is small it's because your people haven't made enough successful interceptions.'

'Oh, absolutely,' Kennedy said quickly. 'That's a reflection of the size of the problem, of course – and the ingenuity and resources of these drug syndicates.' He was not going to be intimidated by this this man, but he had no wish to antagonize him either. 'So you never discovered the full route those consignments took?'

'Nope. We assume the drug in each case was made in the orbiting factory you destroyed recently. From there it would have been sent several different ways.' He sighed. 'There are too many links in the chain. Any one person in that chain doesn't know enough about what goes on before or after they carry out their part. Even if they cooperate it doesn't get us a lot further.' He waved a large hand. 'Look, I don't have to tell you this. You know what we're up against.'

Kennedy managed to sound weary. 'Yes, only too well.' He leaned forward. 'You mentioned cooperation. Some defendants gave evidence in return for lenient sentences. Any idea what happened to them?'

Quenby's right cheek lifted slightly. Kennedy thought it

was the nearest he ever got to a smile.

'You thinking of having a chat to them yourself?'

'It could be helpful.'

'Well you're out of luck. When they're released from prison most of them go underground. The syndicates discourage employees from talking to the authorities. They do this by killing them slowly in various nasty ways. We can give them new identities and they often get plastic surgeons to alter their appearance; then they disappear. In most cases we don't know whether they're alive or dead.'

Kennedy narrowed his eyes. 'In most cases…?'

Quenby shrugged. 'There are exceptions. Larssen, for example – I remember that one rather well. Became something of a hero afterwards, I believe.'

Kennedy had already made a note of the name when he was reading through the files. 'Well, thank you, Mr Quenby. I appreciate your time.' He stood up.

Quenby placed his hands on the edge of the desk and rose ponderously to his feet. 'You people planning something over there?'

Kennedy smiled. 'We're conducting a wide-ranging review, Mr Quenby. Whether that leads to something – well, we'll have to wait and see.'

*

'Larssen? Daniel Larssen?' Henry Leighton straightened up from his desk, eyebrows raised.

'Yes, sir,' Kennedy said, drawing up a chair. 'I've been looking at his record. He has experience in a number of relevant areas, including encounters with Rostov's syndicate. I think he could make a useful contribution to our meetings.'

'Kennedy, I'm trying to keep this whole thing tight.

Someone with that sort of background could leak intelligence straight back to the very people we don't want to have it.'

It was Kennedy's turn to raise his eyebrows. 'Sir? This is the man who transmitted the coordinates of the orbiting drug factory. I know they didn't reach us at the time but that wasn't his fault.'

Leighton frowned. 'Oh yes, I remember now. All the same, I'm not sure. The man has a reputation for being a bit of a maverick.'

'I'm not sure he deserves that. He's a Test Pilot with Space Fleet.'

'Is he, by God?' Leighton's mouth twisted briefly. 'Have you approached him?'

'Not yet, but I will if you agree. Of course it would have to be cleared with his boss – that's Barry Curtis, Director of Earth Flight Testing.'

There was a long silence. Then Leighton sighed. 'All right. I'll ask the Commissioner to speak to Curtis. It shouldn't present a problem – it's only a few meetings. In fact see if Larssen can come to the next meeting. It's short notice, only the day after tomorrow, so it'll be a useful test of his commitment.'

'Thank you, sir.'

Kennedy got up to go. Leighton gave him a doubtful look.

'I hope you're right about this, Kennedy. A man like that... Well, we'll see.'

7

Dan eased the craft into another long turn, out over the Atlantic and back towards New York.

Barry had discussed this assignment with him a week ago.

'It's called a CitySpeed, Dan. An Oregon company called HubAir manufactures subsonics like this one for intercity travel. The CitySpeed's going into service with three East Coast airlines and they want one in New York City now for pilot familiarization.'

'Right. Where do I make the pick-up?'

'At HubAir. They'll send an executive jet here for you. Drop the CitySpeed off at JFK and come back to Armstrong on a scheduled flight.'

'Okay, no problem.'

The CitySpeed was a sweet aircraft to fly. He'd made good time but now he'd been placed in a holding pattern. The forward placement of the cockpit and large windows gave him good visuals, particularly with the craft slightly banked. So in spite of the delay he was enjoying the view: the New Wall Street district with its tall buildings interconnected by a criss-cross of transparent walkways;

the buzzing skimmer lanes on twelve levels, one reserved for the yellow New York taxi skimmers; and the Great Dam, built to protect the city from rising sea levels and a possible tsunami, which had become a tourist attraction in its own right.

An hour later he was still in holding. By this time he'd decided that you could, after all, get tired of the view. More to the point, this was a medium-haul airliner and he was getting low on fuel. If he had to divert to another airport it was really going to prolong the whole assignment. He was on the point of reporting the fuel situation when Air Traffic Control gave him clearance to land. He left the holding pattern, joined Standard Arrival Routing and lined up with 13L, the assigned runway. Minutes later he'd landed, and he was exiting on Taxiway E.

Now where?

He paused on the taxiway, hoping this would elicit a response from Ground Control. This was a busy airport – on the runway over to his right they were landing at a rate of one a minute. They certainly wouldn't want to leave him here.

Ground Control came through. 'New York Ground, taxi to vacate clear of Echo.'

Yeah, glad to, if you tell me where to go.

He said, 'Wilco, New York Ground, advise taxi to park, November-one-three-Romeo.'

It was a courtesy to use his call sign. Ground had assigned him an individual channel during the approach. They knew who they were talking to.

Ground Control. 'Standby. Hold clear of Echo.'

For Christ's sake, tell me where I'm going. I don't know this airport and I don't know where I'm supposed to go.

He said, 'Roger, hold clear of Echo. Unfamiliar. Advise

routing.'

Come on, man, give me a clue.

Ground Control. 'Standby.'

I give up, it's your call.

He said, 'Stopping.'

Ground Control. 'Negative, Continue.'

Continue where, you dipstick? I'm staying here till you sort me out.

He said, 'Unable. Advise taxi to park, request Follow-Me.'

Silence. Presumably consternation. Consultation. A different voice.

'November-one-three-Romeo, vacate left, use Taxiway Bravo, Follow-Me to hangar area.'

He sighed. At last. 'Vacate left, Wilco, November-one-three-Romeo.'

He found the truck with the flashing sign on Taxiway B and followed it to a completely different area of the airport, a wide magnacrete apron behind which there were several large grey hangars. There were also some low office buildings that looked as if they'd been built for temporary use but somehow got left there for the next twenty years. He taxied onto the apron and cut engines. Then he opened the forward exit and pressed a button. A motor hummed and the CitySpeed's stairs deployed.

Just as well the stairs are built in; the way things are organized here they probably expect me to rope down.

He'd just stepped off the stairs and onto the apron when a side door opened in one of the low office buildings. A member of the ground staff appeared, dressed in yellow reflective coveralls. He beckoned and led Dan to an office, where he accepted the handover documents and signed the copies Dan would be taking back with him.

Dan slipped them into a slim document case. 'Thanks, thought I'd be out there for ever.' He jerked his head in the direction of the taxiways. 'Nobody seemed to know who I was or where I was supposed to go.'

The guy shrugged. 'Don't feel bad about it, they treat everyone the same. You ain't with a scheduled airline these people don't have a clue.'

'Can I catch a ride up to the terminal? I have to get a flight back to Armstrong – on a scheduled airline.'

'Sure.' He looked out of a grimy window. 'The Follow-Me is still there. You mind riding the truck?'

'No problem at all.'

Fifteen minutes later he was checking in at Airspeed California for the return flight. He took a soft drink from a dispenser while he was waiting. His return was booked First Class so he knew he'd be getting a decent meal at some stage.

In another thirty minutes he was joining the queue for preferential boarding. The flight would be bang on schedule. It looked like things were going smoothly at last.

8

The problems began during boarding. Dan paused to allow another passenger time to put his hand luggage into an overhead locker and he was just tucking his document case in next to it when a loud voice said:

'Hey, you! C'm here.'

He turned his head out of curiosity, not because he thought this peremptory summons was directed at him. But it *was* directed at him.

The owner of the voice was a stocky figure already seated in the front row. He pointed, then crooked his finger. Dan's insides melted. It was Braggazzi, head of the New York mob, the last person he expected to meet. Also the person he least wanted to meet. The mobster was slumming it to take a scheduled flight, even if he was in First Class. It was incredibly bad luck to come across him like this.

He debated ignoring him and going to his seat but when he turned to look up the aisle he found a heavily built man standing in front of him, blocking the way.

A bodyguard. Braggazzi never travels without them.

The man jerked his head and at the same time unfastened the single button on his leather jacket and flicked it back. Dan had spent enough time around people like this to recognize the gesture.

The man is right-handed. There's a sidearm in a holster on his right hip and he's making sure he can get at it.

He turned back to Braggazzi and saw that another big man was standing in the aisle. His jacket was open, too. No escape that way. He decided to play innocent.

'Sorry, sir, are you speaking to me?'

'Yeah, you. Sit down.'

He patted the seat next to him. Dan hesitated then went over and sat down. He felt his seat back strained by the weight of one of the bodyguards as he put his hands on it and settled into the row behind him. The second bodyguard took the seat on the opposite side of the aisle.

'Name's Braggazzi.' The man was fixing Dan with small, narrowed eyes. 'You're the guy flew us to Nassau a while back. I know your face. I never forget a face. Ask my people here if I ever forget a face.'

Continuing the air of baffled daftness Dan turned to ask the man opposite if his boss ever forgot a face but Braggazzi snarled, 'Listen to me when I'm talkin' to ya. You was workin' for Virgilius.'

Dan's mind was racing. The man did have a good memory; the incident had to be all of four years ago.

'Er, I was freelancing,' Dan lied. 'Just flew where people asked me to. But yes, I did do a few jobs for Mr Virgilius.'

'Yeah, well you was supposed to fly us to Nassau. Only you flew us to some shithole called Veracruz instead.'

'Er yes, I remember now. We had to stop over to check for damage. We'd been through a bad storm—'

'That's a bunch of crap! I had a guy check it afterwards. They said there was nothing wrong with the plane.'

'Ah, but we couldn't know that at the time. The regulations are for your own safety—'

'Safety, my ass. You flew us right through a fuckin' storm.'

'We were very unlucky to—'

'You coulda gone round it. Gave me and my people a bad fuckin' ride.'

'It was unfortunate…'

'Bullshit! I think you done it on purpose. We spent a coupla nights in jail. I don't forget things like that so easy.'

I haven't forgotten it either, you lousy bastard. As you have such a wonderful memory perhaps you remember Kelly. Because I did it for her. I delivered you to Veracruz stinking of drink and your own vomit, and you and your friends reeled into the terminal bad-tempered, aggressive and, worst of all, armed. Well surprise, surprise, they clapped you in jail. I thought they would, in fact I was counting on it. The police in Mexico can be relied on to be highly intolerant of that sort of thing.

'Really I…'

'Give Benny here your seat ticket.' He jerked his head in the direction of the man sitting behind Dan. 'You've changed places with him. Benny, you give him yours. And you keep an eye on this guy, you hear? We got a little business to attend to when we get to th' other end.'

The reply was slow and contented. 'Sure thing, boss.'

'Believe me, Mr. Braganzi—'

'Braggazzi, Braggazzi—wassamatter wit' you?'

'Sorry. Believe me, Mr. Braggazzi—'

'Maybe I believe you, maybe I don't. Only I'm someone who likes to be on the safe side.' His voice hardened. 'So just in case I don't believe you you're coming with us.'

He looked down, and with a sudden, unexpected movement he grabbed Dan's wrist and held it up. Dan caught a glimpse of the man's hand. On each of the short, powerful fingers there was a large ring. He recalled the damage those rings did to Kelly, the once-pretty Casino girl, when Braggazzi and his thugs beat her up. The bruises, the deep lacerations, the broken cheekbone. And that's what was in store for him when they reached their destination. He jerked his hand away.

Braggazzi's thick lips curled in a one-sided smile. 'Nice hands you got. Not strong, but nice, like a lady's. Too bad…'

Dan's stomach lurched as he caught the thinly veiled threat. They'd take a hammer to them. He'd never fly again. He swallowed hard.

How the hell am I going to get out of this?

The cabin crew closed the doors and started to go through the safety routine.

The plane was full of people. He could stand up and tell everyone he was being kidnapped. Braggazzi would say, 'Who said anything about kidnapping? The guy's a loony.' And he and his buddies would laugh their heads off – and still stay close.

Could he leave it until they landed?

The flight would come in at Armstrong's domestic terminal. It was an internal flight: security checks on boarding, nothing on disembarkation. There may be an armed guard somewhere in the terminal but he couldn't rely on one being around when he went through. He could yell blue murder and a few passengers might turn their heads; then they'd walk faster, anxious to get on with their business, anxious not to get involved. It may have been a caring society once but it wasn't now. Not any more.

What else?

The plane took off and began the climb, turning over the Atlantic and setting course for California. He thought quickly. He knew the route. They'd hit a jet stream at operating altitude, which they'd reach in about ten minutes. He waited.

He felt the turbulence start, a series of light shudders that rocked them slightly in their seats. Dan made a grab for the seat pocket. He glimpsed Braggazzi's hand dipping quickly to the left. It was a reflex movement that may have kept him alive in times past. Right now it told Dan he was carrying, too. Better still.

Dan opened the flight sickness bag he'd taken out of the seat pocket and began to retch violently, leaning towards Braggazzi at the same time. He was turning himself inside-out, in fact he surprised himself with how realistic he made it sound.

'Hey cut that out, will ya! What the fuck…! Get to the toilet, asshole!'

Dan got up, holding the bag to his mouth, opened the toilet door and went in, leaving it wide open. He made a lot of noise. Then he looked along the shelf, took the hand lotion, and dribbled some down each side of his mouth and rubbed some more on his chin to make it look shiny. A pair of big blue eyes appeared at the door. One of the flight attendants.

'Excuse me, sir, are you all right?'

He held a finger to his lips and beckoned. As she came close he showed her his ID card. She scanned it quickly. Major Daniel Larssen, Space Fleet Test Establishment. And her employer, Airspeed California, was a wholly owned subsidiary of Space Fleet. She almost certainly knew that. He had her attention.

'Listen to me carefully,' he said softly. 'In the first two rows there are three men carrying sidearms.'

She began to reply in a normal voice. 'Oh no, sir, that's not possible, everyone's been through—'

He hushed her, a finger again held to his lips.

'Probably Glock 90 series, carbon frame, sealed polycarbonate rounds. They're hard to detect in a routine security check. They must have put them in carry-ons and taken them out once they were through.' He glanced at the badge pinned to her tunic. 'Bonnie, this is what I want you to do...'

When he returned to his seat the flight attendant followed him. She was playing her part well. Almost too well.

'Now are you sure you're all right, sir? Would you like some more water?'

He heaved a laboured breath. 'No, I think I'll be all right now.'

'Well, that tablet should settle you. You be sure to press the call button if you need any more help.'

'Thank you. Thank you very much, miss. Appreciate it.'

She continued down the aisle and he blew out his breath noisily, as if after a great effort. 'Sorry about that.'

Braggazzi gave him a sour look. 'What an asshole! Don't do it again, you hear? I don't like people sicking their fuckin' guts over me. Jesus! Wassamatter with you, anyway? You're supposed to be a goddamned pilot.'

'I'm all right when I'm in the cockpit. Up there I can see the whole horizon. It only gets me when I'm a passenger. I should be all right now. The hostess gave me a tablet.'

'You shoulda taken sump'n before, punk.'

'Yes, I know. I'm sorry.'

Dan sank back and reclined the seat, his eyes closed. Braggazzi muttered something under his breath but left him alone. There was nothing to do now except wait until they'd landed and hope for the best.

The pilot delivered an in-flight commentary. A meal was served, which Dan declined. He was hungry but he had to keep up the pretence. Braggazzi had no such inhibitions; he had several drinks and tucked into the meal noisily and with great relish. There was a strong smell of whisky, sweat and overcooked cabbage. Dan started to wonder if he really would be sick.

The seat-belt signs came on and the usual landing announcements were made. The aircraft touched down smoothly, taxied for several minutes, then turned into its assigned bay. Bonnie went to the exit door and appeared to be having a problem. She called to one of her colleagues and they held a quick consultation. Then the other one picked up a microphone.

'Ladies and gentlemen, I'm afraid there is a problem with the forward door. Disembarkation will be from the rear door.'

There was a murmur of annoyance, particularly from the First Class passengers, who would now be the last to leave the aircraft. The engines whined down, the seat belt lights went out, and there was a scramble for the overhead lockers. Then everyone seemed to be in the aisle, facing the rear, waiting, dodging their heads to one side and then the other to see what was happening further down the line.

Dan retrieved his document case and waited patiently. Braggazzi and one of his bodyguards were in front of him, the other bodyguard was behind him. Together with a heavily overweight man towing an overnight case they would be the last to disembark.

The passengers filed slowly towards the exit. The fat man was preparing to go through the door when three airport police pushed past him. One of them held up a hand.

'Routine check,' he said. 'Please stand still, legs apart, arms out.'

Braggazzi muttered, 'What the fuck…?'

They began to conduct a hand search, starting with Braggazzi.

'What's this?'

Braggazzi emitted an injured whine. 'It's nothing. It's for my protection. I'm an important man. I gotta lotta enemies.'

'I'm sorry, sir, I'll have to detain you for unlawful possession of an offensive weapon on a scheduled flight.'

He nodded to a fourth officer, who was standing at the door with an automatic rifle held at the ready. The man nodded back.

They repeated the hand search on the bodyguard, with the same result.

When they'd finished with Dan, one of them said, 'Okay, sir, you can go.'

As he hurried through the exit Dan heard Braggazzi say:

'Listen, Mister, you're making a big mistake. Look, maybe we can come to some arrangement here…'

Dan ran through the jetway, out of the departure gate, along a travelator, down the stairs, and didn't stop running until he was through the main doors and outside the terminal. There he caught one of the waiting skimmer taxis. The cab lifted quickly to Level Four and he settled back with a sigh.

Will Braggazzi come after me again? Probably not. It was a chance encounter and he simply made the most of it. He doesn't know my name and if he tries for a face match he'll be looking for airline pilots; he won't guess that I'm a test pilot. His heart stopped pounding and he began to breathe more easily.

Traffic was light and they covered the distance quickly. He directed the cab driver to the top level of the apartment block, paid him, then rode the elevator down. It was still late afternoon and Neraya wasn't home from work yet. He wouldn't say anything to her about what happened. It was a routine delivery flight to New York, that's all. More than that would only alarm her.

He went into his study. Because Airspeed California was a subsidiary of Space Fleet it wasn't hard to find the staff list on the internal network. Under Personnel – which at one time had been called HR – he found the name of the manager: Norma Bryce. He punched in the number.

'Ah, Ms Bryce. This is Major Daniel Larssen, Space Fleet Test Establishment. I was travelling today on one of your scheduled flights from New York to Armstrong.'

'Excuse me, sir, complaints should be directed to—'

'This isn't a complaint, just the opposite, please hear me out. There were three men on board who were carrying concealed weapons. I want to commend the flight attendant who dealt with it. Her name badge was "Bonnie".'

'Bonnie?'

'Bonnie, yes. This young lady saw the problem and she handled it expertly. I could see what was going on, but none of the other passengers were aware of it.'

'I'm glad to hear that, sir. They are trained to be discreet.'

'Yes, well I just wanted to let you know that she's a great asset to the company. It's not for me to say, but if I had someone like that on my staff I'd want to show my appreciation in some tangible way.'

'We'll certainly take up the suggestion.'

'Thank you.'

'Sorry, sir, may I just have your name again?'

'Yes, Major Dan Larssen. And the flight number was...' he dipped into a pocket for the seat allocation slip and read it out.

'Well, thank you, Major. I appreciate your taking the trouble to call.'

'No trouble at all.'

He clicked off. One good turn deserved another.

You did a great job, Bonnie. You saved my skin and you gave Braggazzi another one in the eye for Kelly. Come to think of it, you look a bit like her. At least, the way she used to look...

It was strange how his past had a way of catching up with him. He was only twenty-seven. He sighed. By rights he shouldn't even have a past.

The screen flashed. There was a priority message from a Special Agent Alec Kennedy, Customs. What the hell did Customs want?

He decided it could wait. He'd remembered something.

He was ravenously hungry.

9

When Dan entered the Common Room the following morning he saw Joe Lau scanning the duty roster. He went over to him.

'Hi Joe. I wasn't around yesterday. Anything new come in?'

'I don't know, Dan, I wasn't around either. Alumni Reunion at Space Fleet Academy.'

'You go to those things, Joe?'

Joe shrugged. 'Before I got this job it was a handy way of networking. I made some good friends. Now it's just fun to meet up with them once in a while. You don't go to reunions then, Dan?'

Dan could have said that he wasn't actually an alumnus because he was thrown out of the Academy before he could graduate. Instead he shook his head.

'No.'

There was a short silence. Then Joe said, 'Your name came up, actually.'

'My name?'

'Yeah, I happened to say you were test-flying with us. It was while I was chatting to Pieter Tyomkin and Carlos

Henriques. They were both in my year.'

Dan nodded. That pair had been about three years ahead of him at the Academy. Tyomkin and Henriques had already achieved god-like status in the eyes of most of the cadets. It was almost unheard of for anyone to get a gold in the final flight exam, yet both these guys had managed it, possibly the first and the last cadets ever to do so.

'They wouldn't have known who I was, Joe.'

'Don't you believe it! Someone told them your final flight exam would be worth watching, so they both went along. You know what they said? How you missed getting a gold for that display they'll never know.'

Dan blew out a breath. He felt both flattered and embarrassed. 'Generous of them to say that, Joe, but it was a fair result. When it came to flying those two guys were in a class of their own.'

Joe smiled and turned to the rotas. 'I don't see your name up here.'

'No, I only came in for a coffee. Barry's released me to go to some kind of meeting later on.'

*

Dan tipped the joystick and the skimmer banked to join the highway, which ran arrow-straight across the desert for another five miles, from the Test Establishment to Armstrong. Traffic was light in mid-morning so he accelerated in boost, then engaged overdrive. At two miles a minute there wouldn't be time to get bored with the featureless landscape. There would, however, be time to think about why he was doing this at all.

Dan had no liking for Customs. His previous experience had led him to conclude they'd been over-zealous in their dealings with him and incompetent in their dealings with everyone else. The belated attack on the orbiting drug factory had only confirmed him in his view. His philosophy had been that the less he had to do with them the better.

Two things had persuaded him to reconsider. The first was his meeting with Special Agent Alec Kennedy. The young Intelligence Officer had made an impression on him. Kennedy was bright, energetic and dedicated. He'd done his homework: he was clearly aware of Dan's history and didn't ask him to expand on any of it. Better still, he was perfectly candid about the strike on the orbiting factory. He admitted it probably hadn't achieved anything beyond its public relations value.

'Of course it hasn't,' Dan said. 'These people don't need two years or more to move somewhere else.'

'The question is where?'

'Wish I could help you with that, but I can't.'

'Maybe you can, in ways you can't see right now. Major, the people we're up against are well resourced. They need reduced gravity to make the drug but aside from that they could have established a new production facility almost anywhere. I think your experience and expertise could be really valuable to us.'

Was Kennedy one of a new breed in the back rooms of Customs? If so, it seemed to Dan that a little cooperation wouldn't hurt.

The second and far more important thing was what they were trying to deal with. Dramatoin was a powerful and fiercely addictive drug; it took only a single exposure to induce dependence. Once hooked, the victims faced years trying to meet the crippling expense of the addiction, all the while undergoing not only physical but mental deterioration. As the drug extended its hold on them, small neurotic tendencies expanded into full-blown psychoses.

They would become progressively more dangerous, to themselves and to everyone else. Eventually, bereft of all reason, abandoned by their despairing families and friends and by the dealers they could no longer pay, they would end up outcasts from society, wandering those vapour-laden streets under the flight lanes. Unfortunately it was highly profitable to deal in human misery, and the wealth it generated kept some of the largest syndicates afloat. They operated behind legitimate façades, of course: international and interplanetary chains of hotels, clubs, casinos, leisure centres. The evidence trail never led to them, and if it did look like coming too near, a team of crack lawyers ensured that prosecutions failed expensively.

He didn't know if he had anything to contribute to this meeting but the mere prospect of putting a dent in that evil trade was sufficient to bring him to the table. If it turned out to be a mere talking shop, a piece of window-dressing like Leighton's attack on that satellite, then he had better things to do. If it looked like they were heading somewhere he'd see where it led.

10

Alec Kennedy met Dan at the entrance to the Customs building and conducted him through security. They went up to Henry Leighton's office, where the meeting was to be held.

When they entered the room it seemed like everyone else was already there, standing around the table, chatting. Kennedy introduced Dan around, starting with the Deputy Commissioner. Leighton shook hands in a perfunctory way without smiling. He was a lean, ascetic looking man, and the lukewarm welcome left Dan ready to reinstate his former jaded views about Customs. Colonel Steven Bell of the Space Fleet Police gave him a hearty greeting and, Dan suspected, had probably forgotten his name already. Captain Lauren Marks was a very different proposition to both of them. A quiet young woman in her thirties, she had dark, intelligent eyes, a firm handshake, and the contained energy of a cat about to pounce. Claudia Zobel was older and more solidly built; he hadn't met her before but he knew of her reputation, which was formidable.

If people like Kennedy and Marks and Zobel are involved, something useful could yet come of this.

Leighton's raised voice gained their attention as he asked everyone to sit down. Kennedy took a chair next to Lauren Marks. Dan sat on the other side of him and across the table from Steven Bell and Claudia Zobel. He took a moment to look around him. Despite the standard furnishings – the desk, the conference table, the chairs and armchairs – the room had an institutional feel to it. It was, he decided, not so much what was there as what wasn't; personal touches like photos, books, plants, even commonplace desktop objects that might have said something about its occupant, were all absent. Possibly the man thought such things were irrelevant or, worse still, self-revealing.

Leighton got down to business straight away. 'You've all met. Could we start with the question I raised at the meeting three weeks ago? We've destroyed an orbiting drug factory. Can we show that it resulted in a decline in the distribution and use of Dramatoin? Claudia?'

She got to her feet and pointed to the short wall at the end of the room. It carried a mural of a woodland scene. 'All right to put something on your wall screen?'

Leighton nodded.

Zobel drew a communicator from her jacket pocket and established contact with the system in the room. The woodland scene disappeared, replaced first by a large blue rectangle, and then by a single graph, which consisted of a thin red line travelling from left to right over an axis marked off in years. She electrodimmed the windows.

'Okay,' she said, walking over to the screen. 'I've had some useful discussions with Philip Sieverts. Phil is a Senior Special Agent with the FBI. He has a special interest in narcotics and the interplanetary syndicates who trade in them, and he works closely with us. We've put together everything we have on Dramatoin use: arrests, hospital admissions, information passed by undercover agents on the streets, and so on. Most of the information comes from this country but we also have some data from law enforcement agencies abroad. Individually, measures like that aren't very reliable. Put them all together and what you get isn't half bad. So this line here is our estimate of the level of use over the last ten years. Let's zoom in on the last year.' She tapped the screen on her communicator and the date axis changed scale. 'Now if you look back six or seven weeks to where that orbiting factory was destroyed you can see it hasn't gone down one little bit. If anything it's gone up. Sorry, but it looks to me like that operation had no effect at all on production. I'd say there has to be another factory churning out the stuff.'

'Or they're keeping things going with existing stocks,' Kennedy said. 'They probably keep stashes in a whole bunch of places.'

'Sure, that has to be a possibility. Let me tell you why I think we can rule it out.' She looked down at the communicator in her hand and tapped some more. Again the graph changed. 'Here's the position seven years ago.'

Dan looked at the heading on the graph and it was as if a shadow had fallen across him. 2148, the year he was thrown out of Space Fleet Academy.

'Seven years ago,' she continued, 'a factory like the one you just destroyed was operating in orbit around the Moon. Space Fleet spotted it, and Customs went out to investigate. The satellite self-destructed just before they got there. We think they were caught by surprise. It certainly looks that way, because the graph shows that Dramatoin use started to decline within weeks.' Her finger traced a downward curve in the graph. 'It continued to go down for the best part of a year. We can assume that corresponds to the loss of production and the running down of stocks. Then it came up again.' Her finger traced the curve upwards. 'Which was, I'd say, when a new factory – the one orbiting Mars – came on line and stocks started to be replenished.'

Dan's mind was working. That was precisely when he was taken on as a pilot for Rostov and flown out to Mars for the pickups. It couldn't have been long after they started to manufacture the stuff in Mars orbit.

Zobel said, 'I think this answers your point about the stashes, Agent Kennedy. Any time drug production stops you'd expect a decline similar to what we saw seven years ago. When the factory in Mars orbit was destroyed there wasn't a sign of one. Why? Because it had already been shut down and production had been transferred someplace else.'

Dan glanced at Leighton. The man's face was a mask.

Zobel added, 'If I could take just a few moments more of your time, we can extract something else from this data.'

Leighton gestured for her to go ahead.

She paused, apparently gathering her thoughts or possibly choosing her words. 'Three years ago an E-class was intercepted by a pirate fleet just beyond Mars.'

Now Dan was bristling with interest. It was *his* encounter she was talking about! When they'd been introduced she'd shown no sign of knowing who he was, nor did she glance in his direction now. Either she genuinely didn't know or she was a consummate operator. He'd place bets on the second.

'There'd been a couple of other incidents in that sector before, freighters that lost communication. It's a fair assumption they were intercepted, too, only in their case no one ever saw them again. It's also a fair assumption that those pirate ships weren't there by chance: they were protecting something.'

'May we guess?' Colonel Bell asked. 'The orbiting drug factory?'

'Exactly. Now the syndicate running that factory was faced with a problem. This interception had gone badly wrong. They had to assume that the coordinates of the attack would be passed back to Earth. That meant manufacture was no longer secure.

'So,' she continued. 'Let's see how the graph looked three years ago.' She tapped and the date axis changed. The line was horizontal. She pointed. 'See this? Not even a hiccup.'

'How do you explain that?' Colonel Bell asked.

'I'd say it went like this. They moved the orbiting factory but kept it operational at its new coordinates until they could begin to manufacture at a new location. Once that had begun they could close everything else down. See? You do it that way you get a seamless handover and no break in production. The orbiting factory we knew about stayed up there, abandoned, doing nothing – until you guys blew it to bits a few weeks ago.' She gestured with one hand, said 'Back to you, Henry', and returned to her seat.

Leighton said stiffly, 'Thank you, Claudia, I believe you've answered the first question. That raises the next question: where is the new factory? Agent Kennedy, you went over the files with the State Prosecutor, didn't you?'

'Yes, sir. There weren't many – it's surprising how few successful prosecutions there've been.'

'Did you get anything useful out of it?'

'I'm afraid not. Some of the defendants gave evidence, but none of them saw more than a small part of the whole operation. And from what Mrs Zobel just said, the period of greatest interest to us would be the last three years. There's been nothing significant in that time.'

Leighton grimaced. He looked around the table. 'Steven, any progress on your satellite census?'

Dan felt his impatience rising.

What? Do they really think the syndicate's set up another factory in Mars orbit?

'Some progress, Henry,' Colonel Bell said, with a sigh. 'But like I said, it's a big job: there are thousands of satellites in orbit round Earth, Moon, and Mars and each one has to be checked against an operating licence. We're maybe a third of the way through. Nothing illegal has come to light so far.'

'Thank you,' Leighton said. 'Keep us informed, won't you?'

For God's sake...

Leighton was looking at his notes. 'Last time we met we discussed the possibility of a factory on Mars surface – that's right, isn't it, Claudia?'

'Yes, in one-third Earth's gravity they could make a product that's impure but still eminently marketable.'

That's more like it.

'Captain Marks, you were looking into this. Any sign of installations on Mars surface?'

Lauren Marks said, 'No, sir. I've studied the most recent satellite surveys of Mars. They're very detailed but as yet there's nothing I couldn't identify as a legitimate construction.'

Someone sighed.

'Sir?' she continued. 'I do have some more thoughts on that.'

'Yes?'

'They could still have a factory there. For example, an

underground factory wouldn't show up from space.'

Absolutely. It's the only way they'd do it.

Zobel was frowning. 'They'd have had to complete it well inside two years.'

Not a problem. They'd just throw a lot of money at it.

'That's not impossible, Mrs Zobel,' Marks said. 'Anyway, I'll keep looking.'

For a few moments no one spoke. Dan had had enough. They were floundering and the whole thing was getting nowhere. He took a deep breath.

'You're missing something.'

11

Leighton lifted an eyebrow. 'Major Larssen?'

Dan leaned forward and placed both hands on the table. 'Go back three years and put yourself inside the heads of the syndicate bosses. They have a very productive factory orbiting Mars but things have changed: it's no longer safe to assume the location is secret. Okay, they move the satellite straight away to a new location. Are they going to launch, or repurpose, another one in case the first one gets hit? I don't think so. These people are not dumb. They know you'll be looking for them in Mars orbit now.'

'Go on.'

'So what's the next best thing? Like Mrs Zobel said: Mars surface. Easier to hide, and they can still turn a good profit on what they make. Better still, you people are all over the place, trying to intercept shipments at destination instead of source.'

Leighton's lips tightened. 'There are good reasons for that policy, Major. In *this* country we can be reasonably sure that outgoing cargo is being monitored in an efficient and professional manner. In *other* countries that may not be the case. In many places – Africa, South America, the

Middle East, for example – bribing officials to look the other way is accepted practice. If we're going to protect our interests the only effective strategy is to examine cargo when it arrives at its destination.'

'Which isn't working.'

Kennedy shifted uncomfortably in his seat. A flush had risen into Leighton's face.

'Are you about to make some sort of suggestion, Major Larssen?'

'Yes, I am. You need to focus on the bottleneck. Look, suppose they *have* set up a factory on Mars. When it comes to moving the product they have a problem. Shuttles can't take off from just anywhere, they need a runway. But there isn't a runway because if there was one Captain Marks here would have spotted it when she looked at the satellite surveys. So what does that mean? It means they have to try to conceal their shipments in amongst legitimate traffic. There's only one shuttle terminal on Mars and that's the one outside Tharsis City. It's a busy spaceport now, because it has to serve not only the main colony but also the process plants and mining settlements at Enterprise and Arestes. Their transports all come along Highway 4 to the shuttle terminal. That's where the drug shipments would need to come, too.'

Leighton's eyes narrowed. 'You're saying if we can't locate the factory directly, we should work backwards from the shipments?'

'That's exactly what I am saying.'

Kennedy was looking back and forth between the two of them as if it were a tennis match.

'That's totally impractical! It's a busy highway. We can't stop and search every freight skimmer coming along it!'

'Of course you can't. You'll have to do it when they're unloading.'

Leighton said, 'Kennedy, you've spent time at the Mars spaceport. Is that feasible?' His tone suggested it was not.

'Um, actually I think it is, sir. "Spaceport" makes it sound grander than it is. Basically it's a complex of big transit hangars. Originally there were two main ones: Hangar A for passenger use only and Hangar B for cargo. As things expanded Hangar B couldn't handle the volume of stuff coming from Enterprise and Arestes any more, so now it only deals with the smaller stuff going to and from Tharsis City. They built a third hangar, Hangar C, specifically to handle bulky cargo from the west.'

'There you go,' Dan said. 'Hangar C is your bottleneck. If drugs are coming along Highway 4, that's where they're going, and that's where you should concentrate your resources. What sort of inspection do you have in there at the moment?'

Again Leighton redirected the question to Kennedy, who said, 'The usual spot checks.'

'Not good enough. You're looking for maybe one container among hundreds. Your hit rate's too low. You need to check everything that comes through.'

Leighton's mouth opened, but Kennedy was nodding thoughtfully. 'It could be done if we had a powerful terahertz source in there. We could scan the containers as they passed through the beam.'

'What about the containers themselves?' Dan asked. 'Won't they block the beam?'

'No, they're made of lightweight reinforced plastic to maximize the payload on the spacefreighters. That material wouldn't hold back the beam from a sufficiently high-power generator.'

'I don't know, I don't understand this,' Leighton said. 'If the technology exists why aren't we using it already?'

'We are, actually, sir. We have one in Hangar B, monitoring incoming cargo destined for Tharsis City in case it contains drugs.'

'Only the one?'

'I'm afraid so. We have a few of the portable terahertz generators but high-power ones like we're talking about are costly. Our resources are limited so, like the Major said, we've concentrated on picking up shipments at the point of arrival. For Tharsis City that's Hangar B, and for Earth it's the shuttle terminals, all of them.'

So typical of these organizations, Dan thought. The people at the sharp end are spread far and wide, strapped for resources. Meanwhile Leighton swans around with a flotilla of C-classes, tossing torpedoes at a derelict satellite. If the man had spent the same money on staff and equipment, he could have dealt with the real problem by now.

He resisted the temptation to voice his thoughts.

Leighton said to Kennedy, 'How long would it take to get another one?'

'Delivery on something like that is several weeks. After that it'd take another three weeks to get it out there and maybe a week for commissioning. You're looking at two months, minimum.'

Zobel seemed to have registered Leighton's pained expression. 'That doesn't sound too bad to me, Henry.'

He sighed. 'You don't understand, Claudia. We're under a lot of pressure here, and I've just undertaken an expensive operation. In my view it was absolutely necessary, but when it comes to tangible results – well, right now we have very little to show for it.'

There was a rare hint of vulnerability in the admission and Dan felt a flash of sympathy. It was true the satellite had to be destroyed – if not it could be started up again at any time – but that was unlikely to cut much ice if it had no obvious effect on the trade. At least not with the kind of people who were breathing down Leighton's neck.

Dan said, 'Look, there's an easy solution. You've already got a powerful terahertz generator in Hangar B. Redeploy it. Put it in Hangar C. Right now it's of more use to you there.'

'If you're right about the route,' Leighton said.

'Yeah, if I'm right. Give it a few months. If I'm wrong you won't pick anything up and you can put your generator back where it came from.'

Kennedy said, 'Excuse me, sir, we could do that. The generator's mounted inside a small truck. It could be taken over to Hangar C and just parked at the side of the entry line. The beam's invisible so no one would know what it was doing there.'

No one spoke. Every head was turned towards Leighton.

The Deputy Commissioner hesitated, then nodded. 'All right, arrange it, would you? The moment it's in place, I want a snatch squad on permanent duty in that hangar. Let's see if the syndicate really is routing drug shipments down that Highway.'

Colonel Bell's face lightened. 'Henry, does this mean we can draw a line under the satellite census?'

'No, sorry. Let's not get too carried away. What we've been discussing is speculative. We have no evidence there's a factory on Mars. Even if we get evidence it doesn't mean they haven't got one in orbit as well. We have to cover every possibility.'

Bell grimaced. 'It's just that it's taking such a lot of resources.'

'Like I said before, Steven, we're all under pressure, and the pressure comes from the very top. The President is deeply concerned about the drug problem. Organized crime is prospering and we have a huge increase in casual crime, ninety per cent of which is committed by people desperate to feed a drug addiction. Of those drugs Dramatoin is the worst by a very long way. The President wants to come down hard on the trade. He also wants to curb the market that drives the trade. You've probably heard about the new Drug Education Scheme, set up to ensure youngsters are made aware of the risks while they're still at school.'

'It's all very well for the President to demand this and that,' Bell grumbled. 'He needs to match the rhetoric with an increase in our allocations.'

Leighton nodded. 'I'm with you there, Steven, but right now we have to operate within the budgets we have.'

Kennedy said, 'Sir, could I go back to what Mrs Zobel said earlier – about the E-class that encountered the pirate fleet three years ago? The pilot did transmit the coordinates of the attack but we didn't act on the information because, as I understand it, it never got through. Do we know why?'

Much as he appreciated Kennedy's tact, Dan was beginning to find this embarrassing. 'Look,' he said, 'I don't mind being up front about this. I was the pilot of that E-class.' The room went very quiet. All eyes were on him. 'I transmitted the coordinates because I suspected there was a factory not far away. Mission Operations for that flight were overseen by one of the directors of Spacefreight, a man called Karl Stott. It turned out he was the one who decided not to pass the message on.'

Kennedy said, 'Why?'

'He claimed the whole pirate business was wild speculation, said he'd have been a laughing stock if he took it seriously.'

Claudia Zobel said, 'We've had our eye on Karl Stott, so has the FBI. We suspect the real reason he didn't pass the message on was that he was in the pocket of the syndicate.'

'But he wasn't charged?' Kennedy said.

Zobel gave the young man a sad smile. 'Do you know who his father is?'

Kennedy's eyes narrowed. 'Not Fleet-Admiral Jurgen Stott?'

'The same. We'd need to have cast-iron evidence before bringing charges against his son.' She shrugged. 'Anyway, all that's water under the bridge. Karl Stott was forced to resign his directorship so I guess he's out of the equation now.'

12

'Can I get you anything else for your breakfast, sir?'

James, Fleet-Admiral Jurgen Stott's butler, gave a deferential half-bow. His matt black tunic and trousers, the standard attire of the Admiral's house staff, were spotless and immaculately pressed.

Stott pushed aside the Agenda and papers he'd been reading.

'No thank you, James.'

'And Mr Karl?'

Karl Stott opened his mouth but his father spoke for him.

'No, he's finished, too.'

Karl winced but said nothing.

'And may we expect you both for dinner this evening?'

'Yes. We'll be in.'

'Very good, sir. The staff will clear the table when you're ready.'

The door closed quietly behind the butler and the Admiral glanced at Karl, then tilted his head and looked more closely, registering the bloated face and pasty complexion. Karl, apparently aware of the examination, looked up. The pupils of his grey eyes were like pinpoints.

Jurgen Stott frowned. 'Are you all right, son? You're not looking well.'

'I'm okay, really. It's just this whole rotten business; it's enough to make anyone ill.'

'It doesn't seem to have affected your appetite,' his father remarked drily, his gaze wandering over the debris on Karl's plate, the remains of a substantial portion of bacon, sausages, hash browns, and fried eggs.

'Food's a comfort for me,' Karl said, rubbing a plump upper arm in what had become an increasingly habitual gesture. 'It's well-known, that, isn't it? People eat when they're unhappy, and I'm unhappy. I've lost my Directorship, my status, my secretary, my staff – everything.'

His father nodded slowly. Then he checked his watch, rose, went over to the window, and stood there, his hands linked behind his back, looking out. A small group of security men were walking down the front drive on their way to relieve the others in the grounds and at the main gate. At the same time an exchange would be taking place in the basement, where a matrix of screens relayed images from cameras throughout the house and grounds. In common with the handful of other fortified mansions in this wealthy outer suburb of Armstrong, the electronic security systems were more elaborate than those of the average bank. All the same, he felt more comfortable having live-in security staff as well. Someone of his influence couldn't be too careful. He turned back to his son.

'My world has shrunk, too, Karl, but we're not isolated. So what if we have our offices here instead of downtown? We have access to all the key networks. We can stay in touch.'

'It's all right for you, you're still on the Board of the Academy and Chiefs of Staff. I wouldn't be considered for anything now – my reputation's in rags. It's all Larssen's doing. You saw what happened in Court, those cheap lawyer tricks. That's how he works. He was always out to get me. He tried at Academy too, only it backfired on him and we got him thrown out.' He gave a satisfied grunt.

The Admiral nodded thoughtfully. 'I had him pegged as a troublemaker back then. I should have dealt with him more firmly. One thing I've learned about strategic warfare, Karl, is the value of the disproportionate response. You can pull the wings off a wasp and it will still turn round and sting you. Best to crush it with your boot.'

A curious light entered Karl's pale eyes. 'That's what I'm going to do, father – crush him like an insect.'

He shook his head. 'Not now, son. You're angry and angry people make mistakes. Take my advice: bottle your anger. Bide your time. Stay in control. Deal with Larssen when the right moment comes, but do it with a cool head.'

*

Maida hastened along the dimly lit corridor, with its perfumed air, deep-piled, plum-coloured carpet, matching flock wallpaper, and antique velvet-and-gold sofas. Although she oversaw the sex parlour in south Armstrong the chain was owned by Hernandez Raoul, the new head of the Rostov syndicate. And Raoul had seen no reason to change the existing management, which was in the hands of Elke Klitgaard.

A door opened and a long-legged girl emerged from one of the many rooms, gathering a sheer peignoir around her. She wiped back a tress of blond hair.

'Zena,' Maida whispered as she hurried by. 'I spotted

Elke coming into the building. Pass the word.'

Zena froze for an instant and her face blanched. Then she nodded and scurried off. Maida felt a little better. She liked to think of herself as a surrogate mother figure – in her teens she'd trodden a similar path to her girls and she knew what it was all about. At least now the girls could make themselves scarce, or as scarce as the needs of their clients would permit. Elke had a reputation for a degree of smiling viciousness, some sort of sexual satisfaction derived from what she called 'disciplining' girls for real or imagined misdemeanours, and she clearly relished the terror it incited in the others. The ones who'd been closeted for a while with Elke never worked again. Maida ran the tip of her tongue round her lips, drew a shaky breath, and turned into the vestibule.

Elke was standing there, dressed expensively as usual, this time in a black trouser suit with a cream silk shirt and cravat. Her lips tweaked in the slightest of smiles.

'Hello, Maida.'

Maida did her best to keep the tremor out of her voice. 'Hello, Elke. Please come through. We'll use my office.'

Almost as soon as Maida had settled behind her desk Elke extended her hand in a wordlessly imperious gesture. Maida took a tablet computer from a drawer and placed it in the waiting hand, then watched anxiously across her desk as the woman crossed her legs and went through the accounts. Maida had triple-checked the figures; she knew better than to allow the slightest error to creep in.

Elke handed the tablet back across the desk. 'No new clients, then.'

'No, it's been quiet. But we have our regulars.'

Elke nodded. 'Including Karl Stott.'

'Yes.'

'It's a while since we had anything useful from him. We need to increase the pressure. Tell Zena—'

'Zena doesn't see him any more, Elke. Only Papillon.'

Elke's thin lips curved in another bleak smile. 'Things are progressing nicely, then. The Blaze—is he still sniffing?'

'Not any more. He had a big problem recently, came to her in quite a state. She grabbed the opportunity and gave him a shot. He really enjoyed that. He doesn't want it the other way any more.'

'Good. Get her to increase the dose. The more they have, the more they want.' Her mouth set tightly. 'I'll make that pompous little sleazeball grovel before I've finished with him.'

'Elke, she's got him on a pretty steep dose already. Increasing it more – well, you know how it can send them right over the edge.'

Elke waved a hand dismissively. 'That's unimportant. If he brings in some useful information it's worth it. If he does go over the edge – well, what has it cost us? A few grams of Blaze, that's all. I'll get you the stuff.'

'All right, Elke. It's your call.'

'Of course it is. Tell Papillon I want it done on his next visit.'

'I'll tell her. She's a good girl. It won't be hard for her, either. She despises him.'

Elke nodded. Then, casually, 'Any problems with the other girls?'

'No,' Maida said quickly. 'We have an excellent team at the moment. They can offer a good range of expertise.'

'Good. We wouldn't want clients turned away because we can't satisfy their tastes.'

'No question of that.'

Elke placed her large handbag on her lap. 'And you would tell me if there was a problem, wouldn't you, Maida?'

Maida eyed the handbag. She knew about some of the things Elke kept in it. Her breathing quickened and she swallowed hard to control it. 'Yes, of course. But there isn't. Not at the moment.'

Elke slipped the strap of the bag over her shoulder and got up. 'Very well. Until next time, Maida. So nice to see you again.'

Maida followed her out to the vestibule, watched her get into the waiting skimmer, then came back to her office, closed the door and leaned against it for a moment, her heart thumping. She took a deep breath, clawed back hair that was damp with sweat, and went to see Papillon.

13

Dan wasn't expecting any further contact from Leighton or Kennedy for the moment. Nothing would happen until the new monitoring system had been set up on Mars, and only then if they picked up a drug consignment. He hoped his idea worked. He had a strong feeling there was a factory somewhere out there on the Martian surface and it would be good to nail it properly.

Meanwhile he had his job to do. They were expecting a special delivery at the Test Establishment this morning and the pilots had filtered into the Common Room to wait.

He brought his coffee over to sit with Andy Cogswell.

'Any news on what's coming in, Andy?'

'Not that I've heard. Unusual for Barry to keep things as tight as this—'

He stopped short and they looked at each other. Both of them had registered the faint noise of engines.

They got up and went over to one of the big windows to watch, joined at the next window by Tim Almond and another pilot, Jan Emans. They were the only four around at the moment; Simon and Raffi were still downstairs in the gym and Joe Lau was away on an assignment. The craft came into view.

Andy grunted in disgust. 'Shuttles!'

'Must be something different about them, Andy,' Tim called out. 'Else they wouldn't bring them all the way from Seattle for testing.'

The two shuttles flew past, straight and level at the same height, one slightly behind the other. They traversed the length of the runway before turning for the run in.

'They don't look too different,' Andy said.

The craft were banking now, the stubby ogival wings a clear silhouette against the sky.

Dan pointed. 'Do you notice something about the fuselage, Andy? A sort of swelling just aft of the wings?'

'Yeah, I see it.'

The shuttles levelled out and approached the runway. Dan's voice rose in alarm. 'What the hell are they playing at? They're going way too slow! They're going to stall!'

But they didn't stall. Instead they slowed to a hover opposite the Control Tower. A cloud of dust rose as they settled gently on the runway. Even through the windows they could hear the rise in the engine notes as the new arrivals taxied to the apron. The pilots looked at each other with bemused expressions. There were plenty of craft with short or vertical take-off and landing capability but no one had ever seen a shuttle do anything like that before. Landing one usually took the entire length of the main runway.

'Well,' Jan said. 'They're different all right.'

Dan's thoughts were racing.

They'd better locate that factory fast. If the syndicate gets hold of one of these babies it'll be a whole new ball game.

Normal test flying was cancelled for the day so that staff could attend the briefing. The two shuttle pilots came into the Seminar Room still in their flight suits. The man with them was wearing a dark blue, high-necked civilian jacket of the type advertised in expensive fashion magazines. Barry Curtis was behind him. The four stood around for a while, talking and drinking coffee in a small group. The staff chatted separately, casting the occasional glance at the newcomers. Simon and Raffi had come up from the gym, and most of the tech staff and ground crew were present, too. Barry clapped his hands to start the meeting and they all took seats.

'Let me introduce Dr Julian Grayston, Deputy Head of Design at BG Aerospace Corporation. He's going to talk to us about the remarkable machines they've just flown in.'

Grayston's boyish features were flushed. He loosened the designer jacket, ran his fingers through a lock of dark hair that was already perfectly in place, and smiled at the audience.

'Hi, everyone. What just landed are the first prototypes of a new shuttle, the C-230 Trojan.'

Dan absorbed the information without surprise. It had a C designation because shuttles were primarily designed for transferring cargo, even if they were trans-atmospheric. The old shuttle was designated C-200 and it didn't have a name, although its pilots had given it plenty, by far the most polite being 'Flying Brick', a reference to its boxy fuselage.

'It's going to need a fresh Certificate of Air- and Space-worthiness, which is why we've brought these two here. My job is to tell you a bit about the design brief and how it's been met.

'Okay, first the brief. I'm sure everyone here is familiar with the shuttle currently in service. Three main thrusters and low-speed manoeuvring with independent auxiliary engines. Frankly a bit of a pig to dock.'

There was a murmur of laughter. Every cadet had to learn to fly shuttles, and docking cleanly and successfully took long, boring hours of training.

'So, Space Fleet wanted a new design, something easier to manoeuvre and dock. But they wanted more than that: VTOL capability. That would mean shuttles wouldn't need five-mile runways, just very simple bases – handy for operating on the Moon or Mars.'

He gestured with one hand. 'What you've seen out there are the prototypes. Externally the craft isn't too different except for an expansion on the fuselage aft of the wings. It has the same cargo capacity and the layout in the cockpit is almost identical. So what's changed? Answer: I've managed to do away with the auxiliary engines. Instead of the auxiliaries I've used vectored thrust, controlled by on-board feedback systems so as to preserve balance, whether the shuttle is empty or carrying a full cargo.'

He looked around the room, evidently expecting a reaction. There wasn't one. He continued, 'Okay, that's the general picture. Internally there was a lot of work to do to make room for the vectoring, rerouting of services, fuel lines, and so on. Don't worry about that part – we did a lot of computer simulation and our own testing shows everything to be on spec. And let me say this. When this project was put in my hands I knew the company had served up a real challenge. But each time I see one of those babies land I get a great feeling, because I know I've come up with a classic design.' Again he looked around the room, this time with a self-assured smile.

Some of those present shifted uncomfortably in their seats or exchanged looks. Crowing about your own achievements didn't go down well at the Establishment.

Grayston seemed unaware of this as he said, 'If you

have any questions, either for me or for the pilots, we'll be happy to answer them.'

Andy raised a hand. 'Apart from the vertical take-off and landing capability, what difference does vectoring make to the low speed handling?'

Grayston said, 'Um, I think Captain Thoreau could answer that.'

He nodded at one of the pilots, who stood up. 'Basically it's just smoother, more predictable. The vectoring is managed electronically, of course, so you're not aware of any of that. You move the throttle to increase or decrease power and you twist to get more vectoring, and that's fed in automatically according to where you've positioned the joystick. The other difference is the power of the main engines. They've been uprated to cope with the vectoring, so when you're on direct thrust you'll notice a real kick in the butt.'

Jan raised his hand. 'What about the vertical landing? Anything special about that?'

The pilot nodded. 'You know how easily one of these babies could stall on you unless you kept the nose up and the airspeed high? Well it doesn't happen any more. the Trojan has the same small aerodynamic surfaces but when you throttle back, the vectoring comes in automatically. It really doesn't take a lot of practice to set one down like we did here today.'

Raffi was sitting next to Jan. 'Are all three engines vectored?'

Grayston fielded that one. 'Actually no, just the top centre one. But, like Captain Thoreau just said, all the engines have been uprated to compensate, mainly by improving the liquid fuel injection system and redesigning the ignition chambers to increase the efficiency of burn. In fact the total thrust from two of these engines isn't far short of the three on the current model. That's why it gives you such a boost when you have all three on direct thrust.'

There were no other questions. Barry went to the front. He spoke first to Grayston.

'I take it you have all the telemetry on board both craft.'

'Absolutely. Standard set-up. You'll be able to monitor every function you want from here.'

'Good. We'll check all that out in the morning.' He turned to his staff. 'Okay, Space Fleet is impatient to get this model into production so we'll start testing properly tomorrow. Normally we'd spend a week or two with the manuals and sims but this model's not a great departure from the previous one and we've been told we can skip a lot of that. Andy? I'd like you to take it on. Dan, you fly the chase plane – use the T-903. Andy, while we've got these two pilots here it would be a good idea for you to go over the controls with them, and maybe get the hang of the short take-off and landing. That's the major new feature. No need to do any more than that just now. Okay?'

'Sure, Barry.' Andy turned to Dan and winked.

Andy's pleasure was written all over his chubby face. There wasn't a pilot in the room who didn't want to get his hands on one of these new machines and he was the one who'd been chosen.

As they filed out of the room Dan moved next to his friend and gave his arm a squeeze. 'Go for it, Andy.'

*

Andy spent a couple of days on the simulator familiarizing himself with the handling of the C-230 Trojan, then told Barry he was ready. When everything had been set up, Dan walked out to the apron with him. The T-903 trainer he'd be using to fly escort had already been towed out and fuelled. It looked very small and sleek alongside the shuttle, which was the size of a large business jetliner but had all the grace of a freight skimmer. They took off together with Dan watching every move from the T-903. They landed an hour later.

'All right, Andy?' Dan asked as they returned to the building.

'Seems to handle okay,' Andy replied. 'Better than the other shuttles I've flown, that's for sure.'

They spent each of the next three days putting the shuttle through its paces. On the third day they had lunch together, consisting of coffee and a Vitabar. They never ate much when they were flying.

'Everything's within spec at the moment, Dan. It flies immaculately. Barry says we should push the envelope a bit this afternoon. Pull some g on the turns, see how it behaves with more extreme handling.'

'No one's going to fly a shuttle like that, Andy.'

He shrugged. 'Routine part of the certification process. They need to know it's always going to be flown well within design limits. You know the score. It's our job to make sure those limits are what they should be.'

'Yeah, well, take it steady at first. Those wings are too small to help much, even in Earth's thick atmosphere. You'll be depending heavily on this new vectored system.'

Andy glanced at his watch. 'They're refuelling now and the ground techs need a break. We'll take off in an hour, okay?'

Dan spent the time dealing with some paperwork. An hour later they rolled out. Andy was using the runway now, a short take-off being more economical on fuel than vertical take-off. Dan was on his wing as they took to the sky and climbed to twenty thousand feet.

Andy spoke to Barry and the ground techs over the comms. 'Target height, straight and level, Mach 0.83.'

'Okay, Andy.' Barry's voice. 'Commence the schedule.'

'I copy. Turn ninety degrees port on my mark. Three… two… one… mark.'

The shuttle tipped over and went into a tight turn. Dan couldn't hold the same radius; the vectored thrust gave the big shuttle amazing manoeuvrability. They levelled out and he regained station.

Andy's voice again. 'Commencing turn ninety degrees starboard. Three… two… one… mark.'

Dan throttled back and managed to pull round behind him. He was watching the craft for any sign of stress. Also by flying slightly above Andy he could usually see when vectored thrust was operating; either there'd be a gush of flame or vapour from the chemical fuel or the ground below would shimmer in the heat from the nozzles. He could see no problems.

They continued to follow each other through banking turns, short and long dives. A loop with a roll out of the top brought a whoop from Andy and Dan smiled. They entered another steep banking turn followed by a dive. The smile on Dan's face faded.

'Andy, I can't see anything from those vectored nozzles.'

Andy's voice came over the comms link.

'Yep, top centre engine's out. Vectoring's gone. Reverting to manual.'

They continued to dive and Dan's pulse quickened.

'Andy, you're too low. Pull up, man.'

A grunt. 'Something's wrong with manual control, Dan.

I'll try some workarounds…'

They were doing six-fifty knots at two thousand feet and the altitude needle on Dan's head-up display was spinning crazily as their height evaporated.

'Andy, for Christ's sake pull up.'

'Still not responding. Trying to restart top centre engine…' His voice was deadly calm.

The ground was coming at them fast. Dan's heart banged in his chest. 'Eject, Andy. Dump the fucker!'

'Can't do that, Dan. It'll come down in Armstrong.'

Dan looked up. The high rise buildings of the city centre were clearly visible on the horizon, five miles away. Andy was right. On this trajectory the craft would plunge into the crowded streets of the suburbs.

'I'm going to roll.'

Dan's back went cold. At this speed there was probably enough control surface on the wings to bank the craft, but without lift and without vectored thrust it would plunge into the ground.

'Andy, try to get clear…'

He watched helplessly, staying with the shuttle as it rolled slowly over and went down.

The runway of the Space Fleet Test Establishment crossed below them. Now they were over open country but Armstrong was ahead, growing larger every second. The shuttle was still going down.

Dan whispered, 'Eject, Andy. Please eject…'

A ball of flame blossomed below him, followed by a rising mushroom of black smoke. The shuttle had crashed two miles short of Armstrong.

Dan pulled out, looking over his shoulder. There was no parachute.

14

Barry Curtis called a meeting at 1100 hours the following day, all staff to attend. It would be held in the Conference Room, which was above the Common Room and had a similar view over the runway.

When Dan went in he saw that the ground techs and several pilots were already there, sitting around the table. Dan joined Craig Allsop, the chief tech. Looking up he saw that Grayston was at the end of the table, with vacant seats next to him. He must have flown in from Seattle earlier.

Barry himself was late. They waited in silence. No one wanted to speak to Grayston; his presence was felt but not acknowledged.

The door opened and Barry entered the room. He flopped into a chair, his features slack with grief and exhaustion. His gaze travelled slowly around the table.

'I've just come from seeing Andy's family. You can well imagine the state they're in. I told them he could have saved himself but a lot of people would have died if he'd let the shuttle crash in Armstrong. He knew that and he chose the hard way. He wasn't just a fine pilot and a superb engineer; he was a goddamned hero.' He sighed. 'The

Trojan's tanks were nearly full of UDMF and oxidant. When I went out there with the second wave of emergency vehicles we drove through a field of debris over a mile in diameter. At its centre there was a smoking crater a hundred feet across. If that Trojan had come down in the city's suburbs there would have been absolute carnage.' His mouth set and he glared at Grayston. 'All right, I want to know why. Why has this "slightly modified" craft taken the life of one of my best pilots and left a woman without a husband, and a young child without a father? Why?'

Grayston fidgeted but said nothing.

Barry's gaze shifted to Craig Allsop.

'Craig?'

The man next to Dan stirred. 'Cause of crash was a flame-out in the top-centre propulsion unit. Left Andy without vectored thrust and for some reason the manual back-up was ineffective. He was on a steep trajectory. He couldn't correct it.'

'Dan?'

'That fits with what I could see. It had been performing normally, but something went badly wrong during the bank and dive. When Andy said it wasn't responding I couldn't see anything from the vectored nozzles. He said he'd lost manual control, too. I told him to eject, but…' Something rose into Dan's throat and choked off the words. He looked down, shaking his head.

'Well, Dr Grayston?'

Grayston ran his tongue round his lips. He said, 'I've looked over the telemetry charts and Major Cogswell's reports following the test flights before the… ah, er… last one. It seems the craft was behaving perfectly up to that point. I can only suggest those final manoeuvres were outside design limits.'

Dan felt the blood rush to his face and he opened his mouth to say something, but Barry responded first.

'They were not,' he snapped. 'I've looked at those manoeuvres carefully. Sure, they were more extreme than you'd get in normal flying, but that's precisely what we're here to do. The accelerometers show the airframe was not unduly stressed. No way does that explain a catastrophic failure of this sort. And any craft like this should have redundant systems. Why did reversion to manual fail?'

Grayston shrugged. 'Look, I'm just as unhappy about this as—'

Barry interrupted and his voice was louder and harsher than Dan had ever heard it. 'No, Dr Grayston, you could not possibly be as unhappy about this as I am – as everyone here is.'

The man swallowed. 'All right, then I have to conclude that there was some fault in the building of this particular prototype.'

Dan stabbed his middle finger on the table. 'Or a fundamental problem with the design.'

'I find that hard to believe. All the simulations, all your own test results up to that point, show that the craft was behaving within specification. The only explanation that makes any sense is that a vital component failed or that something worked loose in those rather extreme manoeuvres. Of course, without the craft we can't verify that.'

Dan took a deep breath. BG Aerospace would deny direct responsibility, wouldn't they? That was to be expected. They had to protect their reputation, and no doubt they were trying to wriggle out of a law suit. He ignored Grayston and spoke to Barry.

'Barry, there's only one way to resolve this. There's a

second prototype down there. Let me take it up.'

Barry's mouth opened slightly and he blinked. 'Are you crazy, Dan? Do you think I'm going to risk another of my pilots in that flying coffin!'

Grayston said, 'Mr Curtis, please, it's not in any way—'

Dan spoke over him. 'Barry, we'll take our time, and I'll go through the same schedule as Andy followed. When it comes to the extreme manoeuvres I'll make sure I'm lined up with the runway, that way I won't be pointing at Armstrong. And believe me, if that thing tries to kill me I won't hesitate – I'll eject.'

'It's too risky. You haven't had any familiarization on it—'

'I have. I've flown it in the simulator and Andy took me over the controls on the second day. I even tried hovering and putting it down. That's not a problem. Barry, please let me do this. It's the only way we'll ever know whether this was a one-off or a basic design fault. We need to find out before anyone else gets killed.'

There was a long silence. Then Barry took a deep breath. 'All right. Joe Lau should be back this afternoon. I'll get him to fly chase. But for God's sake be careful.' He stood and the others rose and filed out without a word.

No one made eye contact with Grayston.

*

'Are you sure about this, Dan?' Joe Lau said, as they walked out to the apron where the T-903 and the second Trojan were standing. 'You know, when these new shuttles were first delivered we couldn't wait to get our hands on them. Now, well not one of us wants to go near the thing. Except for you, that is.'

'Andy was a good friend to me, Joe. I owe him this

much. Stay on my wing. Watch the nozzles, especially the ventral oblique ones. You can usually see some heat shimmer from them. If it looks like they're not cooking, let me know.'

'Those vents are bled from the top centre engine. I could keep an eye on that one.'

'No, I tried that. With the blast from the two engines below it you just can't be sure. Do like I say. And stay with me, okay?' He donned the comms helmet he'd been carrying under one arm. 'Let's go.'

He went to the Trojan, opened a flap on the side, and pulled a manual release, which swung back the nose cone to reveal the docking ring. Immediately behind it was an airlock that provided for crew access on the ground and cargo transfer in orbit. There was no pressure difference at the moment so the airlock was open. He passed straight through it into the forward cargo bay and up into the cockpit. During orbital training at the Academy he'd flown and docked the C-200 more times than he cared to remember, and the cockpit layout was totally familiar. In a gesture that was close to automatic he flicked the lever switches for the motors that operated the airlock and the nose cone. Nothing else would operate until they were closed and locked.

The motors droned softly as he scanned the area outside. There were no ground vehicles around. Over his left shoulder he could see Joe closing the canopy of the T-903.

Inside, the sounds stopped and the red warning lights on the control panel extinguished, signifying that the nose cone and airlock were closed securely. He went through the flight checks, then activated the starter sequence. The engines wound up. Moments later he was rolling forward.

They took off in formation and Joe clung doggedly to Dan all day. The shuttle handled sweetly. It was responsive, and the controls were far more progressive than Dan had ever encountered on the C-200. Although the disaster was never far from his mind he began to wonder if Grayston was right. Perhaps it was, after all, a failure of a component or a structural weakness, something confined to that particular craft. It was certainly hard to fault the one he was flying, and as they entered the second and third days of testing Dan even began to feel a certain affinity with it.

On the afternoon of the third day they reached the stage of pushing the envelope.

'Straight and level, flight level two-zero. Barry, ready to go.'

He could hear the intake of breath. 'All right, Dan. Now for Christ's sake be careful.'

'I will. Commencing ninety degrees turn to port. Three... two... one... mark.'

When the manoeuvre was completed he glanced out of the left side of the canopy, where Joe was appearing again above his port wing.

'Sorry, Dan. Couldn't stay with you.'

'Throttle back, Joe. With vectored thrust this thing can turn on a dime.'

They went through the schedule as before. Dan even copied the loop with the roll out at the top. The time had come to execute the bank and dive, the manoeuvre that had killed Andy. If anything was going to go wrong it would be now. Andy hadn't been ready for it. Dan would be – he had to be. He did a final check. Everything was working normally.

'Commencing bank and dive. Three... two... one... mark.'

During the steep banking turn he lined up carefully with the distant runway. On the horizon over to the right he could see the high-rise blocks of downtown Armstrong peeking out of that permanent haze of water vapour; ahead of him there was just open landscape, mainly desert. If he had to dump it now there would be no casualties on the ground. He moved the stick forward.

The altimeter needle fell back: five thousand feet, four, three…

A red light flashed on the panel. Engine failure, top centre. Small movements of the stick to each side, then up and down, had no effect. His pulse rate shot up.

Joe Lau's voice. 'Dan, you're going in steep and I can't see anything from the vents.'

He swallowed. 'Okay, problem here. Flame-out on top centre engine. Vectoring's gone.'

He tried to pull out, using the control surfaces of the small wings. Nothing seemed to be working. The airframe shuddered slightly with the increasing speed. It was like riding a projectile. He hauled back harder on the stick, then harder still. He detected a small response. Thoughts flashed quickly through his mind.

Fly-by-wire's gone. It's reverted to manual but control's unassisted.

Barry's voice, taut with concern. 'Eject, Dan, while you still have time.'

A curious calm settled on Dan. 'We won't learn a thing if I do that. I'm going to try to land.'

'Negative, Dan. Don't take any chances!'

'Barry, I have to try. I'm cutting coms now, I need to concentrate.'

'Dan—'

He flicked off the comms and focused on the terrain

ahead. The runway was coming up very fast. He hauled even harder, his grip tight, the knuckles white. He'd never exerted this much force on a joystick. It was designed for light servo-assisted manipulation, not this sort of rough treatment, and he just hoped it wouldn't snap off in his hands. He gritted his teeth.

I'm not going to eject.

He was breathing fast and his whole body seemed to be radiating heat. The craft's nose began to ease up slowly, very slowly. The g pinned him into his seat and he could feel the skin of his face taut against the bones.

His eyes flicked to the head-up display: altitude, rate of descent, airspeed... Altitude was dropping away but the rate of descent was falling, from thousands of feet per second to hundreds to only tens of feet per second. But he was travelling too damned fast.

The near end of the runway rushed towards him and passed underneath in a blur. He continued to edge the nose up. He was still flying like a shell out of a gun, only feet above the ground, but at last he'd got it straight and level. A mile of runway passed underneath him, two miles, three...

It was still way too fast. If he overshot the runway he'd be into rough terrain and any attempt to put down there would mean certain disaster. Somehow he had to slow down. Did he dare to lower the undercarriage or would it be ripped off? If it stayed in one piece the extra drag might just do it.

He made the decision and pulled down the levers. The control panel lit up like a Christmas tree but he felt the instant pull of the deceleration, the weight of his body throwing him forward into his harness. There was a heavy impact as the wheels touched the runway, a long bounce, another impact, another long bounce, a lesser impact, and they were rolling.

He came to rest one hundred yards from the end of the runway and switched off the engines. For a moment he remained slumped forward in his seat. Then he straightened up and inhaled deeply.

He switched comms back on. 'Barry, safely down. You can tow this crate in. I'm walking back.'

*

Before his feet even touched the runway the wail of two-tone sirens was already echoing around the airfield. Three fire trucks reached him just a few minutes later. Two stopped, one on either side of the Trojan. The door of the third vehicle opened and the driver jumped down, grinning broadly.

'Hop in, I'll give you a ride back.'

When they reached the Control Tower it seemed like every member of staff was out on the apron waiting for him. They were clapping, and a cheer went up as he got down from the fire truck. He found himself hustled inside, people patting him on the back. Joe was waiting for him in the debriefing room. He held out his arms and embraced Dan, then stood back, holding him by the elbows. There were tears in his eyes.

'Jesus, Dan, for a moment back there I thought you were going the same way as Andy.'

Dan smiled weakly but he could say nothing. His hands had begun to shake uncontrollably.

'Come on,' Joe said. 'I'll take you home. Barry can debrief you in the morning.'

*

By the time Neraya came in Dan had recovered his customary composure.

She joined him on the sofa. 'You're early. Did you have a good day?'

He grunted. 'Took a turn in that new Trojan, the C-230. With luck we'll find out what happened to Andy.'

Her eyes widened. 'You think it was a design fault after all?'

'No question about it. Our engineers will be going over it as we speak. We'll know what the problem is soon enough.'

She frowned. 'It's that unsafe?'

'It behaved itself prettily to start with, in fact I really started to like it. Now? Well if you'll pardon the expression, I think it's a crock of shit.'

'You didn't take any chances, did you?'

He shrugged. 'Erm, not really.'

'Because you have additional responsibilities now.'

He met her eyes and there was a heavy silence. Her mouth crept into a shy smile.

'You're not!'

'I am.' She bit her lip.

'But I thought you were taking...'

'I stopped. I should have said.' She frowned. 'You're not cross, are you, Danny?'

He swallowed. 'Cross? God, no – it's just, it's just such a surprise! I never thought... It never occurred to me...'

His heart surged and he took her into his arms. Neraya had brought such hope and happiness into his life, and now she would bring even more. Again the past loomed up in the back of his mind, reminding him that the good episodes in his life had always proved ephemeral. He closed his eyes and sighed. *Not this time. Please don't snatch this away from me.*

He pulled back, looking at her anxiously.

'Are you all right? Shouldn't you be taking it easy? I should cook tonight—'

She laughed. 'I'm fine – it's a pregnancy, not a heart attack! Of course, my boss won't be pleased. He'll have to do without me for a short while, but there's time enough for him to plan for that.'

'We should be buying things: a crib, clothes, toys…'

'Danny, darling, there's plenty of time.'

He shook his head. 'I still can't believe it. I don't deserve it.'

'Yes, you do,' she said firmly. 'We both do. We lost our families. It's high time we started our own.'

15

Barry Curtis looked up as Dan came into his office.

'Have a seat.' Dan took the chair in front of the desk and Barry leaned back. 'Dan, that was a pretty dumb-ass thing you did out there – you know that, don't you?'

'It may have looked that way from here, Barry, but I knew what I was doing. If I didn't think there was a good chance of landing that heap I'd have ejected, even above the runway.'

'So how did you manage it?'

'You know, I think the designers drew auxiliary power from the vectored engine, so when it went out the window the servo systems went the same way. For a moment I thought it had left me with nothing. I guess that's what Andy thought, too. He tried to restore control. I just used brute force. It was really heavy but it did respond – enough to put it down.'

Barry frowned, then his expression lightened. He smiled ruefully. 'Well, you scared the shit out of me but it brought results. Our guys have been over that second prototype with a fine-toothed comb. The top centre engine flamed out because there was a vapour lock in the fuel line. Space was limited so the designers had trouble routing it, gave it too tight a radius. You wouldn't get it in normal flying, but the bank and dive manoeuvre showed it up.'

Dan set his lips. 'That idiot Grayston better not show his face at the Centre again. If I don't tear his throat out there are a lot of other guys round here who will.'

'Quite. Well, there'll be some red faces up there in Seattle, and I've no doubt Andy's family will sue them for compensation – and win. The company still has to fulfil their contract so they'll have to make modifications and send us another production prototype.'

'If you can get anyone to fly it.'

'Which brings me to the second point. We're a small team here at the Centre, Dan. Losing someone as experienced as Andy is a real blow, not just personally but from a staffing standpoint.'

'You're always inundated with applications, Barry. Are you saying none of them are suitable?'

'Oh they all have sound resumés but I need more than that. Then a few weeks ago I had an applicant who interested me. Silver for flying during his years at Academy and first class marks throughout, with distinctions in several subjects, including engineering and computer technology. He's flown shuttles, then had a few years on freighters, and he's done some passenger work, mostly atmospheric.'

'But that's exactly the combination you need: engineering knowhow and flying experience.'

'It is, but it's unusual to get it in someone who's only twenty-four.'

Dan blinked. He thought *he* was young to be a test pilot. Most of them were in their thirties and forties.

Barry smiled. 'Yeah, I know. All the same I decided to

take a look at him. He interviewed well so I put him on the simulator. I'm telling you, Dan, I threw in some real tough emergencies, ones I've seen more experienced pilots flunk. He did all the right things without a moment's hesitation. Then this disaster with Andy, and all of a sudden I've got a vacancy to fill. I tried to think of a reason for not appointing the youngster but all I could come up with was his age. That was no kind of reason, so I'm giving him a chance. Remember how Andy took you under his wing when you first got here? I'd like you to do the same for this guy. I think you're a good role model – when you're not trying to total Trojans on our runway.'

Dan smiled. 'When's he getting here?'

'Later on this morning. We have some paperwork to go through, then I'll give you a buzz.'

'Okay. What's his name?'

'Richard Hoefler. Likes to be called Rick.'

*

'We've got our replacement for Andy,' Dan said to Neraya that evening. They'd finished dinner, and he was bringing a tray of coffee into the living room. Just as Neraya preferred to cook their meals, Dan liked to go through the motions of making the coffee, grinding the beans afresh each time; they both enjoyed it better that way. Neraya put aside the journal tablet she'd been reading and made room on the sofa for him.

He handed her a cup of coffee, poured one for himself and sat down. 'His name's Rick Hoefler. Barry asked me to look after him.'

'What's he like?'

'Well, certainly not what I expected.' He shook his head. 'The guy's only twenty-four. Great resumé, very good grades at the Academy, Silver for flying, the lot. All the same, the Test Establishment is a top drawer job for a flyer, and an amazing appointment for someone as young as that. You'd think he'd be just a little bit awed. Not a bit of it. I showed him around, introduced him to hugely experienced pilots. He gave the impression he was inspecting the premises – and us – to see if we measured up to his standards.'

'He sounds very arrogant.'

'Arrogant? Maybe that's going a bit far; he's talented and he knows it. I told him he'd better be completely familiar with both the systems and the instrumentation on these craft, because if something goes wrong he'll be expected to fix it then and there if possible. You know what he said? "That's why I took the job." Not even "That's why I applied." You know, like he'd weighed the offer up carefully to see if he should really accept it. He was beginning to piss me off so I threw some questions his way as we were going along. They were things that would have sent me back to engineering texts I hadn't looked at since the Academy. He had the answers right at his fingertips.'

'Danny, you'd been through the ringer several times over before you got this job. He's almost fresh out of the Academy. Of course he's more familiar with that material than you were.'

'I guess.' He sighed. 'Well, we'll find out soon enough. The Silverpoint 700's coming in tomorrow. Barry's asked Rick to take it up.'

'The Silverpoint – the one you tested with Tim Almond? It's a bit early for that, isn't it?'

'Exactly what I said to Barry. He gave me some background. The previous version is very popular with the airlines but now they're looking for something bigger. It would be a big order and several companies are tendering. General Aviation thought they had it in the bag with the 700. Then we uncovered those problems and they've had to pull out all the stops to regain their position.'

'That's all very well, but have they got it right now?'

'They say they have.' He drank some coffee and replaced the cup. 'They were trying to save weight with the wings on the one we tested: new alloys and manufacturing techniques. After what happened they reverted to the standard design. That makes sense; the old one was very reliable and it goes together pretty fast. We're not expecting problems so it's a good one for Rick to start with.'

'Is anyone going up with him?'

'Yeah, me. We'll be on it the rest of this week. Another cup?'

'Thanks.' She held out the empty cup and he poured more coffee for her and topped up his own.

'He may be talented,' she said, 'but can he work as part of a team? That's just as important, isn't it?'

Dan nodded. 'He'll probably do okay. Just seems strange, getting someone like that after Andy.'

'Because he's so young?'

'Not so much that. Andy's – Andy was – solid, experienced. A family man. And modest. This guy's not modest, far from it. And I think he likes to play the field.'

'What makes you say that?'

'Well, I suppose girls would find him good-looking with those eyelashes, long dimples and the rest. And he has an exciting job, so it probably impresses them – at least the sort of girls he's interested in. I spent most of the day with him and at the end of it he asked me if I'd like to go to a club he knows. Lot of nice tail, he said. So I said, "Thanks, but I'm in a relationship." And he said, "So what?"'

She smiled and her voice was low and teasing. 'You could have gone.'

He chuckled. 'You know, there isn't any way I could explain how I feel to a young shaver like that. He probably thinks I'm past it. Well, perhaps I am but if so, boy, am I ever glad!'

She tossed her head back and laughed. 'Oh Danny, what a pair we are!'

16

Dan followed Rick Hoefler out onto the apron. It was the fourth day of testing and so far the Silverpoint 700 had performed according to specification. Dan had commented to that effect when they came in the previous evening.

'Yeah,' Rick had responded. 'Gets kind of boring after a while.'

'It's when you get bored that things can catch you out, Rick. You have to stay sharp.'

Hoefler had engaged Dan's eyes and gave him a lopsided smile that was closer to a sneer. 'No worries, man, I'm always sharp.'

Dan had left it at that. Today they were due to push the envelope a bit. Dan was again flying chase in the big B-90P photoreconnaissance aircraft. Remembering the problems Tim had encountered last time, Dan was keeping close station, the Silverpoint on his right, a mere wingspan away.

The test was going well. Steep banking turns to left and right had been completed without incident. They accelerated to transonic speeds, through to supersonic and back, and Rick reported that handling was neutral throughout and there was no flutter. Dan relaxed. They'd completed the day's scheduled manoeuvres and it was time to return to base. He wouldn't separate yet, though; it should be reassuring for Rick to have him there, escorting the test plane down.

They shed altitude and commenced final approach. Without warning, the Silverpoint reared towards him.

In that instant Dan felt his whole life pass before his eyes. All the risks he'd taken, all the dangers he'd faced, and here it was, ending in a mid-air collision. He couldn't bank left for fear that his rising starboard wing would contact the looming aircraft. Instead he put the nose of the Ninety down. The Ground Proximity Warning System immediately went berserk: 'TERRAIN, TERRAIN, PULL UP', and 'SINK RATE, SINK RATE' sounding in his ears and flashing red on the panel in front of him. The ground was coming up fast. He had just enough free air to pull out of the dive and side-slip away.

The crisis was over as quickly as it had begun. He looked up, breathing fast, his heart hammering – to see the Silverpoint complete a barrel roll. Hoefler's chuckle came over the comms link.

'Bit slow there, weren't you, Larssen? I thought you were supposed to be flying chase.'

A surge of fury swept through him.

You stupid little...

He was about to give vent to his feelings, but everything he said would be recorded and transmitted. What he had in mind would sound less than professional when played back in Post-flight Analysis, so he'd save it until they'd landed. He kept it short.

'Quit grandstanding, Rick. Just land, will you?' And then, for the benefit of the control tower, 'B90. Going around.'

As he circled he saw the Silverpoint sink towards the runway, then make a perfect air cushion landing. He completed the circle, lined up the Ninety, landed and taxied in. The engines died, and a few minutes later Dan opened the cockpit and climbed down to the apron. The fear he'd felt earlier had now been transmuted into a cold rage. He stood in front of Hoefler, blocking his way. The young man's cocky grin faded.

'What the fuck was all that about?'

'Ah, lighten up, will you, Dan? It was just a bit of fun.'

'A bit of fun…? Look, I don't give a shit if you want to break your own neck, but I'd prefer it if you didn't take me with you.'

'What are you talking about? Before you even reacted I was moving away from you. You were never in danger – you panicked, is all.'

Dan took a deep breath. 'I did not panic. I reacted to an unexpected situation. These craft haven't been pronounced airworthy yet. Last time we tested that Silverpoint you were flying, a bloody trim tab came off. I thought something like that had happened again. Instead it was just you playing silly buggers.'

'Get yourself a sense of humour, man—'

Dan's left hand darted forward and before Hoefler could recoil he had the flight suit bunched around his neck and he was lifting hard enough to bring the young man onto his toes. 'Now just listen to me for a change. What we do here determines whether or not an aircraft is safe to fly. It's not a job for clowns. If you can't take it seriously, do us all a favour and find yourself another job.'

He let go with a push that sent Hoefler staggering backwards, turned on his heel, and walked into the building.

He was still seething when they joined Barry in Post-Flight Analysis.

'I caught your comms at the end, Dan, something about grandstanding. What happened?'

Hoefler smirked. 'Just a little manoeuvre to round things off.'

Dan's lips were set tightly. Barry looked at him and his eyes narrowed. Then he turned back to Hoefler.

'You're to stick to the agreed schedule, Rick, no more, no less. Understood?'

Hoefler shrugged. 'Sure. Whatever.' He gestured to the room. 'Look, do you need me for this? It was all within spec.'

Barry hesitated, then said. 'No, just go and write your report.'

Hoefler went out, pushing past a tech, who was coming in with the memory squares from the B-90. Dan and Barry sat down to scan through the multichannel telemetry, listening to comms and pausing to examine the camera records whenever the multiple lines snaking across the screen showed a significant excursion up or down.

They came to the final comms exchange.

'Bit slow there, weren't you, Larssen? I thought you were supposed to be flying chase.'

'Quit grandstanding, Rick. Just land, will you?'

Barry rewound and switched to the video. The cameras had captured the Silverpoint banking abruptly towards the chase aircraft, then away and into a barrel roll. He hissed 'Jesus, the stupid bastard' between his teeth. When he turned to Dan his voice was deadly calm. 'I'm sorry, Dan, I made a mistake. Just seemed to me the guy had a lot of talent.'

'Oh, you weren't wrong, Barry. He has heaps of talent.

You saw that manoeuvre. It's no small thing to barrel roll something as big as a Silverpoint and he did it perfectly. Talent's not the problem, it's attitude.'

'Rick's still in his probationary period. You're entitled to lodge a formal complaint. If you do, he's out.'

Dan drew a deep breath. 'I'd hate to be the one who loses the guy his job. He's immature, that's all – over-confident, not frightened enough. Someone or something needs to put the fear of God into him.'

'I can do that all right.' Barry said. They sat in silence for a moment, then he sighed. 'I guess you're right. He's young still, maybe we should cut him a little slack. I'll give him a good talking to, tell him how close he came to being shown the door. I'll also tell him that from now on I'll be watching his every move like a damned hawk.'

*

Next morning Joe Lau and Dan were the first ones in the Common Room. After they'd checked the duty rotas they made for an autochef. Dan spoke the order.

'Two regular coffees, black, no sweetener.'

The machine dispensed the coffees and they picked up the beakers. Dan took an armchair next to him.

'Saw you leave with Rick last night, Joe. Do anything interesting?'

'He asked if I felt like going to a club with him. I said okay. Thought it might be fun.'

'And was it?'

'Nah, he dropped me like a hot brick the moment we got there. He wanted to work the room, especially the girls. The guy certainly gets around – they all seemed to know him. I had a few glasses of juice and left. Wasn't my age group anyway.' He sipped his coffee and swallowed. 'I'll tell you, Dan, I used to be young like him, but only once. Rick wants to do it three times over. I don't know how he lives at that pace.'

'So long as it doesn't affect his work I guess we don't need to worry about that, Joe.'

'I guess not.'

*

Dan said nothing more about the Silverpoint incident, and so far as he was aware Joe didn't mention the night club business to anyone either, but it was a closed community and in some indefinable way things got around. The other pilots were cordial enough towards their young colleague but they maintained a certain distance, and the atmosphere in the Common Room changed in a subtle way whenever he strolled in. Barry appeared to treat Hoefler like anyone else, but Dan knew he was still examining carefully every flight he logged. Evidently there were no more unscheduled departures from his allotted tasks because when his probationary period passed he was still in a job.

If Hoefler had sensed a change in attitude towards him he showed no sign of it. All the same he tended to steer clear of Dan, and fortunately – or more likely thanks to Barry's tactful scheduling – they weren't asked to fly together again. It was an unusual situation but Dan didn't expect it to last. A free spirit like Hoefler would weary of any job, even one as good as this. He'd leave sooner or later and their paths would never cross again.

It would be several years before he found out how wrong he was about that.

17

'What's this guy's name again?' Tim Almond asked.

'Eden Lavister,' Barry replied. 'He's the CEO.'

'The big honcho himself. What does he want?'

'I don't know. He said he'd like to show me round the plant. Said I could bring two of my staff.'

BG Aerospace Corporation, the company that made the Trojan shuttle, had invited a small delegation from the Test Establishment to visit their plant at Seattle. Barry was taking Dan and Tim Almond. They were the sole passengers in one of the company's own executive jets.

Dan asked, 'Barry, is this visit connected with the Trojan that killed Andy?'

'Must be. That's why I chose you two. Apart from me, Tim knew Andy longer than anyone else, and you were up with him when it happened.' He shrugged. 'Well, I guess we'll find out what's on his mind soon enough.'

As they came in to land Dan caught a fleeting view of low, grey, shed-like buildings and a high perimeter fence that continued on either side of the runway. It was the size of a small town. Some Air Force bases were like this.

They'd start with a couple of hangars and an accommodation block for the staff. Then there'd be a change of purpose that called for more aircraft or bigger or more specialized ones and they'd add more buildings to cope with pilots and maintenance and office staff and equipment and spares. You'd end up with a tangle of structures with paths zig-zagging between them, so that walking from one to another was like negotiating a maze. BG Aerospace had probably gone the same route, a small company that had expanded as it became more successful. Now it was a global player and this facility was its hub.

The BGStream touched down, made a short run, turned and taxied back. The perimeter fence passed by on either side, tall, topped with razor wire, with high-intensity lighting installed along its length. There were square boards at intervals, presumably notices warning of electrified wire or dog patrols. Dan had a faint sense of privilege at being inside such barriers. At the same time he was wondering what made that degree of security necessary.

The aircraft came to rest opposite a four-storey building with a lot of glass, which distinguished it from virtually every other building on the site. The flight attendant opened the exit door and deployed the steps and they emerged from the cool, subdued interior of the cabin into dazzling sunlight and air that was hot on their faces and dry enough to sting their lungs.

A young man was waiting for them at the foot of the steps. 'Welcome, gentlemen, I hope you've had a good flight. I'll take you straight up.'

*

The CEO greeted them in a fourth-floor office that would have commanded a decent view if it hadn't consisted mainly of low grey roofs. Barry introduced Tim and Dan, and they gave him guarded nods. They all sat down and a secretary served coffee.

Since Andy's fatal crash Dan had built up a head of steam about this company and he wasn't unwilling to vent it on the grey-haired, expensively dressed man in front of them. But it was Lavister who took the initiative.

'Look, let me say to you at the outset that I'm absolutely mortified by what happened to your colleague. That shuttle should never have left this plant. We've built up a reputation for working to the highest standards in this organization. Reputations like that are hard to acquire and they're all too easily lost. Grayston had a large team working on the project and it amazes me that no one pointed out the design problem and the lack of adequate redundancy in the control systems. He headed the section and he has to take primary responsibility. I've sacked him, and I've told every member of that team that unless they wake their ideas up they'll be out of a job as well.'

Barry's mouth tightened. 'Andy Cogswell was a good friend, Mr Lavister, and a valued member of my staff. He'll be sorely missed.'

'I do understand and I'm sure your impression of the company has been tarnished by the whole dreadful incident. That's why I invited you here. I thought it might reassure you if you had a tour of the plant, saw the detailed design, planning and testing we undertake, and the quality of our manufacturing facilities. If you've finished your coffee we can start right away.'

Lavister stood up and they followed suit. He took a freshly laundered white coat off a peg for himself and handed one to each of them before opening the door. Dan slipped his on, aware that it was more to identify them as visitors than to protect their clothing. As they filed out Tim raised his eyebrows at Dan. He shrugged in return. There was nothing to say.

They walked along the corridor. Lavister said, 'It's all offices on this floor and the one below: administration, finance, paperwork of every sort. All boring stuff for you people, I'm sure, so we'll start on the second floor.'

The second floor was occupied by a single, open-plan space, lit diffusely by glow panels in the ceiling and the electrodimmed, electrogenerating glass in the large windows. More than a hundred operatives were in there, working at computer terminals or big touch screens. The walls were hung with flow charts and drawings. There were some tall pot plants, probably artificial.

'The design office,' Lavister explained. 'All the projects start here, of course.' He gave them a few minutes to walk around, looking at the work stations. Then, 'Okay, downstairs again.'

On the floor below they entered a similar space, this time for testing and simulation. There looked to be just as many operatives as upstairs, all seated at terminals. Again he gave them some time to look around, then they reassembled.

'What conditions can you simulate?' Barry asked.

'Anything that's likely to be encountered, on or off Earth,' the CEO said. 'Laminar or turbulent flow at any speed in any weather with any atmospheric composition. At one time we'd have had to do it with a model inside a huge wind tunnel. These days the flow codes we use are very advanced. We'll be seeing the supercomputer downstairs in just a moment, but with the computing power that gives us we can test every possible condition, all in real time.'

'Everything,' Dan remarked drily, 'except for flow in

fuel lines.'

'Ah, Major, I take your point. Look, we deal with aerodynamic behaviour here. It's the engine suppliers who investigate things like fuel flow. They send us a complete specification. To be fair, it's well known that their specifications tend to be on the conservative side and it's tempting to push the boundaries. Grayston succumbed. He paid the price.'

'So did Andy,' Tim breathed.

The CEO led them down to the basement and into a room full of large cabinets. It was cool here, and the only sound was the faint hum of ventilator fans.

'Conventional data banks and servers for the whole site and an Athelstan cluster capable of 100 zetaflops.'

Tim whistled softly.

'There's back-up to data banks off-site as well, of course,' he continued, pointing to some racks. They walked over to some large cabinets and Lavister placed his hand on one. 'Auxiliary power, in case of an outage. If it's prolonged we have our own generating plant as a fall-back. All right? Let's have a look at some of the manufacturing facilities now.'

They went up the stairs and came out of the office building into the heat of the day. He led the way between buildings, and after several turns they entered one of the hangars. Inside were four large aircraft in various stages of assembly. Dan recognized one of the almost completed ones as a Stratoflier, a long-distance supersonic on which wings merged imperceptibly with fuselage. The aircraft dwarfed the dozens of people working on them, probably women as well as men, although it was impossible to tell beneath the complete protective clothing.

'Quite a few personnel,' Barry commented. 'Don't you

use robots?'

'We do on some of the sub-assemblies. A lot of the components are outsourced, particularly the electronics. The suppliers test them but we have to make sure, so we inspect them and test them here, too. I'll show you that later.'

They surveyed the work in progress then began to walk between buildings again.

Down a side path Dan spotted a pale grey hangar which looked newer than the other buildings. The entrance was covered by a short vestibule and there was someone in it. Two people in fact, because one now detached himself to come out and look at them. To his surprise he saw the man was armed.

Dan stopped and pointed. 'What's in the building over there?'

Lavister said, 'It's another assembly plant. High security.'

'I thought this whole place was high security,' Tim said.

The CEO smiled. 'This is higher security.'

Dan said, 'Can we see inside? We're all Security Class A.'

'Ah, afraid not. Your Class A is government security, designed to protect the national interest. This is company security, designed to protect the confidentiality and commercial interests of the client. It would be quite unethical for me to take you inside.'

Dan's eyes narrowed, but Lavister turned and walked on. End of conversation.

Tim pulled a face at Dan and spoke out of the corner of his mouth. 'Quite unethical, Dan. And we wouldn't want that, would we?'

They grinned at each other like a pair of rebellious

schoolboys.

Dan liked Tim a lot. But then he'd liked Andy a lot. Sometimes it didn't pay to get too close to people in this game.

*

The tour over, they went out to the same aircraft that had flown them in. After take-off they sat around a table and the flight attendant served them coffee. Then she withdrew discreetly to the cockpit and closed the door.

'Interesting tour,' Tim said. 'The guy seemed genuinely sorry about Andy. He didn't have to show us around like that.'

'Oh yes he did,' Barry said. 'Space Fleet is by far their biggest customer. Whatever his feelings about Andy it was a commercial disaster for the company. He has to mend fences quickly. He'll probably be conducting all the Space Fleet top brass round the plant during the coming weeks.'

Dan sipped the coffee. It was fresh and strong. 'I'm curious about that high security project. It was the only hangar I saw with an armed guard on it.'

Tim nodded. 'Must be pretty special. Military, probably.'

'Almost certainly,' Dan said. 'Who would commission a project like that?'

'Who has the resources, you mean?' Barry said. 'China builds their own. The Middle East prefers to buy stuff that's already proved itself in service. The US Air Force could commission aircraft at one time but they're too strapped for cash now. That leaves Space Fleet, either in the hope of selling it or for their own use.' He drank some coffee, then rubbed his lower lip. 'Could be the Morningstar, I suppose.'

'Never heard of it. What is it?'

Barry shrugged. 'I don't have any details but I remember it coming up. I keep an eye on Space Fleet's invitations to tender – gives me a heads-up on what could be coming down the line in a few years' time. This one stuck in my mind because I thought the spec was impossible. Very fast, very agile, multi-role with all-atmospheric capability, including near-vacuum.'

Tim blinked. 'You'd need mega-powerful engines for something like that! Who got the commission?'

'BG Aerospace – that's what I'm saying; they tendered with something called the Morningstar. And that's all I know. Space Fleet keeps a tight lid on the whole thing.'

'Hell of a spec,' Dan said. 'The company must have had to put their top designer on it.'

Tim nodded. 'I hope he's better than Grayston. Dan, press the call button, could you? I could use some more coffee.'

18

Rory Mitchell, Chief Test Pilot for BG Aerospace, gripped the stick and with a subtle flexing of the wrist eased it back a fraction to regain lost height. The engines responded by screaming and the Morningstar rocketed upwards. He was pressed back in his seat, the altimeter on the head-up display spinning crazily, tens of thousands of feet whisking by in seconds. It wasn't exhilarating, it was terrifying. Forty thousand feet, fifty thousand feet, sixty... The sky darkened from a peach colour through brown almost to black. He cast a quick glance at the attitude sensor on the instrument panel and saw that the craft was on its back, turning over at the apex of a gigantic loop. Now it entered the descending limb. The altimeter wound down even more rapidly than on the ascent. The darkness evaporated and stripes of light scanned across the interior of the small cockpit. He touched the controls and began to pull out of the dive. The ground continued to rise quickly towards him, then it fell back and the horizon came into view. The forces relaxed; he was in level flight again. One thousand feet below him the landscape passed in a blur, a desert landscape the colour of tanned leather, littered with rocks and craters of every size. He was going ludicrously fast but he hardly dared to throttle back. Olympus Mons appeared ahead and moments later it was dominating the forward view, towering to the height of three Mount Everests. He touched the stick to turn and bank. Instead the horizon tilted violently and continued to roll over and over, height dropped away and the ground rose up. Panic drilled out along every nerve. He struggled with the controls.

Too late.

The canopy went black.

He took off the special helmet, placed it in a box at the side of the footwell and pressed the button to raise the canopy. For several moments he remained seated, sweat trickling down his neck, his heart banging in his ears. Then he took a deep breath and climbed out of the cockpit of the simulator. He paused on the platform outside to regain his balance, his senses still reluctant to accept reality. Then he took the short flight of steps down to the hangar floor. A couple of engineer technicians were standing close by, watching him curiously. He strode past them without a word. Still in his flight suit, his gauntlets in one hand, he emerged into the open air, went down the path to the next building and up the stairs.

The secretary looked up in alarm as he banged open the door of the Design Office.

'Where's Franc Tomazic?' he demanded.

'Sir, he's in the Special Assembly Plant. Can I—?'

'Don't bother, I'll find him.'

He strode down to the pale grey hangar with the covered vestibule. The two armed guards recognized the Senior Test Pilot but politely indicated the reader at the side of the entrance. He passed his ID card near it, recording his arrival. One of the guards pressed a button and a heavy door slid back.

He entered a large, brilliantly lit hall. Dominating the area were three partially assembled aircraft, swarming with workers wearing white overalls and white, padded overshoes. There was little noise, just an occasional snatch of conversation, the crackle of an arc welder, the buzz of a power tool. The air was cool and odourless; this was a controlled environment. The door slid shut behind him.

He walked alongside the nearest aircraft, unable to keep his eyes off it. The Morningstar was without doubt the most beautiful machine he'd ever set eyes on. It was slim, flattened in the fuselage tapering to a point at the nose. The nanocarbon coating that rendered it invisible to radar made it appear black, yet more than black, as if it were sucking the very light out of the air. He walked past the delicately tapered nose and the stubby wings with their long trailing edges. From this angle the light caught the numerous perforations in the metal skin, vents that redirected the thrust of the engines to give the craft its lift and aerial agility. He slowed, then paused for a moment to look back at the tail pipes of the two massive engines, shrouded to minimize the infra-red signature. Preparing to blast through those openings were twin Wheldons, top-secret propulsion units, each with the power of a rocket and the endurance of a turbojet.

He shook his head slowly, turned and strode on.

He spotted Tomazic talking to one of the senior engineers and went straight up to him.

'Can we talk?'

The two turned in surprise. Tomazic said, 'Hallo, Rory. Sure, come over here. Sorry, Bob, back in a moment.'

He led the way to a small glass-enclosed office area and

closed the door.

'It's unflyable, Franc!'

Tomazic smiled patiently. 'What do you mean?'

'I can't say it more clearly than that. What you're building out there can't be flown.'

Tomazic gestured with the flat of a hand for him to lower his voice. 'Now tell me, what is the problem?'

'I've just come from the sim. Crashed again. I'm telling you, the machine is uncontrollable.'

'It will take getting used to—'

'Look, Franc, I've been flying for thirty years, ten of those as a Test Pilot. I have flown everything from mile-long spacefreighters down through hypersonics, supersonics, rotaries, and straightforward atmospherics. I have never encountered anything I couldn't fly – until now. If I say the Morningstar is uncontrollable, take it from me, it is.'

'Rory, you have to understand. This is a completely new design philosophy. Those engines are immensely powerful—'

'You can say that again.'

'They have to be. We've designed—'

'What you've designed, Franc, is an engineering triumph, a thing of beauty, an aeronautical wonder – and an ergonomic disaster. Human reflexes are just not fast enough to cope with that speed of response. You don't want a man in that pilot's seat, you need a goddamned robot.'

Tomazic shook his head from side to side, the patient smile still there but wearing thin at the edges. 'If I'd been asked for a pilotless craft I'd have designed something completely different.'

'Then use the avionics to damp down the performance.

Good God, man, the controls are like hair triggers! I try to do a leisurely turn and an instant later I'm pulling six g! For Chrissake, you've got to take into account human limitations.'

'If we slowed up the response with the avionics we'd lose the wonderful handling characteristics. Look, Rory, Space Fleet wanted this craft for manned operation anywhere in the solar system. The three Morningstars out there are close to completion and they've been built to that exact specification. Very soon they'll be sent to Mars for flight testing. The company needs someone to go out there with them, as chief test pilot and senior instructor—'

Rory snorted derisively. 'Well I don't know who the hell you're going to get. I can tell you this, it won't be me. I'd sooner resign than take off in that...' he slapped his gauntlets on the desk. 'That death trap!'

And he stormed out of the office.

19

The Martian night was dead and deep and black. At the edges of the highway Pat Coyle could just make out a white frost of frozen carbon dioxide. Beyond that the landscape on either side was shrouded in utter darkness. But in the rear-view monitor, Highway 4 could be seen snaking back across the desert, its course revealed as a diffuse glow created by dust blown up by the convoy of freight skimmers and illuminated by headlights. He no longer looked at it. He was tired, so tired there was a danger that the steady moan of the engines would send him to sleep.

In front, partially obscured by dust, was the freight skimmer he'd been following ever since he joined the line of vehicles on the highway, his speed held steady by cruise control, his separation maintained by forward-pointing radar, which was housed in the broad, smooth nose of all these vehicles. Holding a good distance was important because the fog of suspended dust along the highway limited visibility, which would have posed a distinct risk of collision. Just as important was the danger of a small rock being thrown up by the vehicle in front and puncturing the thick, reinforced glass of the canopy, the only thing that separated the driver's microenvironment from the tenuous atmosphere outside. If ever that barrier were breached the best he could hope for was to hold things together with the emergency gas cylinders until help arrived. That was the best scenario. The more likely scenario was that the pressure difference would blow the cabin apart, with a similar effect on him. He knew all about those risks but they'd long receded to the back of his mind; he was more concerned about what reduced gravity had done to his body. He used to be proud of his build. Now, despite regular sessions in the company gym, his legs were so thin he hated to look at them. Still, what could he do? – the job paid well and he had a family to support. In any case, the six months were nearly up and then he could go home.

The backs of his eyes ached and the edges of his vision shrank to that tube of illuminated dust ahead of him. It gave him a feeling of claustrophobia, as if he were travelling down an ever-narrowing tunnel. Back on Earth he would have called a halt long before this, taken a nap. You couldn't do that here. He blinked hard, trying to shake it off.

The radio crackled. *'Pat? Jeff, at Jepson. Where are you?'*

'Not far off now, Jeff. A few miles at the most.' His own voice sounded loud in his ears.

'How long to base?'

'Depends how busy it is in the hangar. Maybe thirty minutes?'

'Okay. See you then.'

The radio went dead and the cockpit was silent again.

He grimaced. They ought to do these runs with robotic skimmers.

Even as the thought ran through his mind he dismissed it. A robot could manage the boring night-time drive along the highway but when the journey there and back included as much free landscape as this one had it wasn't remotely practical. Why these process plants had to set up so far from the highway he had no idea. It was probably something to do with whatever minerals they were working with.

The sky ahead was beginning to glow with the lights of Tharsis City. Between that and the pall of headlight-illuminated dust it was impossible to see the stars except for the few that made an intermittent appearance directly overhead.

A second glow appeared to the right, the floodlit bulk of Hangar C – at last. He sighed. Another run nearly over. Soon he'd be making the short drive back to Tharsis and crawling gratefully into his bed.

*

Hangar C was equipped with separate entry and exit airlocks, each of them evacuated and repressurized swiftly by giant pistons. It operated like a ferry: freight skimmers approached along the access lane and entered the long airlock in single file, ten at a time. The airlock was closed and brought up to pressure, the inner doors opened, and the skimmers came into the unloading bay on a moving belt. Their big blunt noses followed each other in like a train of cargo planes, each one cut short behind the cabin to furnish a flat open loading platform for the containers. When the belt stopped moving, the inner airlock door closed and the cargo handlers moved in to check the manifests. After the containers had been hoisted off and taken away to a holding area by forklifts, the moving belt conveyed the skimmers to the exit airlock, the movement bringing in a new batch for unloading. Powerful fans circulated the internal air through filters to remove the dust that came in with the vehicles.

Agent Gordon Baker and two other Customs officers wandered among the containers in the holding area, making spot checks on the cargoes. It had been a busy night, the big signal lamps on either side of the entry airlock cycling repeatedly through the sequence – red for evacuation of air, green for repressurization, red, green, red, green – and on each cycle another batch of freight skimmers came through, were unloaded, and moved on. Baker picked up a cargo manifest, then tensed as his communicator sounded a specific snatch of tune. It was a call from the special vehicle located near the entrance, the one that was scanning incoming cargo.

He took the communicator from his pocket. On the screen was a still of a freight skimmer. What looked like a silver paint job was just visible under the light coating of red dust, and it had 'Jepson Heavy Haulage' in black letters on the side. The open back was loaded with two containers, of a similar silver colour. Inside one of them something had responded to the probing, broad-spectrum terahertz beam with the characteristic signature of Dramatoin.

He beckoned to the other two officers and they walked purposefully along the line of vehicles. The freight handlers saw them coming and moved out of their way. Baker pointed; it was the sixth from the front. They stopped at the cabin.

Baker shouted, 'Out!' and banged it with the heel of his hand.

There was no response and the canopy remained closed. Baker drew a sidearm and levelled it at the canopy. He jerked his head at one of the other officers. 'Open it, then stand clear.'

The canopy was operated hydraulically on a thin-atmosphere vehicle like this. The officer opened a red hatch marked 'Open in emergency', grasped the handle inside and pulled it down. There was a hiss from the seal and the canopy opened.

The driver was slouched over the controls. Baker approached and nudged him with the muzzle of his pistol.

'I said "Out"!'

But the man didn't get out. Instead he slumped over sideways, and one arm dangled loosely out of the cab.

20

Dan was just leaving the Test Establishment for the day when his communicator buzzed. It was Agent Kennedy.

'Major? Are you tied up right now?'

'I was just leaving work. Why?'

'We have a situation on Mars. It would be really helpful if you could be here when we discuss it. Could you possibly make it over to the Deputy Commissioner's office?'

'When, now?'

'If you can.'

He hesitated, then said, 'Okay, I should be there in about ten minutes.'

He clicked off and hurried to the skimmer park.

What did he mean by 'situation'? Have they made a successful interception?

*

Deputy Commissioner Henry Leighton was sitting behind his desk. As Dan came in he gave him a brief nod and indicated an empty chair next to Special Agent Kennedy and Captain Lauren Marks.

Kennedy turned to him and murmured, 'Thanks for coming.'

Leighton placed his hands on the desk. 'All right, Kennedy. You'd better tell them.'

Kennedy drew a breath. 'We redeployed the big terahertz source from Hangar B to Hangar C. It's been in operation for a couple of weeks now and I've been monitoring the results daily. Two nights ago a man named Pat Coyle drove a freight skimmer into Hangar C. One of the containers scanned positive for Dramatoin.'

Marks clenched her fist and hissed 'Yes!'

Dan felt a flush of satisfaction.

Kennedy went on, 'I wanted Major Larssen to be here, sir, because this was his idea, and this arrest shows he was absolutely on the money. There must be a factory on Mars surface and they're mingling containers of the product with the traffic from the process plants and the mines to get the stuff through the shuttle terminal.'

Marks said, 'Did the driver say where he made the pick-up?'

Kennedy heaved a sigh. 'The driver is dead.'

She closed her eyes, then reopened them. 'Our people?'

'Apparently not, he was dead when they opened up the cab. He'd driven as far as the airlock, so whatever it was it must have happened very quickly.'

'Cause of death?'

'No obvious injuries, no blood. His lips were blue. They thought he'd had a heart attack.'

'Oh yes,' Dan said sarcastically. 'He gets a heart attack just when he might have told somebody where he'd made his pick-up.'

'That's what I thought.'

Marks said, 'You think he committed suicide?'

'Well, it was either that or he was knocked off,' Kennedy said. 'Obviously we had to establish cause of death so I told them to take the body to the Medical Center in Tharsis City for a whole-body multi-scan and autopsy.' He turned back to Leighton. 'That's how things stood when I spoke to you last, sir.'

'Right,' Leighton said. 'Have you received the autopsy report yet?'

'Yes, we have now. He was poisoned.'

Dan heard an intake of breath from Lauren Marks. Leighton blinked.

Kennedy said, 'The scan revealed something in the stomach and they retrieved it at autopsy. It looked like this.'

He dipped into a pocket and placed something on Leighton's desk. It was a capsule, rounded at one end and blunt at the other.

Leighton looked at it. 'What is it?'

'It's a swallowable capsule, a commercially available device for remote release of therapeutic material. Physicians use it when dose delivery needs to be timed very precisely. I spoke to a biomedical engineer over here about it. Apparently there's as much chemistry as electronics inside. There's a receiver coil – that's what showed up on the scan. It receives a signal and sets off a series of small biochemical reactions, each one amplifying the one before. The last one activates an enzyme which dissolves the thin cap,' he pointed to the blunt end, 'and that releases whatever's inside.'

Marks said, 'And what was inside was a poison?'

'In this case, almost certainly. They're still working on the analysis, but from the symptoms the medical examiner at Tharsis thought it was probably a neurotoxin. Paralysed him. He couldn't breathe.'

'What was it doing in there?'

'That we don't know. But it's a fair bet that all their drivers have taken one.'

Leighton threw up his hands. Kennedy and Marks watched him get to his feet and walk over to the window. Dan ignored him.

'You mentioned a receiver coil,' he said to Kennedy. 'So this was set off by a transmitter somewhere. How close would that have to be?'

'Close. The engineer said these devices have to be activated by radiofrequencies of around a megahertz; higher frequencies don't penetrate the tissues efficiently enough. That means the range is quite short, just a few metres at most. It could have been the driver of one of the other skimmers or it could have been one of the freight handlers. There are a lot of people milling around. If our officers looked like they were going to stop a driver and someone just happened to stroll by at that moment with one hand in his pocket, no one would notice.'

Leighton returned to his chair and began to drum his fingers on the desk. 'Damn these people,' he said. 'Always one step ahead of us. What happened to the container, the one with the Dramatoin?'

'Still in custody, so far as I know.'

The room was silent for several moments, the only sound the quiet, rhythmic thudding of Leighton's fingers.

Dan said, 'We need a change of strategy.'

Leighton gave him a dead look. 'Obviously.'

'What did you have in mind, Major?' Marks said.

'First, suspend further interceptions.'

Leighton stopped drumming. 'Are you serious? We're

just getting results! Why stop now?'

'The syndicate may accept this incident as a spot check that struck lucky, but repeat the performance once or twice and they'll know how you're doing it. They'll adopt another tactic for trans-shipment, or worse still, move the factory. We'll have thrown away our best chance of locating it.'

'That won't matter if we get a driver who'll talk to us.'

'Drivers can't talk to us if they're being killed as soon as we try to arrest them. All we'd be doing is giving the bosses time to work out what's happening. We'll have lost the initiative.'

Leighton scowled. 'You said "first". Is there a "second"?'

'Yes. I think we should locate the company that owned that freight skimmer – the papers will be on board. We'll tell them the driver has died of a heart attack. We've accepted the consignment and we'd like them to come to the hangar to collect their vehicle.'

Leighton's eyes widened. 'Accept the consignment? I can't do that! I can't just stand by and let a container load of Dramatoin find its way onto our streets!'

'We won't be standing by. We'll radiotag the container before it goes on the shuttle. Then it can be picked up when it arrives back on Earth. We'll do the same for any other consignments we detect. Except we'll do the radiotagging out of sight, so the syndicate has no idea we've picked it up or how we managed it.'

'Kennedy, what do you think? Can that be done? I thought these syndicates ran their own transport systems throughout.'

'They used to, sir, including the spacefreighters. But we only had to pick up one freighter and they lost maybe a year's production. These days they tend to transport the stuff in smaller quantities. It isn't economical to do that themselves so they conceal their material by transporting it with legitimate cargo. They use conventional hauliers to put it on commercial shuttles, which in turn transfer it to commercial freightliners.'

'So we'd have access once the skimmer's been unloaded?'

'Yes, all we have to do is move the container where we can deal with it without being observed.'

Leighton sat forward. 'What about the driver who delivers it to Hangar C? He's the one I really want.'

'That's the third thing,' Dan said. 'No uniforms inside the hangar – we don't want to raise suspicions. Video him secretly with his skimmer and get a separate team to follow him afterwards to make the arrest.'

Kennedy nodded enthusiastically. 'If we do it that way the syndicate won't think anything's wrong. It'll give us a chance to spirit the driver away to a safe place. From there we can take him back to Earth. And we do the same with the next driver, and the next, until we get one who'll talk to us.'

'And then,' Lauren Marks said, 'maybe I'll know where to look for this factory.'

Leighton's eyes flicked from Kennedy to Marks and back to Kennedy. Dan could almost see his mind working.

He doesn't like where the suggestions are coming from. Why? What has he got against me? I was right before and I'll be right this time. Maybe that's it, I'm undermining his authority.

The room was silent again. Leighton sat stiffly behind his desk. He picked up a pen and turned it end over end between his fingers. They waited, watching him.

Eventually the tightness around his mouth slackened, and the shoulders lowered just a fraction.

'All right, we'll try it. Set it up, would you Kennedy?'

As they got to their feet he looked up, tapping the pen sharply on the desk, 'I hope to God we can nail those consignments on arrival, that's all. I shudder to think how much damage even one of them could do.'

Kennedy saw Dan to the entrance, where they stopped and shook hands. He said, 'Thanks again for coming. I'll start getting all that in place.'

Dan nodded. 'Good. Let me know how it works out, Alec. Sounds like they're moving a production batch at the moment, so with luck it shouldn't be too long.'

21

Hangar C at the Mars shuttle terminal was buzzing with activity as usual. Hoists running on overhead rails unloaded cargo from freight skimmers that were continually entering and leaving. Rubber-tracked fork-lifts were transporting containers through to the holding area, close to where the freight shuttles docked on the outside. The air was full of noise: the hiss of the big airlocks opening and closing, the clanking of machinery, the hum of electric drives and, as a constant background, the steady drone of the big circulating fans. The smell of metal, oil, and an occasional whiff of ozone hung in the air. Workers in blue coveralls went to meet the incoming drivers, checked their consignments and oversaw the handling. One of them paused, suddenly alert. He slipped behind a stack of containers, drew out a communicator and looked at it. Then he punched a key. While he waited he moved his baseball cap up a little, dropping a finger casually on his ear to shield the device within the canal from ambient noise. He spoke almost inaudibly, his voice picked up by the vibration sensors woven into his collar.

'Hayes, Garcia, it's Fletcher. You receiving?'

'Hayes here, go ahead.'

'Vehicle is grey under the dust. Name on the door is 'Allbright Freight Transport'. Two containers. Both of them just checked positive for Blaze. It'll be coming through the exit airlock in a few minutes.'

'Allbright Freight Transport. Okay, I copy.'

He glanced up at a mobile elevated platform. His colleague there nodded and brought up a small video camera.

A regular freight handler was already on his way over to the grey skimmer but Fletcher held up a hand in a casual gesture.

'It's okay, I'll take this one.'

He straightened his baseball cap with the Mars Cargo logo, a reddish-brown circle with an elliptical orbit around it, and waited. The canopy hissed open and the driver vaulted down with the practised ease of someone used to moving in one-third normal gravity. He was lightly built and long-limbed, but not young – maybe late forties – and the pale, lined face looked strangely at odds with the dyed yellow hair and the two small silver rings in his left ear lobe. He presented a smart card, which Fletcher took from him and placed over his tablet while the spy camera concealed behind the logo in his baseball cap recorded more video. He strolled round to the back, looked at the two containers and down at the details now displayed on his tablet, which declared the contents to be crushed mineral-bearing rocks. He returned to the driver.

'Okay, put your thumb on this spot.'

The driver frowned. 'Thumbprint? Never had to do that before.'

'New identity procedure. We had a bit of trouble about a month back.' He showed him the tablet. 'It just says

136

you're a bona fide representative of the company and you're happy to hand over the cargo to us for transport.'

The driver shrugged and placed his thumb in the corner of the tablet screen.

Fletcher signalled to a hoist operator and a grab moved into position to unload the crates. He pointed to the ground, indicating that the operator should place them there for a fork-lift driver to pick up. Turning back to the blond driver he tapped a symbol on the tablet screen.

'Okay, I've transmitted the receipts to your company HQ. You're clear to go.'

The driver said 'Thanks, mate' and climbed back into his cabin. The canopy came down and sealed. A few minutes later the line of skimmers moved into the exit airlock.

Fletcher went over to the fork-lift driver who was handling the crates and indicated an area shielded from the rest of the hangar by stacks of boxes. When both crates had been delivered there and the fork-lift had left, he picked up an electric drill that was tucked under an empty box and drilled a small hole next to a rib in the first container. He pushed a slim radiotag through it and sealed the hole with a plastic compound. He rubbed it with a finger to transfer some of the red Martian dust still clinging to the container, and blew to even out the layer. He repeated the process with the second container, then straightened up to admire his handiwork.

These two wouldn't have to be scanned; they'd signal their presence loud and clear.

*

The grey open-backed freight skimmer emerged from the airlock and moved away from Hangar C. When it had advanced fifty yards down the service road an unmarked black skimmer pulled out and followed it along a small road that ran parallel to Highway 4. After about a quarter of a mile the freight skimmer passed a sign for the Allbright Freight Transport Company, took a right turn, and paused briefly at a security cabin. Ahead of it was a tall wire-netting fence. A pair of gates opened and it went inside and headed towards a pressurized hangar.

Agents Hayes and Garcia waited in the black Customs skimmer. Twenty minutes went by. Then a small skimmer, a Rondeo, emerged from the direction of the hangar. The gate opened and it came through.

Hayes checked the two screens on the central console: on the left a still from the video transmitted by Fletcher in Hangar C, on the right the output from a night vision scope which he'd focused on the vehicle.

Garcia said, 'That's him.'

'Yeah, it's him all right.'

The Rondeo passed and, after a suitable pause, the black skimmer followed.

*

With the Allbright Freight Transport Hangar behind him, Jason Lennox turned right to join the continuation of Highway 4 that led to Tharsis City. He yawned and flicked the Rondeo into overdrive. The company vehicle was a piece of crap but it was okay for the short ride to and from the City. Right now his main object was to get some sleep.

Unlike the Highway from the west, which he'd just left, the stretch into the City was almost deserted in the early hours. It was just as well. He knew he wasn't as alert as he should be; his eyes ached, his neck and shoulders ached, his back ached. He fumbled in the central cubby to see if he'd left some gum or mints in there. Nothing.

Not for the first time he wondered if he'd done the right thing, coming out to Mars. A six-month contract, transport out and back, free food and accommodation, and double the normal salary – sounded all right, didn't it? Allbright's were always advertising these jobs with their drivers Earthside, and a lot of the guys had taken them. He'd never felt like asking one if he thought it was a good or bad thing to do, but even if it was tough it was only for six months.

Right now he'd done three of those six months and he couldn't wait to get back. It wasn't just the gravity; that didn't do you a whole lot of good but you sort of got used to it. The dust was a pain, too. Not even the filters could take all of it out. He could taste it in the food he ate, feel it in his clothes – even found it between his toes when he took a shower. But worst of all was being cooped up like a bloody bird in a cage – inside the City, inside the freight skimmer, inside the hangars – everywhere cooped up. Back on Earth when he took a truck out onto the open highway he had a feeling of freedom. If he was getting tired he could pull over somewhere, maybe have a sandwich or a Vitabar, or just sit in a field for a while, chewing on a stalk of grass. The memory of it made him sigh.

Ahead of him the brightly lit geodesic dome of Tharsis City grew larger all the time. Once you were anywhere near it you completely lost the night sky, which was a shame because it could be quite something. He'd read up a bit on it. You needed it to be really dark, like out in the rough where he'd just come from. It was tricky viewing it through the canopy of the freight skimmer, but Earth was easy enough to spot, and he could recognize Deimos now, which was about as bright as Venus was from Earth, and Phobos, which was even brighter. They weren't stars, of course, they were moons – in fact they weren't even proper moons, just a couple of asteroids captured by Mars some time way back. If he thought about it, the night sky was the one thing out here he did like but you just didn't get it here in Tharsis City.

He was approaching the dome now, close enough that he could no longer see the top.

How was his mother coping? He'd never been away from her this long. He remembered the last time he was down in Kent, how she'd gripped his hands in both of hers.

'Don't do it, Jay, please. Whatever am I going to do with you millions of miles away?'

'It's only for six months, Ma.'

'I could be dead in six months.'

'Come on now, you'll be fine. You got your carer, the nurses, food, entertainment – everythin's on tap in this place. But you have to understan', Ma, it costs to keep you here. This job'll make it a lot easier on me. And I promise I'll call you, make sure you're okay.'

Call her! He snorted. Try holding any sort of conversation with a four-minute lag! It was hard enough for him and she certainly couldn't get her head round it. They'd end up with a jumble of words that simply didn't connect.

The City airlock came into view. His was the only vehicle to enter, so he didn't have to wait long. In another ten minutes he was guiding the Rondeo into the multilevel belonging to his apartment block. Allbright's rented a number of apartments here. Very small and basic, but right now he could have slept standing up. It'd been a long night.

He found a parking place and the engines whined down. Then he yawned again, stretched, opened the door and got out – to face two men wearing helmets and black uniforms with red trim. One was pointing a multirifle at him.

'What the…?'

'Customs,' the unarmed one said, holding up a badge. 'Hands on the skimmer, legs apart.'

'What the fuck—?'

The muzzle of the rifle jerked. 'Just do it.'

He turned, placed his hands on the gritty surface of the skimmer. One of them patted him down while the other one scanned the licence spot on the Rondeo's windscreen. Out of the corner of his eye Jay saw him show the tablet to the one behind him. There was a pause, then:

'Jason Charles Lennox, I'm arresting you for trafficking in a proscribed drug. You have the right to remain silent. Anything you say can and will be used against you in a court of law. You have the right to an attorney. Do you understand?'

Lennox took his hands off the skimmer and turned around slowly. 'Did you say drugs?' He gave a short laugh. 'You must be jokin'. Not me, pal. You made a mistake.'

'No mistake, sir. We can go into this back at the station.'

'You serious? I only just got in—'

'Sir, I have to tell you that right now you're in serious danger.'

Lennox cocked his head to one side. 'Oh, now you really are shittin' me, right?'

'I'm afraid not, sir. Did you swallow a capsule when you made your last pick-up?'

He frowned. 'Well, yeah… The controller said solar radiation was bad right now. He gave me a Ligasin.'

'I'm sorry, sir, that capsule does not contain Ligasin, it contains a fast-acting poison. Unless we get you to a safe place quickly you could be dead in a few minutes.'

Lennox felt his jaw go slack. He blinked, then his shoulders sagged and he allowed the two men to lead him to a black skimmer. One got in the back with him. He'd swapped his multirifle for a pistol.

'You can put that bloody thing away,' Lennox said. 'I'm not goin' to give you any trouble.'

The man smiled, but there was nothing friendly about the smile; it merely rearranged his features in the prescribed way. 'I'll keep it handy all the same, mister. Okay, Hayes, let's go.'

22

In his office at the Test Establishment Dan was writing up a report. Engine noise rose outside as an aircraft taxied in. He didn't look up; from the sound alone he knew it was the T-903. That would be Joe Lau, and it meant they'd got up to the mid-morning part of the rota.

A light blinked in the comms panel on Dan's desk – his secure line. He pressed a button. Outside, the noise of engines died.

'Larssen.'

'Major, this is Alec Kennedy. I hope you don't mind me using this line.'

Dan straightened up. 'Not at all, Alec, that's why I gave you the code.' Dan had been encouraging the agent to use his first name as well, so far without success. 'What's up?'

'My people have arrested a driver on Mars. He had a cargo of Dramatoin. They're bringing him back here under armed guard.'

'Does the syndicate know you've got him?'

'We think not – at least, not yet. He works for a company called Allbright Freight Transport. The officers who made the arrest sent a medical certificate to Allbright's to say he'd been taken ill and had to be returned to Earth for treatment. They'll probably buy that for the moment, and if the syndicate starts asking questions, that's the story they'll get.'

'Well done. Did they ask him where he made his pick-up?'

'No, they're not authorized to interrogate him. At this stage the idea is just to let him know how much trouble he's in. That way he'll give us more reliable information if he does start to talk.'

Kennedy's probably right. The officers are obliged to tell this guy why they're arresting him. The moment he finds out he's been carrying illegal drugs he'll realize the danger and clam up. They'll need to put a lot of pressure on him. He knew from bitter experience how that felt.

'Well, I hope he cooperates when he gets here.'

'Yes, in fact that's why I'm calling. Major, er Dan, I hate to revisit what must be a painful period in your life, but I was wondering if you could tell me who represented you, I mean, after you were, um, detained in similar circumstances.'

Dan smiled at the attempt at delicacy. 'Yes, I can tell you that. It was a guy called Julian Romero. He was appointed by the State. I think he often defended no-hopers like me who couldn't afford an attorney of their own.'

He thought he heard Kennedy swallow. 'Julian Romero. Right, thank you very much.'

'Why do you want to know?'

'Well, it's very important for us to persuade this man to give evidence.'

'I see, Romero successfully entered a plea bargain for me, so he may be able to do the same for this guy.'

'Um, yes, that's about it.'

'Fair enough. Things didn't work out wonderfully for me, but that wasn't his fault. He's a good lawyer, and you can trust him.' Dan paused for a moment, thinking it through. He said, 'I take it you'll be approaching him yourself?'

'Yes.'

'Can I give you a word of advice?'

'Please do.'

'If this driver says he'll give evidence Romero will take that to the Prosecutor. He'll do the best he can for him, but he can't negotiate with one hand tied behind his back. You need to give him the whole picture.'

'My boss won't like that.'

'I'm sure he won't. But that's the only way.'

'Understood. Thanks, Dan. I'll keep you posted.'

*

Julian Romero entered the interview room. It was a plain, windowless chamber, white walls, glow panel ceiling, grey composite tiled floor. In the middle there was a small table on which he dumped his document case. He drew back a chair, sat down, opened the case, and took out the relevant papers to read while he waited – legal materials were always printed to avoid tampering. Opposite him an empty chair stood ready for his client.

He scanned the charge sheet for Jason Charles Lennox: the evidence, the circumstances of the arrest, and a brief statement, a more or less verbatim record of his client's protests of ignorance as to what he'd been carrying. It was a familiar story.

Romero sighed. He was prepared to believe this man, just as he'd believed many of the others he'd defended.

They were the innocent victims of ruthless criminals. But sympathy wasn't in the nature of State Prosecutors and many of these people ended up spending years in jail. The law was clear: they'd committed a serious offence and they had to be punished. The best answer was to nail the big players, the syndicate bosses. That was why he'd always try to plea bargain for his clients if he could. Most weren't interested. They had little faith in witness protection programmes and they were probably right; at least in jail they had a chance of staying alive. Still, he'd had some successes.

Larssen, for example – that was a real success. What is it that sets apart those few like Larssen who are prepared to give evidence? Indignation, perhaps? More like anger. Right now Lennox is probably upset but he won't be angry, not angry enough. Can I make him angry?

The warder opened the door and came in, gripping a man by the upper arm.

'Jason Lennox,' he announced, and added, 'I'll be right outside.'

The door closed and Romero got to his feet.

'Mr Lennox, I'm Julian Romero, your attorney.'

'I never asked for an attorney.' The voice was distant, weak.

'You're facing serious charges, Mr. Lennox. The State has to appoint someone to look after your interests. They've appointed me.'

'Yeah, well, I can't pay you.'

'You don't have to worry about that. Won't you have a seat?'

Lennox shuffled forward. Romero watched him sit down slowly and carefully, gripping the edge of the table, the way they always did when they'd just returned from a zero or low gravity environment. Lennox's dyed hair was black at the roots and looked dirty and uncombed, he had several days' growth of beard, his eyes sat in darkened hollows, the lids red-rimmed. He looked like he'd hardly eaten or slept since he was arrested more than three weeks ago. He sat quietly, studying his hands.

'Now, Mr Lennox—'

'Jay! F'r Chrissake drop this "Mr Lennox" crap, will you? – no one calls me that.'

'All right. Jay, do you know what you're charged with?'

'Somethin' about illegal trafficking in drugs. Load o' bollocks.'

'Jay, you were recorded on video in that Mars hangar delivering two containers destined for Earth. Your thumbprint is on the transfer document. The cargo you handed over contained Blaze.'

'Blaze? Jesus!' For the first time he engaged the lawyer's eyes. 'Are you on the level?'

Romero nodded grimly.

'How the fuck did I know? The cargo manifest said something about minerals. I thought that place was a process plant.' His speech became hurried. 'Look, this is nothin' to do with me. I go where I'm told, pick up a container or two, drive it to the terminal. That's my job. End of story.'

'The fact is, Jay, you were carrying drugs, and the penalties for doing that are severe. You could be facing twenty-five years in prison.'

'What?' Lennox's face sagged, then he dropped his head into his hands and wagged it from side to side. 'This ain't right. They can't do this to me.'

'I'm afraid they can, Jay.'

Romero waited in silence. Eventually Lennox

straightened up with a shuddering sigh. There was desperation in his eyes and his voice sounded broken. 'Listen, can you get me out of here for a bit, like on bail or somethin'? It's me old mother – she's in a care home back in the UK and I ain't seen her for three, nearly four months. I really need to see her.'

Romero absorbed the information without a change in expression.

An ageing mother. Interesting. This man is already under pressure.

'I'm really sorry, Jay. They'd certainly oppose bail in a case like this, especially if it involved leaving the USA.'

He ran his tongue round his lips. 'You gotta help me. I tell you, I had no idea what was in them containers – I swear it! I'm just a driver, just tryin'-a make a decent living.'

'The State Prosecutor won't be satisfied with that, I'm afraid. Did the people who made the arrest ask you about a capsule?'

Lennox's face darkened. 'Yeah, I told them and I'll tell you. I did, I took a capsule. A guy at the plant gave it me. He said it was Ligasin – you know, for radiation. I said it was kind of big, and he said it was a special slow-release formulation, more effective.'

'And did the Customs people tell you what it was?'

'They told me it was some sort of deadly poison. That's why we never left straight away. They watched me every time I took a dump until they said it'd passed through and I was safe. I don't know – who am I supposed to believe?'

'Jay, did you know a driver by the name of Pat Coyle?'

'Pat? Yeah, I knew Pat. Worked for Jepson's. We met up once in a while, had a jar or two together – alcohol-free o' course. I heard the poor sod died of a heart attack. Must be the low gravity. Does funny things to you.'

'It wasn't a heart attack, Jay. Pat Coyle was killed by the same people who loaded those containers onto your truck.'

'What?'

'Yes. He took a capsule, one just like yours. His truck was spotted by Customs, also just like yours. But he wasn't as lucky as you; the organization got to him first. One of their members used a remote device to release the poison in the capsule he'd swallowed. That's what killed him, Jay, not a heart attack.'

'Why? He was just an ordinary, decent bloke. Why kill 'im?'

'Because they didn't want him to talk to Customs, that's why. These people aren't just drug traffickers, Jay, they're murderers. They're the ones who should be convicted, but the court doesn't have the evidence so they go scot free. The court has evidence against you, so you'll have to do. Do you think that's fair?'

Lennox's eyes narrowed. He gritted his teeth and his voice descended to a growl. ''Course it ain't fuckin' fair. What you gettin' at?'

Anger is good, Jay. Keep the anger.

'What I'm saying is, if you were to give evidence, evidence that might lead to the conviction of these people—'

Jay threw his head back. 'You're jokin'! Listen, I wasn't born yesterday. They couldn't get at me before, they'll sure as hell get at me after. I'm better off in jail!'

Romero said, 'Let's not be too hasty, Jay. If I can go back to the State Prosecutor with something useful he could go easy on you.'

'But—'

'Look, it's your decision. Just remember, these people killed Pat Coyle and they'd have killed you, too. You want to go to prison for maybe twenty-five years while they get away with it? You want to take the fall? Fine. I'm your attorney. If that's what you want I'll do my best for you. Maybe I can get the sentence reduced to twenty years, fifteen if we're lucky. Think it over. I'm going to leave you now. I'll come back tomorrow and we can talk about it then. Okay?'

He was aware of Lennox's eyes following him as he picked up his document case and walked to the door.

23

Julian Romero knocked lightly on the door and entered the State Prosecutor's office. James Quenby was at his desk. He lifted his head slowly, as if it weighed too much.

'Going to waste my time again, Julian?'

Romero drew back a leather chair in front of the desk and sat down. 'Did I waste your time with Dan Larssen – the guy who gave you Mikhael Rostov's head on a plate?'

Quenby scowled. 'That was – what? – five years ago? You've brought me nothing as good as that since.'

'I'm bringing you something as good as that now. Better.'

'Are you really?' Quenby raised one bushy eyebrow in an expression of clear disbelief. 'Do tell me more.'

'Jim, I'm sorry to have to ask you this, but do I have your word that this conversation, and anything that flows from it, will be kept absolutely secret?'

Quenby's face reddened. 'Good God, Julian, that's plumb offensive! Do you think I'd be sitting here,' he waved a hand around the luxurious office, 'if I couldn't respect client confidentiality?'

'I'm not talking about client confidentiality. Look, I can imagine the sort of pressure you're under to deliver results on crime, the drug trade in particular.'

'You can't, but go on.'

'What I'm saying is, if the Attorney General himself asks you what progress you're making, this conversation didn't take place, mustn't even be hinted at. There's too much at stake.'

'This a new ploy to grab my interest, Julian?'

'Not at all. The success of this whole operation depends on keeping it tight until it's all over.'

'This whole operation,' Quenby repeated, and his eyes narrowed. 'Would this, by any chance, have something to do with a young Customs agent, name of Kennedy, who came here asking questions a month or two back?'

'In a word, yes. But that was just part of it. There's a lot riding on this, Jim. That's why secrecy is vital. Can we agree on that?'

'Yes, yes, of course. Now I haven't got all day. Get to the point.'

'Okay, here it is. Larssen gave you Rostov and you put Rostov away. Wonderful. What happened to the drug trade? Nothing. Raoul Hernandez took over the syndicate and the drugs kept flowing.'

'But Customs knocked out their orbiting factory recently, didn't they? It was all over the news.'

'Didn't achieve anything, Jim; production had already been moved. And right now no one has any idea where they moved it to.'

Quenby's lips tightened and he nodded. 'One step ahead, as usual. So?'

'My client, Jason Charles Lennox, has been driving freight skimmers on Mars. Just over three weeks ago he picked up two containers from a factory somewhere out in the desert. The *manifest* said processed minerals.' He paused for effect. 'There was Dramatoin in those containers, Jim – a large consignment of it.'

Quenby was watching him closely now. Romero leaned forward and tapped on the desk. 'You see? Without realizing it, this guy has been to the syndicate's Dramatoin factory. He can tell us where it is! It's a rare break, Jim. If that factory is destroyed the supply of the drug dries up.'

Romero could almost see the man's mind working.

Quenby clasped his hands together. 'What do you want, Julian? A reduction in sentence for this man in exchange for information?'

Romero shook his head. 'Not good enough. He's angry, but not that angry. He's aware of the risk he'd be taking. When that factory is hit the syndicate will know just who gave us the information and they'll come after him. Even with witness protection we can't guarantee his safety.'

'What then?'

'Lennox has an ageing mother. She's in a care home in the UK. They're evidently very close and he wants to be with her. Acquittal, Jim, on the grounds of insufficient evidence. A new identity, and travel for Lennox and his mother to a remote – preferably a warm – place.'

Quenby slapped the desk and got to his feet. The blood had risen to his face. 'Are you crazy, Julian? The man transports two containers of Dramatoin and we let him go scot free? Have you any idea what would come down on me if I agreed to that? They'll think I've gone soft in the head!'

'When that drug factory is destroyed, people won't be looking over your shoulder, Jim, they'll be celebrating. You're one of those who'll get the credit. After a coup like that they're not going to quibble about an innocent man who was duped into taking a consignment, one that he thought contained minerals.'

Quenby glared at him, his face like thunder. 'And what happens if the operation fails, eh? What then? We end up with nothing and I lose my job.'

Romero shook his head. 'You saw what they did to that orbiting factory. These people are serious. They're not going to pass up a golden opportunity like this one. Failure simply isn't an option.' He sat back. 'Well that's it. What do you say?'

24

Lauren Marks looked up in surprise as Henry Leighton entered her office. She half rose from the desk but he waved for her to remain seated.

'Marks, you remember the driver they picked up three weeks ago? Jason Charles Lennox?'

'Yes, of course, sir.'

'He's in custody here now. The attorney appointed for his defence has persuaded him to give evidence. He's prepared to reveal the route he took. I plan to be there when he makes his statement and I want you to come with me.'

Her face lit up and she nodded quickly. 'Thank you, sir.'

'Bring some detailed aerial views of the terrain served by Highway 4. See if he can show you exactly where he collected his consignment.'

'When are we doing this?'

'Two o'clock this afternoon. Come up to my office; we'll take my skimmer.'

He closed the door behind him.

Her pulse was quick with excitement. She'd studied that terrain until her eyes ached, all to no avail. Now, at long last, the answer was within her grasp.

*

Alec Kennedy looked at the distraught face on his videocomm.

'I've been looking and looking ever since we came back from the prison, Alec. There's nothing there! Not a thing!'

He took a deep breath and said, 'Okay, Lauren, take it easy now. I'll come down.'

She sighed. 'Thanks. Make it Presentation Room 1, my office is too small. Five minutes.'

The image disappeared. He sat there for a few moments. Lauren had been in high spirits when she told him Jason Lennox was going to give evidence. He knew how hard she'd studied the Martian terrain for that factory, and with how little result. This promised to be the big break. It would be very disappointing if Lennox's evidence led nowhere, especially for her. He had to support her.

This wasn't the first assignment they'd worked on together, pooling their different areas of expertise. On one occasion after a particularly exhausting stake-out he'd gone to bed with her. The following day she'd discussed it with him in a rational, matter-of-fact fashion. It had been very nice, perhaps even necessary, but it was unwise. They were both very focused on their careers and they occasionally needed to cooperate professionally, so it would be best simply to remain good friends. He'd agreed, of course. What else could he do? What remained was a mutual regard and an attachment-at-a-distance of the type you might find between a once-married couple who'd divorced without acrimony. All the same, each time he saw her he couldn't help recalling the firmness and power of that lithe body, and his loins would stir at the memory.

When he entered the presentation room Lauren was already standing there, staring at an image she'd displayed on the wall screen. As usual, her hair was tied back. She was wearing a white uniform shirt with the two silver bars on the epaulettes. The black trousers, which fitted snugly, emphasized her slim hips. He walked past ten rows of empty seats and joined her at the front. She turned and shot him a rueful smile. Although her voice was flat now, it carried a trace of relief.

'Thanks for coming.'

'No problem.'

'I'm going to show you—'

He held up a hand. 'Lauren, before we start just remember *you're* the terrain specialist, not me. Can you walk me through this slowly?'

'Okay.' She held up a sheet of e-paper. 'This has the maps I took along to the prison.'

'To show to Jason Lennox?'

'Yes. I printed them from the most recent satellite survey. This one is the whole of the Eastern Tharsis region, just to give Lennox his bearings. It's like a view from thirty thousand feet. Even so, you can see Highway 4, here,' she pointed, 'and the mining works and the cluster of factories at Enterprise and Arestes, here.' Now she dragged a finger across the sheet. The map followed it, uncovering another. 'This is a higher resolution view of the western end of the Valles Marineris: the Noctis Labyrinthus. It's where he said he made the pick-up.'

Kennedy looked at a bewilderingly complex pattern of intersecting canyons. She pulled across another map, this one with a pink line twisting and turning through it.

'This is a closer view. I gave Lennox a stylus and asked him to trace the route for me. So according to him this is where the factory's located – here, at the end of this valley. With me so far?'

'Yes.'

'Right, now take a look.'

She used a console at the front desk to dim the windows slightly and they turned to view the three-dimensional image on the wall screen. It was a detailed view of the same part of the Noctis Labyrinthus, the colours ranging from amber through tan to a dark brown in the shadows. For a few moments they studied it in silence. She turned to him, gesturing at the screen.

'See?' She slapped one hand down on her thigh. 'I thought he'd given us the factory and there's nothing there.'

'Did he tell you what it looked like on the outside?'

She shook her head. 'It was night when he made the pick-up. It's pitch black in those deep Martian valleys and as soon as the sun disappears over the rim the temperature drops like a stone, so there was quite a bit of mist.'

'Condensing carbon dioxide, most of it.'

'Yes. When he arrived, a shutter peeled back and the light from the inside lit up the mist so he couldn't see anything to the left or right or above or below. He drove in and the shutter came down behind him. Then a bigger door closed and that's when he realized he was in an airlock. He knew he wouldn't have to go through – the containers were standing there in the airlock with robot handlers ready to load them. As soon as the pressure was up to one bar a guy came in to do the paperwork with him. He was the one who gave him the pill. They exchanged documents and he turned round and by that time the containers were already on his skimmer. He got back in and sealed the canopy. Then they depressurized the airlock, lifted the shutter, and he drove off.'

Kennedy pointed at the screen. 'Can you go in any closer?'

'Sure.' Her fingers flicked expertly over the console and the picture enlarged, the resolution so fine he could barely detect any loss of detail. They were looking at the end of a deep valley. He studied it carefully but still he could see no sign of anything resembling a man-made structure.

He pointed. 'Will the software let you put contours on it?'

'Yes. Just a minute.'

Again she tapped at the console for a while. He watched the screen and a pattern of thin blue lines appeared, closely spaced on the sides and end of the valley and wide apart over the base. That confirmed the visual appearance: it was a steep-sided canyon with a flat bottom, like many in this area. And still nothing artificial showed up.

'And you're sure that's where he said?'

'Look for yourself.' She widened the view on the screen again and showed him the e-paper map with the pink line. He looked back and forth between the screen and the sheet, comparing the patterns. They were identical.

He shook his head. 'He must have pulled a fast one. He wanted to get treated leniently but he was too scared to hand over the goods so he just drew something at random.'

'I guess so.' She clicked her tongue and shook her head. 'You know, I'd have sworn he was being straight with us. He gave us all that detail about how it looked inside when he went in to make the pick-up. And he was so confident of the route he'd taken. He's been hauling freight all his life, he said, and you need a good memory for routes, just in case you have to go back to the same place again. It was very convincing.'

'You know, there's something I don't understand. If the syndicate is so concerned about preserving the secrecy of that factory, how come they're using ordinary commercial drivers?'

'Yes, I wondered about that, too. Apparently these freight jocks are tough and there's a sort of macho indifference to the jobs they do. If it was you or me we'd say, 'God that was a tough trip!' but that's the one thing they'll never discuss. It's a sort of built-in security, and the syndicate evidently knows it. The advantage is, they're dealing with a legitimate transport company, so the handlers at the hangar and all along the way are dealing with documentation from an accredited source and there's less chance the consignment will be picked out for inspection. The main risk is a random Customs check, and in the unlikely event of that happening they have that radio-controlled pill as their insurance policy.'

'Well, it looks like you'll have to go back and pressure this guy harder. That or wait for the next one.'

'What? They've only just delivered two containers of the stuff. They can't be producing it that fast. It could be ages before they ship out another batch.'

'The containers weren't full,' he said. 'Our people picked up the two radiotagged ones that Lennox was carrying. They sent a report to Leighton and he copied it to me. The contents were crushed mineral-bearing rocks, all right, Lauren; the Blaze was in bags, concealed in the middle. You'd never have found it with a normal inspection. Larssen's idea of using the big terahertz generator was inspired.'

She ran both hands back over her hair, then dropped them to her sides. 'Well, it makes no odds. Even if there is more on the way we'd have to wait at least another three weeks before we could get our hands on the driver, and with every day that passes the syndicate has a better chance of finding out what we're up to.' She sighed. 'I'll just have to ask Leighton if we can go back to Lennox. Damn!'

Kennedy studied her. Agitation had brought more colour to those high cheekbones and her fine lips were pressed tightly together. Then their eyes met and her expression softened. She shrugged apologetically.

'Thanks, Alec. I needed to share it.'

Yet again he felt that strong draw, the mutual attraction they'd so sensibly, so frustratingly, set aside. He swallowed. 'I'd better go.'

'Yes, okay.'

He left her standing there, her head bowed in thought. He'd just reached the door when she shouted, 'Wait a minute!'

He turned. 'What?'

'I've had an idea.'

'Go on.'

'Let's have a look at that region in the first detailed Mars survey, the one they did before we started to colonize.'

'The first survey? Why?'

'Bear with me, okay? I think it's still on the data banks... Yes, here it is. I'll put in the identical coordinates.'

The picture went up on the wall screen and they examined it carefully.

He shrugged. 'It's the same.'

'Let's try it with contours.'

The blue lines came up. They stared, then looked at each other.

A slow smile spread over her face. 'So that's how they did it!'

25

Dan was in the Common Room, about to get a coffee from one of the autochefs, when he heard the door open and Barry came in.

'Hi, Barry.'

'Ah, I was looking for you, Dan.'

'Why, what's up?'

'I don't know exactly. There's some top brass just came in with Dr Trebus. They want to see you. I put them in the private conference lounge. Can you meet them up there?'

'Sure.'

Barry hurried away.

Dan stood there for a moment. Dr John Trebus was a straight dealer, one of the few directors of either SpaceFreight or Space Fleet he would trust. But who were the top brass, and what did they want with him?

*

The private conference lounge was the quietest and most comfortably furnished room in the Test Establishment building – and the least used. It had been placed on the opposite side of the building to the runway, and active interference cancelled out any residual noise. Instead the windows looked out onto an adequate, but hardly inspiring, landscape of lawns, shrubs and trees. Taller specimens served to screen parts of the high wire fence at the perimeter.

The centre of the room was occupied by a long table of polished wood. Deeply upholstered chairs were spaced uniformly along either side of the table. Currently only the end three were occupied, the first by Dr Trebus, and the second and third by the two men he was talking to. One was Henry Leighton. Dan didn't recognize the other man, but four silver stars on each epaulette made an adequate impression. Trebus made the introductions:

'Major Larssen, I believe you've met Deputy Assistant Commissioner Henry Leighton.'

Leighton nodded curtly. He didn't smile.

'And this is General Hugh Norton, Air Force.'

An officer of that superior rank would not be expected to get up or shake hands, but the General's forward posture and welcoming smile emanated warmth. The grey hair and heavier build suggested someone a lot older than Leighton.

Trebus motioned Dan to sit down.

'Dan,' Trebus continued. 'What we discuss here has to remain between these four walls, all right?'

Dan shrugged. 'All right.'

'Have you heard of the Morningstar?'

'Morningstar?' Dan's mind quickly ran over the conversation with Barry and Tim on the way back from BG Aerospace. 'Heard of it, yes. I gather it was built in response to a call for a super-fast, super-agile, all-atmospheric craft. That's all I know. I understand the project's very hush-hush.'

'Do you think you could fly one?'

'Yes.'

The Air Force General said grudgingly, 'You seem remarkably sure of that.'

'Well, General, I haven't yet come across an aircraft I can't fly.'

'All right. If you can, given suitable training, and if you're interested, we'd like you to flight-test one with some interesting modifications.'

'An all-atmospheric craft? Where were you thinking of testing it?'

'Mars.'

Dan frowned. 'The Morningstar's a military aircraft. How can you get away with flying it on Mars?' He was thinking of the International Convention on the Militarization of Space.

'Fair question,' the General replied, 'but it's all entirely within the law. We've known for a long time that Mars would be the proper place to test the aircraft, so we applied for an exemption early last year. The licence was granted. The flight simulators and the first three production models have just arrived there, so everything's in place.'

Dan felt a flush of excitement. The Morningstar, the craft with the impossible specification! It was a tempting prospect. But what was the reality? Another trip to Mars, cryosleep, the effects of weeks of reduced gravity on his bones and muscles...

He looked at Dr Trebus. 'We agreed I could work in full gravity at the moment. My contract says I don't have to do any off-Earth flight testing for the first year. I've only been in post a few months.'

'This would be outside your contract. You don't have to do it.'

Dan looked at the three expectant faces in front of him. He was starting to smell a rat. Why were they here? Why hadn't this come through Barry?

He turned back to Norton. 'So you want me to volunteer to go out to Mars and flight-test a top-secret military craft. Why me? I'm a civilian. Why don't you get one of your military pilots to do it? And where does Customs come in?' He jerked his head in Leighton's direction.

Trebus leaned forward to speak to the other two. 'Gentlemen, I think it would be best to lay this out properly, don't you? Would you like to explain, Henry?'

Henry Leighton took over.

'I believe Kennedy told you we had a driver in custody: Jason Lennox. My people intercepted him after he left Hangar C at the Mars spaceport. The cargo he'd just delivered consisted of two containers that scanned positive for Dramatoin.'

Strange how all my suggestions now sound like Leighton's idea, Leighton's initiative.

'Yes, he told me. Last I heard he was hoping the guy would plea bargain.'

'Well, he did. Based on the information he provided we've been able to locate the factory that's been making the drug on the surface of Mars.'

Dan received the news with mixed feelings. On the one hand he was pleased that his hunch had been correct. The strategy had paid off and they knew now not only that there was a factory on Mars surface, but also where it was. On the other hand he felt guilty for placing a presumably innocent driver in an unenviable situation.

That poor bastard will be looking over his shoulder for the rest of his life, unless...

'What steps are you taking to protect the identity of this

man? I'm asking because I was just turned loose with the syndicate thirsting for my blood, and he may not be as lucky as I was.'

Leighton gave him a tight smile. 'Lennox gave us valuable information. In return we persuaded the State Prosecutor that no useful purpose would be served by bringing the case to court. The official line is that he had a medical condition which had to be treated Earthside. The company has been informed that, on medical advice, he will be unable to undertake future assignments in a low gravity environment. He was released with a new identity and relocated somewhere in the South Pacific.'

It was the best they could do, Dan thought. All the same the syndicate would be mad as hell when they discovered what had happened. Lennox wasn't entirely out of the wood.

Leighton's manner became more brisk. 'Let's go back to your own case. Your evidence led to the conviction of Mikhael Rostov. There were two possible heirs within his organization: Raoul Hernandez and Tony Navarro. It seems they worked it out between them. Navarro took a small part of the operation and set up in South America. It was Hernandez who got the lion's share.'

'Including the manufacture of drugs?'

'Yes, Dramatoin in particular. It's a big organization. They're almost certainly the only ones with the resources to make it, at least make it in significant quantities. We believe it was their orbiting factory we destroyed. As we've learnt since, they'd transferred production elsewhere by that time.'

'To Mars surface.'

'Yes, they've built a cleverly concealed factory and warehouse at the western end of the Valles Marineris.

Hernandez and his people don't yet know we arrested their driver or that he told us where he made his pickup. When they do find out they'll move production again, and quickly, so we've got to strike fast. We don't intend to miss our chance; we want to destroy that factory, completely and utterly. Even if we can only keep Dramatoin off the streets for a year or two we're going to save thousands of unfortunates from an ugly death. And it goes further than that. This drug is an important – perhaps the most important – source of revenue for Hernandez and his people. Few things would hurt them as much as a total loss of production.'

Dan's thoughts raced ahead. It wouldn't just be Raoul Hernandez's syndicate that would feel the pain. Hernandez would be marketing the stuff at the top level to every major syndicate there was. They in turn would be selling it down the line through complex channels of distribution that ended up with the street dealers. If the supply dried up, the big operators would be especially vulnerable: people like Braggazzi's New York mob, with its own peculiar brand of vicious, mindless violence. Drugs were their main source of income too, along with cyber fraud and prostitution, so something like this would hit all of them hard.

'That,' Leighton concluded, 'is why we've set up a combined operation between Customs and the Air Force, headed up by myself and General Norton.'

'Fine. But there's a problem, otherwise you wouldn't be here. What is it?'

Norton's lips tightened briefly. 'We want to use the Morningstar, but the licence granted to us under the Convention is for flight testing. It doesn't cover military operations.'

'It's a legitimate use of military force. Couldn't you

apply for another exemption?'

'No time for that. The applications have to come up before an International Panel and the process takes months. And that's not all. We have good reason to believe that the larger drug cartels have infiltrated governmental organizations in some of the countries represented on the Panel. They'd almost certainly get early warning if we went that route. Our only chance is to take action now. That, Major, is the problem.' He paused and took a breath. 'There is, however, a solution. Our existing licence does allow us to flight test the Morningstar as a weapons platform, so long as the weapons carry dummy warheads.'

Dan gave him a sardonic smile. 'I get it. Someone quietly swaps the dummy warhead for a real one, and—' The smile vanished and he looked from Norton to Leighton to Trebus and back to Norton. The penny had finally dropped. 'So that's it! I'm not just a civilian pilot flight testing the Morningstar. You want me to swoop down like a lone avenging angel and dump a bomb on the factory's doorstep!'

'Not "lone",' Norton said quickly. 'You wouldn't be on your own.'

'Oh?'

'Look, I don't want to understate the size of the challenge: this assignment calls for some exceptional flying. We need pilots of the highest calibre, so we made discreet enquiries at the Space Fleet Academy. Two names came up immediately. Both have been approached and both are now on board: Pieter Tyomkin and Carlos Henriques.'

'Tyomkin and Henriques?' Dan couldn't conceal his surprise. 'You guys are serious. Who else is involved?'

'No one else. Just the three of you.'

'And I suppose you're approaching me because I've

been involved in the preliminary discussions and you don't want to let any more people in on it.'

'Not at all,' Norton answered. 'The operation calls for three outstanding pilots and we asked Tyomkin and Henriques to suggest the third. Neither one hesitated. They both named you.'

For a change Dan was lost for words. He glanced at Leighton. The man's expression was sour.

What is it with this guy?

'I told them we'd sound you out,' the General continued. 'You see, Major, you've earned something of a reputation for your flying abilities. From my point of view you're also one of the few with non-terrestrial combat experience. I should tell you first, though, that Pieter Tyomkin will be leading the operation. Do you have any problem with that?'

'None at all. Why? Should I?'

The General pursed his lips wryly. 'Let's just say you also have a reputation for being someone who kicks against authority.'

'Put me in a life-threatening situation with an incompetent fool in charge and you might have a problem. Put me under the command of someone like Pieter Tyomkin and you have no problem at all.'

'Good. Well, there's no point in going into more detail at this stage,' there was a note of finality in the General's manner. 'There'll be a proper briefing at oh-nine-hundred tomorrow. In this room. Then you'll leave immediately for Mars. We only have time to give you a week's flight training on the Morningstar, I'm afraid, but if you're as good as they tell me you are, one week should be more than enough.'

'Hey, hey, hold on, you're going too fast. I haven't said

I'll do it yet. It sounds bloody dangerous as a matter of fact, but you still expect me to volunteer, just like that.'

A heavy silence followed. It was eventually broken by Leighton. His voice was hard. 'Look, Larssen. By your own admission you made two deliveries for Rostov's organization before you were picked up. That's a lot of Dramatoin let loose on the market. You may not have known it at the time but you're still responsible for a good deal of human misery. We're giving you the chance to wipe the slate clean.'

Dan saw red. Leighton's attitude towards him had been close to hostile from the start and now he understood why. So far as Leighton was concerned he was still a criminal. Well, it was true he'd flown two freighters loaded with the stuff, but he'd suffered agonies for it. It was outrageous to exploit a naïve mistake for the sole purpose of manipulating him.

He spoke through gritted teeth. 'You seem to be forgetting – *Leighton* – that it was my advice, my strategy, that gave you this target in the first place.'

Leighton's eyes flashed and two red spots blossomed high on his cheeks. Dan was pleased to have shaken the man's composure. He wasn't Leighton's underling and he had no intention of being spoken to like this.

Leighton was opening his mouth to speak, but Dr Trebus intervened. 'Gentlemen, gentlemen, please. Let's not lose sight of the big picture. Major, you're under no obligation whatever, the decision is entirely yours. All we're saying is that you possess the rare skills needed for this operation, and we're hoping you'll want to be part of it.'

'And remember,' Norton put in, 'Pieter Tyomkin and Carlos Henriques have already agreed to sign up and both of them have said you're the person they'd most like to have with them.'

That, at least, is an acceptable argument. Flying's my profession, and there's nobody more respected in the profession than Tyomkin and Henriques. If I backed out now I'd lower myself badly in their esteem – and my own.

He considered it for a moment.

'Has this been cleared with Barry?'

'Barry Curtis?' Trebus said. 'Not at this stage. But Space Fleet wouldn't want to stand in the way of this operation. If you agree to go I'll tell him you're being seconded for a special project, that's all.'

'All right, I'll attend the briefing. That's as far as I'm prepared to go at the moment. I presume Tyomkin and Henriques have had the chance to discuss it with their partners. I'd like to do the same, and if she really doesn't want me to go or if I don't like the sound of it when we're given more details tomorrow, I'm out.' He glared at Leighton. 'Without penalties or recriminations.'

'Does your partner have a security clearance?'

Dan was pleased that Trebus had had to ask. He and Neraya had gone to some trouble to protect their privacy, and if a director of the company they both worked for didn't know about them, they'd obviously succeeded. He replied:

'Yes. Class A.'

Dr Trebus raised his eyebrows and turned to General Norton. The General responded.

'All right. Agreed. There's one thing I can't stress enough, though. If you do decide not to take part, it's absolutely vital that no one gets the slightest hint of what has been said here. If that happened, the lives of the other pilots would be in serious jeopardy. We're relying on you to exercise the utmost discretion.'

Discretion. That word again! Now he really knew he was in trouble.

26

'I don't understand, Danny,' Neraya said. 'Why are you even considering this?'

He opened his hands. 'Look, if it was another piece of political posturing by Leighton – like the overkill on that satellite orbiting Mars – I'd tell them to go to hell. But this is different. It's a fully operational factory, Neraya, quite possibly the only one, and it's churning out Dramatoin. Just in the few weeks they've been monitoring cargoes with the big terahertz scanner they've picked up several containers of the stuff. Knocking this factory out would clear the streets of Blaze for years.'

'All right, it's a strategic target. Let them use someone else, a younger man, someone without ties. Why does it have to be you?'

'They haven't given me any details yet but they say the mission is going to take some pretty fancy flying. They said they want the best. It wasn't Leighton who put my name forward, it was Pieter Tyomkin and Carlos Henriques.'

'How kind of them to volunteer you!'

'They didn't volunteer me. They just said I was the one they'd most like to have with them. Pieter and Carlos aren't any old pilots, Neraya. They've become legends in their own lifetime.'

She threw up her hands. 'I see, so it's a great honour to go on a suicide trip with them.'

'Of course not—'

'How have you left this?'

'There's a full briefing tomorrow. In the meantime I said I was going to consult you.'

'Fine. You know my answer.'

He shook his head. 'It's not as simple as that.'

'Yes it is! Danny, it's dangerous. I can feel it in my bones. Why do you feel you have to go?'

He closed his eyes. 'Because I'm guilty, Neraya. I transported freightloads of that drug to Earth. A lot of people have suffered because of me.'

'You can't blame yourself for that – you mustn't! You had no idea what you were doing. And you paid your debt to society. They put you on probation but you spent months in prison before that! Your problem, Daniel Larssen, is you have too much of a conscience!'

He met her eyes and saw them suddenly bright with unshed tears. She wiped angrily at them with the back of her hand. He seldom saw her in such distress and his chest ached with the thought that he'd been the cause of it.

When she spoke again her voice was low.

'Danny, listen to me. When Mummy and Daddy died, something inside me died, too. I thought I'd never be able to open my heart to anyone ever again. Then I met you. I've found happiness with you, Danny. If you died... I don't think... I'd ever be happy again.'

He put his arms around her. She was quivering.

'Neraya, darling, listen. I want you to be happy, of course I do. But this thing haunts me. You know when I have bad dreams and wake up in a sweat? You thought it was the Saturn run. It wasn't the Saturn run. I'm seeing them all over again, those poor people in the streets below the flight lanes, dying slowly from Blaze addiction.'

She swallowed her tears. 'Why didn't you say? You should have told me.'

'Maybe I should have, but it's my private hell and I didn't feel I had any right to ask you to share it. I'm only telling you now because I want you to understand why I'm taking this seriously. This mission could set me free.'

She looked up at him. Her belly was quite rounded now. It would have been all too easy for her to remind him that she was carrying his child, that he had a duty to her and to their unborn baby. Leaving the issue unspoken made him feel even worse than if she'd confronted him with it. He was almost overwhelmed with his love for her.

He drew a deep breath. 'Look, I'll go to the briefing tomorrow. If I think it's not worth the risk I'll turn it down. But if I think it can be done, I'd like to give it a shot. You wouldn't want me to live with nightmares for the rest of my life, would you?'

She sighed and laid her head on his chest.

'Oh, Danny. That's the man you are. I suppose you have to do what you think is right.'

27

They were standing alone in the private conference lounge, chatting. Both looked round as Dan came in and went over to them.

'Pieter Tyomkin? Dan Larssen.'

'I know who you are.' He was very tall, with fair hair and piercing grey eyes. He barely smiled as they shook hands but Dan could sense the charisma, the mixture of warmth and authority that makes some men natural leaders. He put his hand on the shoulder of the other pilot. 'This is Carlos Henriques.'

Henriques was a head shorter than Pieter and good-looking in a slightly feminine way: large dark eyes, long eyelashes and masses of curly dark hair.

He shook hands quickly. 'Rico,' he said. 'Good to meet you, Dan.'

'Look,' Dan said. 'I want to be up front with you guys. I'm not committed to this thing, not yet.'

Pieter said, 'Neither are we.'

Dan looked at him in surprise, then shifted his gaze to Rico, who was also shaking his head. He returned to Pieter.

'They said you two had signed up for this.'

Pieter's lips twitched. 'They call it the art of persuasion, Dan. No way am I signing a blank cheque. Nor is Rico here.'

'Goddam right,' Rico said.

They obviously knew each other well. Joe Lau had said they were in the same year at the Academy. There would be a lot of competition between cadets at that stage and competition often brought out the best in people, so perhaps it wasn't so surprising that they were both awarded golds for flying. These two must have become good friends and stayed in touch after they graduated.

He was about to say something more when the door opened and Dr Trebus came in, followed by General Norton and Deputy Assistant Commissioner Leighton together with several others Dan hadn't seen before. He noted the mixture of uniforms, Customs and Air Force. Combined op.

They gathered round the table and sat down in the comfortable chairs, looking along it at Leighton, who remained standing at the end. Leighton started by introducing himself. He didn't introduce anyone else, and Dan concluded that he didn't know all the Air Force personnel present, even if he knew his own staff.

'Now,' Leighton said, 'before we start the briefing I must warn everyone of the highly sensitive nature of this operation. Success will depend on swift, positive action and total surprise. If any of you so much as breathes a word of what we're planning you could be responsible not just for a breach of national security but for the failure of the mission and possibly the death of some of your colleagues. I'm sure none of you want any of that on your conscience. So the watchword is absolute secrecy, not just before but after the mission. If we fail, no one must know we even tried. If we succeed there will be no publicity, no medals, just the personal satisfaction of having done something we can all be intensely proud of. Is that understood?' He looked around, engaging each person, waiting for a nod or a mumbled 'Yes' or 'Of course' before going to the next.

Pieter stared straight ahead. Rico caught Dan's eye, shrugged, and grimaced, and Dan nodded back, tight-lipped. Everyone in the room must have been warned about confidentiality well before this meeting. All Leighton had achieved with his little homily was to create an atmosphere of tension and discomfort.

The Deputy Assistant Commissioner handed over to General Norton and took a seat. Happily, the General was more business-like.

'This isn't the first combined op between Customs and one of the services, and I'm sure it won't be the last. It happens that the Air Force is best suited to this job and we're one hundred per cent committed to its success. I know both teams have been working against the clock to put everything together, and I want to thank you all for your efforts. Now the floor is yours. Captain Marks, could you kick off by briefing us on the geography? Captain Lauren Marks is a planetary terrain specialist with Customs.'

'Thank you, sir.'

Dan watched Captain Marks walk to the front. It was the first time he'd seen her since the meeting in Leighton's office, and again he was aware of the contained energy in the young woman. Now, observing the powerful grace and balance of her movements, he placed a mental bet that she was skilled in one or more of the martial arts. She picked up a remote and activated the wall screen to display an aerial view of a Martian landscape. She took up a position to one side.

'This is part of the Noctis Labyrinthus valley system. Just to orientate you, Tharsis City would be up here to the north-east...' she used the laser pointer on the remote, 'and the rest of the Valles Marineris would be over here to the east.' She pointed to a valley, 'This is the target.' She zoomed in twice and the image enlarged, its three-dimensional quality intensified. 'Looks like a pretty ordinary slice of undeveloped Martian scenery, doesn't it?'

They nodded. It certainly did.

'Let's put some contours on it,' she said. She overlaid a series of thin blue lines on the rust-coloured image. That made it clearer. They were looking at a flat-bottomed valley, bounded on either side by steep mountain slopes that curved around to meet each other at the southern end. At the northern end the valley was just one of a series of intersecting valleys. 'This image comes from a recent satellite survey. All right, now here is another image of the same area, taken from the detailed aerial survey of Mars that was completed some years ago, before the colony at Tharsis City was established. We can add the contours to this one, too.' Again a pattern of blue lines appeared. Dan saw the point immediately, but to make it obvious she began to alternate between the two images. Each time she went back to the older image the contours at the southern end of the valley floor leaped sideways in a series of U-shapes. 'Do you see? What the late Mr Rostov's clever gang has done is to roof over the floor of this end of the valley.' She pointed to the blind southern end. 'They probably put up an active camouflage net first, then erected a more permanent structure underneath. A few rocks and some dust scattered on the top and you'd never know it was there – unless your attention had been drawn to it. Which, of course, is precisely what our informant has done for us. Now here's another image, which we took a few days ago from a high altitude survey ship.'

The view was towards the blind end of the valley, but this time it was oblique and the sun was a little lower, so that the mountains threw their jagged shadows across a third of the valley. On the sunlit portion of the valley floor a pattern of short black streaks indicated the presence of boulders that had cast shadows of their own. Again she zoomed in twice. Now they could see it: a rectangular shadow between the true valley floor and the roof that had been constructed to look like the valley floor.

'This is the only way in and out of the facility. Freight skimmers come here during Martian night, go in, load up, and come out again.' She switched back to the aerial view. 'Here's the entrance,' an arrow appeared on the screen, 'and this is the route they take.' She superimposed a thick yellow line that started at the entrance and lengthened, as she was speaking, to snake slowly through the branching valleys. 'They travel north along the valley floor to this intersection, turn east into this valley, then along here, up this valley and finally out across the plain. That's where they join Highway 4, which links process plants and mining settlements like Enterprise and Arestes to the spaceport and the main colony at Tharsis City. That's all I have to say. Any questions?'

Pieter asked: 'How solid is that information on the route?'

She nodded. 'Our informant picked up a consignment at the factory a little over three weeks ago and that's the route he told us he took. When he reached the shuttle terminal he drove the consignment into Hangar C, where the drug showed up on our terahertz scanner. The cargo was loaded onto one of the commercial shuttles for trans-shipment to Earth orbit on a normal freightliner. We'd tagged it by that time, and it was picked up over here when it was shuttled to the delivery point. We also picked up the drivers sent to collect it, although, like our informant, they seemed oblivious of what they were transporting. However, that part of the operation doesn't concern you. We need to focus here on the facility, because that's the source of the stuff. General Norton?'

Norton nodded. 'Thank you, Captain Marks. Special Agent Kennedy, can you give us the intelligence report?'

Captain Marks went back to her seat, and on the way handed the remote control to Kennedy. Their eyes met as they passed each other.

'As Captain Marks said,' Kennedy began, 'the skimmer route was included just for background. We're not concerned here with the transport details, we need to concentrate on the factory. If we hit it right we'll get the source of the drug, we'll destroy all the current stock, and there's a good chance we'll take out the people on the syndicate's payroll who know how to manufacture more.' He put up on the screen a schematic of the front elevation of the facility and settled the green dot of the laser pointer on it. 'There's nothing ordinary about this roof. A span like that would have to be strongly constructed and heavily reinforced. We've consulted civil engineers and demolition experts about it – they weren't told more than they needed to know, of course. They thought it was likely to be a standard design borrowed from military underground bunkers. If so they would have used autonimetic materials, ceramics that adopt physical and chemical properties very close to those of the surrounding rock. It looks like that's exactly what they've done, and it would explain why it doesn't show up from space with magnetometry, deep radar, or anything else. We know a lot about this type of construction. It's very robust, so the only way we can be absolutely sure of destroying the entire facility is to fly a missile *under* the roof, through the entrance you see here.'

'Excuse me,' interrupted Rico, 'but what do you need us for? You could fly an unmanned smart missile up the valley and into that slot, no problem.'

General Norton answered the question. 'No good. It'd be picked up by the Mars surveillance satellites and straight away we'd have an international incident on our hands. The only way to do it is to have a legitimate exercise, with ostensibly unarmed craft, so that when they're picked up flying through the valleys people know, or think they know, what they're doing there. All right?'

Rico nodded and sat back. Kennedy switched to a new drawing and continued. 'This is a rough plan view of the installation.' He moved the laser spot over the screen as he spoke. 'The entrance is here and the end of the valley is back over here. According to our driver the entrance is behind a shutter. Presumably that provides additional protection when there's a dust storm. At other times it could well be up, as it was when that high-altitude survey picture was taken. Behind the shutter is the outer airlock door. It was already open when he arrived and he took his skimmer truck straight in. The cargo was waiting for him in the airlock, which is big, so we think this serves as warehouse space. The door closed and they pressurized the space so he could exchange documentation while the cargo was loaded by robot handlers. Then they depressurized, the door opened, and he came out again. He didn't go anywhere else. He says there's a wall at the back, but he doesn't know what's beyond it.'

'Do we?' Rico asked.

'Yes, we do. The wall will be the inner door of the airlock, sealing it off from the core of the facility: the laboratories, production facilities, offices, communications rooms, and living space. When they've produced a batch of stuff they'll place it in the airlock to await collection. Some of this is guesswork, of course, but it's informed guesswork; we've looked over similar, legitimate facilities on the Moon, close to Serenity. Pressure changes in the airlock space are probably managed the same as elsewhere, with two or more large pistons to evacuate the air and store it during each cycle. The technology's expensive but it's around. These people didn't have to invent it for themselves.'

'What about internal walls?' Pieter asked.

'Some will be weight-bearing, to support the roof. The rest won't be anything special. You'll get maximum damage if your missile penetrates both the outer and inner walls of the airlock and travels some way in before detonating. That way the roof will contain the blast. As I said before, we've consulted civil engineers and demolition experts about the construction of the roof. We asked them what would happen if the weight-bearing walls were taken out. It seems that even a roof of that construction would probably collapse, because of the span involved. That would be a bonus but we're not counting on it. We know this much: with the charge we have in mind the shock wave and the heat produced in the space under that roof will not be survivable – by materiel or personnel. All right?'

'What if the shutter's down?' Pieter asked.

Kennedy gave a grim smile. 'The shutter's designed to keep out dust, not missiles. If it is down you'll go through it like it's not there.'

He sat down. General Norton said: 'Thank you, Kennedy. Colonel Stansfield, would you like to take us over the Attack Plan?'

28

Colonel Stansfield wore several campaign ribbons on his Air Force uniform as well as the bird on each epaulette. He had white hair, a black moustache, a slightly ruddy complexion, and a parade-ground voice and manner. He turned the display screen off.

'Three Morningstars,' he said, 'each carrying a single Blue Lance.'

Rico pursed his lips in a soft whistle.

'Officially these are test flights, and the missiles carry a dummy warhead. On the day they'll actually be fitted with a Telonite warhead with a hardened penetrating tip. The missile will home optically on the image you have in your sights at the moment you launch it. Obviously that image needs to be the entrance to the installation. Detonation will be triggered by first impact, and delayed just long enough to let it go through the outer and inner airlock walls and well into whatever lies beyond them. Then it blows.'

'Colonel, can we vary the delay from the cockpit?' Dan asked.

His eyes narrowed. 'What do you want to do that for?'

'I don't know if I do want to. A pilot just likes to know what's under his control and what isn't.'

'Well you can't faff around with the delay – we'll set that on the ground. You can turn it off, that's all. If you do it'll detonate immediately on impact. All right?'

'All right.'

'Now, I don't know how familiar you are with Telonite, but just one of those warheads is more than enough to destroy the target. And I do mean completely. You go in one at a time – you can sort out the order between you. If Number One misses, Number Two goes in. If Number Two misses, Number Three goes in. If Number Three misses, you've failed, there won't be any more chances. As soon as one of you slots the target you come back home with the missiles that haven't been fired. All of them, understood? No target practice, this isn't a pigeon shoot. If you can slot it first time that's the best result. The roof will contain a lot of the blast and with luck nobody else will notice.'

'It'll show up on seismology,' Rico pointed out.

'Captain Marks, do you want to answer that?'

Captain Marks said, 'For logistical reasons Rostov's people needed to site the facility with reasonable access to a major highway, in this case Highway 4. If you remember, when the engineers constructed the first stretch of Highway 4 they followed the route of the old dust road from Tharsis City to the mining operation at Arestes. Mining is still going on there and it's near enough for your explosion to be taken for a quarry blast. In fact that could be the reason no one noticed the noise of drilling or other construction activity when they built the facility.'

She nodded at Stansfield.

'Thank you, Captain,' the Colonel continued. 'As I was saying, you should aim to get it under the roof. That's what we're hoping for, and that's what you'll train for. If you do miss and the missile explodes on the surface it'll make a king-sized mess and we may have some explaining to do.'

'Is there any way of aborting detonation if we miss?' Pieter asked. 'That way you wouldn't have a king-sized mess.'

'Good question. Answer is no, and I wouldn't want you to, even if you could. The last thing we want is a Blue Lance sitting out there on the ground, much less with a Telonite warhead on board. That'd be a worse outcome than if it exploded on the surface. All right?'

'Are we carrying any other armament apart from Blue Lance?' asked Rico.

'No. Look, I thought you people had got the message by now. These craft are supposed to be unarmed. We're licensed to flight test them as a weapons platform. For that purpose they can only be equipped with one weapon at a time. If we send them out bristling with lasers and shell-throwers somebody, somewhere, is going to smell a rat.'

'What about the target? What countermeasures do they have?' Dan asked.

'None, so far as I know.'

'What does that mean?'

'It means what I said. We don't know of any. Their main defence is the fact that the installation's nigh on invisible. They may have surface-to-air missiles in bunkers but I doubt it. They'd only be good against high-level attack and they know perfectly well we can't set up something like that without breaching the Convention. As for low-level attack, well, their situation – at the end of a valley with a wall of mountains behind them – provides a perfect natural defence. There isn't a craft in existence that could mount such an attack and still be able to climb out in time. With one exception.' His eyes made brief contact with Pieter's, Rico's, and Dan's in turn. 'A Morningstar in the hands of a really expert pilot. That's why we've brought you in. All right?'

He sat down and General Norton said, 'Lieutenant-Colonel Cameron will now cover Mission Training. Cameron?'

Cameron was younger than Colonel Stansfield but equally direct.

'You'll leave for Mars on Monday. We've chosen a small executive spaceliner and you'll be the only passengers. I recommend that you don't put yourselves in cryosleep; we can provision the ship accordingly. That way you'll have plenty of time to study the flight manuals and terrain maps on the way. We can't do much more than that until you get there. As soon as you arrive you'll start training on the flight simulators. You can make your mistakes on those. And don't think there won't be any. Morningstar's not like anything you've ever flown before.'

'Excuse me, Colonel, can you say what you mean by that?' Rico said.

Cameron looked at Colonel Stansfield, who answered from his chair. 'As I understand it, the controls – joystick, rudder pedals, and so on – are conventional. That's to give the pilot a familiar interface. What they actually do is another matter. Flying in thin atmospheres depends on a totally new concept. Ordinary control surfaces – ailerons, elevators, and so on – wouldn't work, and there aren't any. The Morningstar gets its lift and manoeuvrability by managing the airflow with vents all over the airframe, not just in the wings, but the whole fuselage, the tail assembly, everywhere. That puts huge demands on the propulsion system. It's up to it. In the cockpit you won't be aware of any of that. What you will notice is that the craft is extremely sensitive, and it can be a handful. That's why you need time on the simulators. Okay?'

Rico shrugged. Dan glanced at Pieter, but his face was impassive.

Cameron continued, 'The Morningstars are already out there, waiting for you. On Day 3 you start to fly them for real. Over the next two days we'll take you through a graduated series of exercises. In the evenings, you'll work on the simulators. We've entered a terrain map of the target area into them so you'll be able to practise. That's important: for this operation you'll have to fly to the target along the branching valley system.'

Dan straightened up. *Fly through that system?*

He put up his hand. 'I take it this craft has a low-speed capability.'

Again Cameron looked to Colonel Stansfield for an answer. 'Nope. Like I said, the Morningstar manages its own airflow. The faster it goes, the more efficient the system is, and the sharper the handling. You'd never be able to negotiate that system at low speed. It's got to be at five hundred knots, minimum.'

Dan blinked. He glanced at Rico, whose mouth was open.

Pieter grunted. 'That sounds damned dangerous. Why can't we just dive in at the end of the valley?'

'That's even more dangerous. The valley's not that long. To dive in, sight the target, deliver the weapon, and climb out is probably too much, even for a Morningstar. If you come in via the connecting valleys you can enter at the correct height. That'll give you more time to line up your sights on the target. And if you go in one after another the second and third craft can get their shot in if the lead craft misses the target.'

Pieter shook his head. 'It's asking a lot to expect anyone to do that on the basis of a bit of practice on simulators.'

'I know,' Cameron said. 'We've identified a similar system of valleys about 250 km to the east of the target. We're calling it Zone X. It's not exactly the same, of course, but it'll help you to hone your skills. You'll train there on Days 6 and 7. On Day 8 you'll take off at dawn and hit the target. From your reputations I'd say you guys will be ready by then.'

He looked at each of the three pilots in turn. They said nothing.

'One final thing,' Cameron said. 'For the purposes of this operation you will each be given the honorary rank of Full Colonel. That means you'll comfortably outrank anyone else in sight except for Major General O'Farrell, who's in charge of our operation on Mars. If you need something, ask. If it's humanly possible we'll lay it on. We've invested a lot in this operation and we're committed to seeing it resourced properly. That's all.'

He sat down. General Norton nodded to Leighton and the Deputy Assistant Commissioner came to the front. 'That concludes the presentations,' he said. 'Any questions?'

Rico wagged a finger between Leighton and Lauren Marks. 'This driver. From what Captain Marks said, you got him, you intercepted the consignment when it arrived, and you picked up the drivers who came to collect it.' He waved an open palm. 'It's not going to take the syndicate long to figure out what's happened.'

'Precisely. That's why we have to move fast. Anything else?'

'Yes.' Dan's hand was raised. 'What's our cover story?'

'Cover story? I don't follow you. If anyone starts asking what you're doing there – police, Customs or military – we'll pull a bag over their heads.'

'I'm not bothered about police, Customs or military. I'm bothered about Rostov's people. If all goes according to plan they'll lose stock representing months, maybe years, of production, the entire manufacturing facility, and the people who know how to run it. They're going to be seriously pissed off. They'll certainly want to know who whacked them. If they get to hear that three well-known pilots were flown in one week before the hit they're going to put two and two together and they'll come after us. I've been in that position before. I don't want to go there again.'

Pieter and Rico caught his eye. They were obviously glad someone had thought of that angle.

'Point taken.' Leighton looked thoughtful. 'Cameron, could we fly them out separately?'

Lieutenant-Colonel Cameron shook his head. 'I really think it would be better if they flew out together. They're going to have little enough time to prepare for this mission as it is. If they travel together at least they can make use of the journey time.'

There was a short silence. Then Dr Trebus spoke for the first time. 'Henry, may I make a suggestion?'

'Please, John, go ahead.'

'As I understand it there are three of the company's test pilots out there at the moment, still training on the simulators. We could spread it around that our three here are going out to Mars to give a special training course on orbital docking and medium-gravity landings. I can arrange for us to fly out the best of the fifth-year cadets from Space Fleet Academy to attend the course. Once our men get there they can change places with the test pilots. The test pilots can do the actual instruction; the cadets won't know the difference. How does that sound?'

'That's an excellent idea. What do you think, Larssen?'

Dan nodded. 'It's good but I'm not sure it's strong enough to cover the return journey. If we've hit the syndicate's factory they'll be on high alert by then, and they'll probably be staking out the terminal. The three of us are going to look pretty conspicuous coming through there.'

Cameron said, 'The return journey's a different proposition. No reason at all why we can't bring you back separately. And we don't have to use a commercial route, either.'

Leighton turned to the pilots. 'All right, that's agreed. You can fly out together but we'll bring you back separately, and we'll arrange things so as to attract the minimum of attention.' He paused. 'I think we're all aware of the importance of this operation. If you three succeed in this mission you'll paralyze one of the most dangerous crime syndicates on the planet. And if the supply of Dramatoin dries up, there'll be fewer addicts, and that means fewer people committing crimes to support their habit and eventually killing themselves with it. That's all.'

Pieter got to his feet. 'Would you mind if we consult in private?'

He barely waited for Leighton's startled gesture of consent before he turned and made for the door. Dan and Rico followed him out.

Pieter waited for them a short distance down the corridor.

'So that's the size of it,' he said.

'They're crazy,' Dan said. 'Narrow canyons, ninety-degree turns, all at five hundred knots.' He huffed. 'There isn't a craft in the world that could do it.'

'I tell you,' Rico said. 'I'd sure as hell like to fly anything that could.'

'They say this Morningstar can,' Pieter said.

'But do they really know?' Dan asked. 'This whole thing sounds to me like a computer simulation.'

Pieter nodded. 'I agree. Even the pilots they sent out there to test it are still on the simulators. I don't believe anyone's been up in it yet.'

Dan said, 'So they want us to fly three completely untested craft through the Noctis valley system at speed. Sounds reasonable.'

Rico grinned.

Pieter said, 'Well if the three of us can't do it, they're not going to find anyone else who can.'

'Damn right,' Rico said. 'This is the dream team, man.'

'That's what bothers me, you know,' Dan said. 'I loathe that drug trade. I'd hate to see an opportunity like this one pass me by.'

They fell silent. Then Rico looked at Pieter.

'What do you think, Pieter?'

Pieter was gazing into the distance. After a pause he said, 'I think we should call their bluff.'

He put his proposal to the others and then, at Rico's prompting, they shook hands all round and went back into the conference room.

Leighton and Norton waited expectantly while the three pilots unhurriedly took their seats.

Pieter's voice was calm and deliberate. 'The success or otherwise of this operation depends entirely on the handling of a prototype aircraft. You've been at pains to tell us that it's different to anything we've flown before. In the circumstances we think it's unreasonable to expect us to give you a yes or a no. But we understand it's an important opportunity and we're aware of the urgency. We're willing to go ahead, on the following understanding. When we've completed the training on the simulators and in the air we'll make our own assessment as to whether or not it's feasible to carry out the mission. If we think it is, we'll go ahead. If we don't, we'll withdraw. I'm afraid that's a decision only we can take, based on our judgement, made on site.'

There was a moment's silence. Then Norton said gruffly, 'Can't say fairer than that. Henry?'

Leighton looked like he was winding up to protest, then he subsided and gave a reluctant nod.

General Norton stood. 'All right, then. We'll see to it that the cover operation is in place before you leave. Good luck, gentlemen, and thank you.'

29

It was late afternoon, the time of day when the clients would start arriving at the south Armstrong sex parlour, and it was important to give them the welcome, the comfort, and all the services they expected. Maida bustled down the dimly lit corridor to carry out a final check of the reception areas. She went into each waiting lounge in turn, plumped up a few cushions and inspected the drinks cabinets. This evening's appointments all came from established customers, and she carried their preferences in her head. In this room there was a tray on the low table with a carafe and cut crystal glasses. She made sure the glasses were clean and filled the carafe from a bottle of single malt from the cabinet. With a last look around she went back down the dim corridor to her office.

She unlocked the door and went in. As she was settling into the chair behind her desk there was a quiet buzz from her videocomm. She looked up, saw who had appeared on her screen, and her back went cold. She swallowed.

'Yes, Elke?'

'Maida, this man Stott. It's his day today, isn't it?'

'Yes, we're expecting him now.'

'Good, I want to speak to him. Tell Papillon to take him to your office when she's finished with him. I'll be there in an hour.'

*

When Elke Klitgaard arrived she went straight to Maida's private office and asked her to leave immediately. She felt a small glow of satisfaction at the look of relief on the woman's face as she withdrew. Then she took the chair behind the desk, making the office her own.

While she waited she allowed her mind to stray to her meeting earlier that morning with Raoul Hernandez. He'd shown an impressive grasp as they went over the collected figures for the sex parlour chain. Raoul understood very well that the rise in revenue wasn't simply due to an increase in the number of client visits. Elke had put a stop to the petty thievery, falsification of figures, and diversion of funds that used to be rife. He was pleased. He was also pleased with her other little projects, which often brought in information useful to the organization. Projects like Mr Karl Stott. True, he had not been very forthcoming of late, but that was precisely why she'd come here this evening.

There were voices in the corridor, then a light knock at the door. It opened and Stott came in. She glimpsed a girl behind him, presumably Papillon, before the door closed quietly. Even Elke was surprised to see how much the man had deteriorated. His grey eyes were watery and dull, the pupils reduced to mere pinpoints, the face bloated, the complexion pasty. She bestowed an acid smile on him, one that reflected the genuine pleasure she took in his condition.

'Hello, Mr Stott. I trust you're well?'

She made no attempt to get up from the desk but waved him to the seat opposite.

Puzzled, Mr Stott? Wondering why I've asked you here when, as usual, you don't have anything for me? You've not been keeping your side of the bargain, have you? You pompous little shit, I've got your nuts in a crusher and in just a few moments I'm going to start turning the screw.

'Thank you so much for dropping by. You're a busy man so I'll come straight to the point. I'm sure you follow the news, Mr Stott. This Government is clamping down hard on businesses such as ours. They are enjoying some modest success. Times are difficult. We have to make economies where we can. We've decided to let most of our consultants go. I'm afraid our little arrangement must come to an end now. I'm so sorry.'

Stott's eyes widened. 'What... all of it?'

'Yes, all of it.'

His tongue flickered over his lips.

She smiled again.

You can't envisage life without the stuff, can you? You can do without the sex now, but you need your fix and you need it more often than ever. Whatever are you going to do?

'You can't do that!' he blurted.

The room went quiet.

Klitgaard examined her fingernails. 'You know,' she said deliberately, 'I find it a tiny bit irritating when people tell me what I can and can't do.'

A slight sheen of sweat had formed on his forehead. 'I'm sorry, I didn't mean... Sorry, it's just that, er, Papillon's been a big help to me. Professionally, I mean, of course. I'm under a lot of pressure. She helps me relax, er, gives me something to help me relax. Can I, er...?'

'I really don't know what you mean, Mr Stott. This is just a sex parlour. We do not offer any... ah... other services.'

He swallowed hard.

It hasn't worked, has it, Mr Stott? You'll have to try another tack.

He stretched his neck and ran a crooked finger around the collar of his tunic. 'You said you were... er... letting most of your consultants go. Who... er... who are you keeping on?'

'Well of course we want to maintain our contacts with people who can help us with really valuable information.'

'But... but I held back the coordinates of your Mars orbiting factory. That's got to be worth something.'

'Oh, I'm not saying for a moment that you haven't been very helpful to us in the *past*, Mr Stott, and don't think we're not grateful. But all that was some time ago. Of course, I'd like to accommodate you, if I could, but the question is: can you keep coming up with information like that? Resigning from the Board of Directors as you did must surely mean you no longer have access to the sort of privileged information we need.'

'Oh I do have access, I do. I can still get stuff. Only it's harder now. They've tightened up security. But I can try.'

She smiled, but her voice was hard. 'Why don't you try, then, Mr Stott? Why don't you try really hard?'

30

The hull of the small spaceliner trembled and the g force from the deceleration burn pressed Dan back into his seat. Pieter and Rico sat across the aisle from him, gazing straight ahead. Facing them from a seat mounted on the forward bulkhead was Amrita, their flight attendant, a tall, exotic-looking woman in her late thirties. They were the sole passengers.

It was nearly an hour since they'd been asked to fasten their harnesses. Then the spaceliner's pilots had turned the craft end for end and fired up the main engine for the approach to Mars. Oddly enough, the flight plan would have been no different for the massive E-class spacefreighter: acceleration from Earth orbit at 1g for one hour to a cruising speed of 81,000 mph, and a corresponding one-hour 1g deceleration burn commencing 40,000 miles from the destination. The main difference was that this light, compact passenger craft could manage it with a single plasma propulsion unit smaller than either of the twin engines on an E-class. The other difference was that it could accomplish the journey in much greater comfort. The chartered executive liner was fully furnished: spacious accommodation, exercise facilities, individual sleeping quarters – even a small conference area.

Dan checked the countdown on the overhead display panel. Less than a minute to go.

Abruptly the pressure eased, the trembling stopped, and the interior of the cabin was flooded with peach-coloured light from the starboard windows. All three pilots detached their harnesses, floated free, then grabbed the guide rails and hastened to the forward viewing ports. Dan had been to Mars several times before, as had the others, but once again he felt the thrill of seeing that lambent orange sphere filling the space where earlier there'd been only a magnificent tapestry of stars. His eyes traced the dark scar of the Valles Marineris to the western horizon, where it disappeared into the milky haze of the planet's thin atmosphere. There, just out of view, it would branch into an intersecting canyon system, the Noctis Labyrinthus. And at the end of one of those canyons was the object of their mission.

They remained there for a while, observing and pointing out landmarks. The broad features were familiar enough to them – Mars geography was a first-year topic at Space Academy. What none of them could have realized when they were cadets was what an intimate knowledge they would now have of the Noctis Labyrinthus.

It had taken three weeks to fly from Earth to Mars. Had it been a normal trip they would have passed the journey in cryosleep. This was not a normal trip, and every available minute was used to equip themselves for the task ahead. They studied detailed maps, memorized the names of the valleys, and gave names to the valleys that didn't have them. Then they tested each other to exhaustion on the distances, timing, and turns. As Pieter said: 'If we're going down those canyons at speed there'll be no time to consult maps or even head-up displays; we need to be carrying the route in our heads.' When they'd done that they examined Zone X, the practice terrain which had been picked out for them, and planned a route that was similar to the one they'd be using during the operation. Between these sessions they spent time on their own, studying the Morningstar flight manuals until they knew them backwards. Much still depended on the unknown handling characteristics of the Morningstar. If the aircraft wasn't up to it the option to abort the mission was still open to them, but there was no further talk of it at this stage. All three were prepared to give it their best shot.

A woman's voice, that of the copilot, came over the sound system. 'Gentlemen, we are go for orbital insertion. Please return to your seats and fasten your harnesses.'

The manoeuvres turned out to be brief; the pilots had calculated course and deceleration accurately and only small corrections were needed. A second announcement came.

'Insertion into orbit completed. Please be ready to embark on the shuttle in thirty minutes.'

They gathered up their things, making very sure nothing had been left behind. Amrita helped them to carry out a final check. Of course she could have no idea why they were being so careful. She'd left them alone for much of the journey, making her periodic appearances only to serve food and drink, to ensure that they were comfortable, and to prepare the sleeping accommodation on a twenty-four hour cycle. This personal service was part of the chartered exec package, but they didn't take it for granted. It was no trivial matter to accomplish these tasks in zero gravity over a period of three weeks. It took someone of her experience to do it, and they were genuinely grateful. They took their leave in turn. Rico, a head shorter than she was, even managed to give her a hug, which made all of them smile. Only Rico could have got away with it.

They went forward to the viewing port. They didn't have long to wait. The thin atmosphere did little to obscure the landscape below, and the shuttle was easy to pick out as it moved over the lightly cratered plains and rose quickly towards them.

'A C200M,' Dan said, noting the large aerodynamic surfaces.

'Passenger variant,' Rico said. 'See the windows?'

'And unmarked,' Dan grunted with approval, ever alert for any lapse in security.

The shuttle disappeared from view during its final slow approach; then there was a thud and a metallic echo and a brief shudder travelled through the airframe as it docked. The two spaceliner pilots emerged from the flight deck to bid them goodbye.

Rico shook hands with each of them. 'Nice ride,' he said.

Dan followed him and murmured his own thanks.

Pieter shook hands but said nothing, merely inclined his head. Typically, his extraordinary charisma seem to say more than words could have conveyed. Finally they crossed into the shuttle, took seats, and strapped themselves in. The shuttle pilot went up into the cockpit, above and forward of them. Two minutes later the craft rocked a little, and Dan knew the airlock had been closed and they had undocked. Faint vibrations told him the nose cone was now swinging into place and locking; then the craft commenced the controlled descent towards Mars surface.

As they lost altitude, bands of light passed across the

interior of the shuttle. Looking down Dan saw that they came from the geodesic dome over Tharsis City, on which sunlight was flashing fiery reflections from successive panes. The shuttle wouldn't be putting down at the terminal there, though. Instead the flight continued south-west and ended in a wide circuit of a runway that stretched five miles into the desert. At five hundred feet, banking with the port wing down, they flew past an L-shaped block located next to an apron at one end of the runway. Close by, the outline of a second building emerged for a moment, then seemed to disappear. The pilot completed the S-shaped manoeuvre, levelled off, and landed. The shuttle rolled to a halt on the apron and the noise from the propulsion units ceased abruptly.

Dan pressed close to the window, looking for a pressurized disembarkation corridor or transit vehicle but there was nothing to be seen. The pilot came down and opened some lockers.

'Okay, guys, time to go. You'll have to suit up; there's nowhere to dock here.'

The space suits were made heavy and bulky by the short-duration air supply, which was accommodated in an extra layer on the back. Here, in one-third of Earth's gravity, the weight was less of a problem than the bulk. They struggled into the suits, donned the helmets, and the pilot checked each of them carefully before giving all three the nod to enter the airlock. Minutes later the outer airlock door opened. Dan stepped out and looked around. Despite the anti-glare coating on the helmet's visor the magnacrete apron was glaringly bright, although the sun itself appeared shrunken in the sky. The others set off across the apron and he followed, moving awkwardly. Nothing was said, and the only sound inside the helmet was the hiss of his own breathing.

On the way they passed a hangar-like building covered in fine netting. It was similar in colour to the reddish-brown landscape and dotted with occasional dark patches. This was the building he'd half-seen during the approach. From a height it would be almost invisible.

The block they were heading for was L-shaped and painted silver-grey. There was an airlock on the end of the shorter arm of the building. Pieter operated the outer door and they entered. Once the chamber had repressurized and the inner door had opened, they emerged into a changing-room, where they removed the helmets and extracted themselves from the one-piece suits. They were just beginning to wonder where to go next when the door to the changing-room opened and a short, stocky man bustled in. He shook hands with each of them.

'O'Farrell,' he said. 'Welcome to Mars Testing. Everyone all right? Journey satisfactory?'

They nodded and shrugged.

'Good. If you're feeling up to it I'll give you a tour. It won't take long.'

They followed him into the complex. There was something about Major General O'Farrell that suggested to Dan he'd reached his career grade at two stars. He had an energetic manner, and he might have passed for a younger man but for the creases on his face and neck, which spoke of life experience, military or otherwise, that had taken its toll. The centre of his head was totally bald but a patch of slack dark hair remained on either side. His accent was British with a slight burr that suggested either Irish ancestry or the product of years in the States.

As he led them off, he said over his shoulder, 'No need for suits once you're inside; the whole complex is pressurized. The only way in and out is that airlock you just came through.'

He showed them the briefing room, then paused at the comms room to introduce Adrian Buick, the Communications Officer. Adrian was obviously civilian; he wore a grey T-shirt and his straw-coloured hair was tied back in a pony tail. He got up from a console and came over to shake hands.

'Welcome aboard,' he said.

Dan pointed at the bank of electronic equipment behind him. 'Nice setup.'

Adrian looked over his shoulder, as if seeing it for the first time. 'Yeah, and we need every bit of it. 'Course, for routine stuff, like talking to Mars Weather Centre, we can transmit and receive in clear. Anything else is secure, on a different frequency each time, and heavily encoded. Means you have to stay on top of things, y'know.'

O'Farrell said, 'Thanks, Adrian. We'd better get on.'

'Sure thing. See you guys.'

They continued the tour, through the office accommodation, the mess, and the sleeping quarters. Whenever they met staff O'Farrell introduced them and they shook hands. One of them was József Kusz.

'József came out here at the same time as the Morningstars,' O'Farrell explained. 'He's worked with the design team right from the start. He'll be fitting you out later with the special helmets and lightweight g-suits.' He glanced at his wrist communicator. 'Shall we say in an hour-and-a-half, József?'

József nodded.

The group moved on. Pieter said, 'This is a sizeable establishment. I thought there'd be more people around.'

'Quite right, normally there are,' O'Farrell said. 'For

security reasons we've reduced the base to a skeleton staff while this mission's in progress. The people here are the bare minimum we need to keep the place operational. But don't worry. All of them have been thoroughly vetted.'

They ended up peering into a hangar-like area with exposed metal beams and a magnacrete floor. Standing there, in splendid isolation, were three identical simulators. They looked quite conventional, each one shaped like the sawn-off front section of a single-seat training aircraft, and supported on a complex system of hydraulic struts. A staircase led to a raised platform that extended alongside all three simulators, providing access to the cockpits.

At the Academy Dan had undergone initial flight training on sims not unlike these. Externally they'd bear no resemblance to the actual aircraft. Internally, the illusion would be pretty much complete. The controls and panel displays would duplicate the ones they'd encounter in the aircraft. The canopy, which looked opaque from here, would be a continuous screen that would display the world outside exactly as it should appear to the pilot, however he moved the controls and wherever he directed his gaze. Soon enough he'd be that pilot, climbing into one of those simulators and learning what it was like to fly a Morningstar. He felt a surge of excitement. He could hardly wait.

O'Farrell interrupted his thoughts. 'When the complex was built we didn't expect to be testing more than one craft at a time. This,' he waved a hand around, 'is big enough to take one good-sized craft, two smaller ones at a pinch. Then we heard three Morningstars were coming out. Three! The Morningstar's got a short wing span but the fuselage is long. No way could we accommodate three in here, so we had to think and act fast. They delivered the hangar outside in prefabricated sections. Standard design, very basic, unpressurized, but it does the job. Do you like the camouflage?'

They murmured their approval.

'My idea, in case some bugger gets curious about what's going on. Well, can't be too careful: three Morningstars and three Blue Lances in there – not to mention the bloody warheads, dummy and real. At least we had room in here for the simulators. Got any questions?'

They shook their heads.

They left the hangar through the double doors at the entrance and started back into the main building. O'Farrell paused and pointed to a door on the right. 'That's the changing-room for the simulators. József says you need to wear the full outfit, even for the simulator. Always use the outfit assigned to you. We'll put them in separate lockers, with temporary labels on the doors; obviously we'll take the labels off and destroy them when this is all over.' He rubbed his hands briefly and clapped them together. 'Right, that's it. We'll have a bite to eat, then József can fit you up with the helmets and flight suits. After that you can get some shut-eye. You'll need it. You start on the simulators first thing tomorrow.'

31

The horizon rotated over and over, the altimeter wound down, and the ground came up. Dan wrestled with the controls but it was too late. Everything went black.

He sat there for a moment, breathing heavily. Then he glanced at the time on the display and flicked a switch to bring up the lights inside the cockpit. He placed his helmet in the box on the floor, then ran his gloved hands up over his face and through his hair, which was damp with sweat. With a sad shake of the head he opened the canopy and climbed out of the cockpit onto the platform outside. He walked along the platform, down the stairs and crossed the floor of the big hangar to the changing-room just outside the entrance. There he stripped off the special lightweight g-suit, hung it in his locker, and looked at it for a moment. He wondered if he'd ever be wearing it in an operational role.

Rico came in. Dan's eyebrows asked the question, but Rico shook his head.

'Am I getting too old or something, Dan?' he said, as he carefully took off the g-suit. 'They used to say I had reflexes like lightning but this thing's controlling me, not the other way round. Five times I lost it this morning.'

'Me too,' Dan said. 'I don't understand it. On the way out I studied those flight manuals until I could recite them by heart. I've listened to what anyone's ever said about the Morningstar, and I still wasn't ready for it.'

They turned as Pieter came in.

'Any good?' Rico asked him.

Pieter shook his head. He peeled down the top half of the g-suit and paused to look at them. 'I wasn't expecting this. It sure is a handful.'

'You can say that again.'

One of the service staff appeared at the door. 'General O'Farrell sends his apologies, gentlemen. He had an urgent communication to attend to. He asked me to take you through for lunch.'

Pieter hung up the suit and said, 'Okay, lead on.'

*

They were left alone at lunch, talking it over. None of them ate much. They pushed their chairs back.

'I've never known a sim like this one,' Pieter said. 'I'm beginning to wonder if they got it right.'

Rico nodded. 'It's like a computer game some idiot made too difficult.'

'Well this craft's supposed to have special handling characteristics,' Dan said. 'But how the hell can we learn to fly it if the simulator design's been botched?'

Pieter heaved a sigh. 'I suppose we have to persevere for a bit before we can be absolutely sure.'

Just as they got to their feet O'Farrell came in.

'Sorry I couldn't join you for lunch,' he said. 'Have another session on the sims and then I'd like to get together with you. Make it four o'clock in the briefing room, all right?'

On the way to the changing-room Dan was wondering whether this whole thing was a futile exercise. The morning's session had certainly taken the edge off the eager anticipation he'd felt to start with. He sensed the same lack of enthusiasm in the others.

There was no further conversation as they donned the g-suits. They gave each other a desultory wave as they went out to the simulators.

Two hours later Dan returned to the changing-room. Pieter and Rico were already there, hanging up their g-suits. They exchanged glum glances.

Dan shrugged. 'I don't know,' he said. 'I gave it my best shot.'

Rico said, 'Best I could do was get off the runway without crashing. And then the goddamned thing went into a loop and I couldn't hold it.'

Pieter looked at his wrist communicator. 'We'd better get to the briefing room. O'Farrell said four o'clock.'

*

The briefing room was a simple affair: white walls, plastic chairs, and a glow panel ceiling. Beyond the heavily glazed windows the Martian desert stretched away for hundreds of miles to an irregular brown skyline, the faint hint of distant mountains. The sky above them was the colour of parchment, pale and featureless.

They stood around until Major General O'Farrell arrived a few minutes later.

He gestured with an open hand. 'Have a seat, gentlemen.'

The three dropped into chairs. He scanned their faces

and evidently decided there was no need to ask them how they'd got on.

'All right,' he said. 'You've had your first taste of the flight simulators and you realize you have a job on your hands. Right?'

They all started to speak at once. Dan and Pieter gave way to Rico.

He shook his head. 'Sir, I have flown many different aircraft. If this one goes anything like the simulator I am not sure it can be flown.'

Dan said, 'I agree, General. I've been in simulators where they reverse the effect of all the controls half-way through the test. That was tough enough but it was a lot easier than this.'

Pieter nodded. 'The controls are too light, too responsive. Every time you try to do something it goes too far. Whoever designed this didn't have much idea about human reaction times.'

O'Farrell held up a hand. 'Okay, okay. Let me tell you who did design it. His name is Franc Tomazic. The word is he's the most original and outstanding aircraft designer in the world. I'd like you to meet him.'

'He is here?' Rico asked.

'Not in person, no. But he asked me to show you this video after you'd had your first sessions on the sims. All right?'

They nodded. O'Farrell dimmed the windows and the wall screen started up.

They saw the head and shoulders of a man in his forties, blond hair, grey eyes. He seemed to be unaware of the camera; it was as if he was speaking directly to them.

'Okay, you have been on the Morningstar simulator and you think it is not possible to fly it. You are not alone. This is not an ordinary aircraft. An ordinary aircraft you take the controls, you tell it what to do, it responds, sometimes quite slowly. If it's too much you can correct it and it comes back – yes? Morningstar is different. Let me explain.

'József has fitted you with the flight helmets. These helmets are special. They are designed to detect the weak electrical and magnetic fields which are generated by your brain activity. It's nothing new – eh? – these signals have been used by neurologists for many years to diagnose problems. Also they are used to control robotic limbs, and this is more like what we do here. We use the signals from your pre-motor areas to detect the movements you *intend* to make. These are translated almost instantly into action. In other words, the Morningstar is responding even before you do.

'So, you may think: why do we need controls in this aircraft at all? Why doesn't the pilot just think what he wants to do?' He smiled. 'Don't believe we didn't try this – we did. It wasn't precise enough. You need to feel you are making the actual movements. And this is your problem. You are trying to make a manoeuvre that the aircraft is already carrying out. It means you overdo it and crash.

'So what is the solution? You must be as aware of the Morningstar as you are of your own bodies. In physiology it is what they call "proprioception". It's the information sent to your brain by all the receptors in your body, the touch receptors in the skin, the receptors in the muscles and joints, your eyes, the balance organs in your inner ear. All these tell you where your limbs and your body are in space, how hard you are gripping an object, and so on. When you drive a skimmer or another vehicle for the first time it seems very large, and you have to be careful not to hit things when you park it, yes? After a while you extend your awareness to the limits of the vehicle. It doesn't seem so big any more. You know what you can get through, where you can put it. If you are patient this is what will happen with the Morningstar.

'Okay, why didn't I tell you all this before you made a mess of things in the simulator?'

Dan murmured 'You read my mind' and heard similar grumbles from Rico and Pieter.

'I admit it: at first I thought pilots would get used to the handling in the simulator without me having to tell you. It didn't work. But I still wanted you to make your mistakes on the simulators, because otherwise you would not believe how responsive the Morningstar is. The controls on this aircraft react so fast it is like your fingers, like a musical instrument, like playing the piano. Don't try to take control of it. Think yourself into it. Become part of it. Don't look at it as an obstacle that must be overcome; learn to love it. When you succeed, it will be a sensation you never had before in your lives. Good luck.'

The wall screen went blank.

O'Farrell looked from one to the other. 'Any questions?'

'Yes,' Pieter said. 'Has that guy ever flown a plane?'

'No idea. Next.'

Rico said, 'How come we don't get any instructors?'

'I don't know, but I can hazard a guess.'

'Nobody flew it successfully yet?'

'That's my guess. The three pilots we had out here until yesterday got no further in the simulators than you have.'

Dan pointed to the screen. 'Did they see this video?'

'Yes, and it didn't make any difference. You see where that leaves us? These Morningstars have come straight off the assembly line. They're the only craft even remotely capable of accomplishing this mission. You three have the reputation of being the best pilots ever to come out of the Academy. I'm hoping you can get the hang of it, because if you can't there's no mission and we've gone to a lot of trouble for nothing. But no one's asking you to get yourselves killed, least of all me. See if you can manage on the simulators and we'll take it from there. All right? Now take a short break, and then would you like to have another go?'

32

They went back to the simulators. Dan climbed in. He picked up the special helmet and this time he examined it more carefully, turning it back and forth in his hands. Sure enough the lining was patterned with a complex webbing, denser at the temples, which glittered as it caught the light.

Electrodes of some sort. This is beginning to make sense.

He donned and fastened the helmet, then flipped a switch to close the cockpit. He was about to reach for the button that activated the start-up sequence but he stopped himself. Instead he paused to think about it.

If this guy Tomazic is talking through the top of his head none of us are going to fly this machine, even if we are the best. But suppose he's not talking through the top of his head? If he's right, then Pieter or Rico may get the hang of it before I do. How will that make me look?

At the same time as he had these thoughts he realized that Pieter and Rico were probably thinking the same about him. They were all being manipulated – and there was nothing he could do about it.

Again he reached for the button.

All right, you sonofabitch. Let's see if I can—

He sat back.

Wrong mind set. You heard what the guy said: it's not a battle, it's a love affair.

A love affair. There was only one girl he'd ever loved, and that was Neraya. He closed his eyes and thought of the two of them in bed, the feeling of her warm body pressed against his, the softness of her skin to his touch. He remembered her love, her loyalty. He thought of the life that had started in her belly, that she was carrying with her. He would love that child, too, whether it was a little Dan or a little Neraya. A feeling of warmth and comfort flowed through him.

He opened his eyes but kept the feeling. All right, my love. Here we go.

He pressed the starter button. The cockpit vibrated slightly then settled as the engines wound up to speed. He released the brake. Ahead of him the apron began to move, passing under the aircraft. The runway came into view and he eased onto it and turned to line up. He advanced the throttles a little and the long ribbon of the runway began to roll towards him. He drew back a lever to activate the air cushion and retract the undercarriage. Then he took a deep breath, felt his way out into the aircraft, and eased the throttles forward. The runway unreeled rapidly towards him, he rotated, and soared into the air. Still in control, he climbed to altitude, banked gently to perform a circuit and landed.

He'd done it all without crashing! As the engines wound down and the vibration through the hull abated he felt like punching the air. He could hardly believe it! He ran his tongue around his lips and quickly set the craft up for a repeat performance.

He crashed on take-off.

He sat back with a sigh.

*

By the end of the first day he'd crashed twice more but he'd also managed three successful flights. It was progress, of a sort.

'The way I see it,' Pieter said, as they compared notes afterwards, 'you have to put the whole idea of controlling the craft out of your head.'

'You're right,' Dan said. 'I found if I simply decided where I wanted to go I could get it to respond, almost without thinking what my hands and feet were doing. But the moment I started to assert myself things went pear-shaped.'

Rico nodded. 'It's hard to explain, no? But it's real good when it works.'

O'Farrell was pleased. 'I've watched the recordings. I'm no pilot myself, I'm afraid, but it seems to me you're doing well. Still, we don't have a lot of time. To stay on schedule you'll have to spend tomorrow trying more advanced manoeuvres.'

Pieter said, 'Steep banking turns, climbs, dives, rolls and loops. We're not there yet. Not by a long chalk.'

Rico said, 'Is it okay to go back on after dinner?'

O'Farrell smiled. 'Of course, the more time you can spend on the sims the better.'

Pieter and Dan nodded at each other. No one wanted to be left behind.

*

They spent the whole of the second day on the simulators. The atmosphere in the changing-room had changed; it was almost jubilant. O'Farrell came in to meet them.

'Bit happier now?' he asked.

'It's wild,' Rico said, with a grin. 'But let's face it: this isn't real.'

'Can't be,' Dan agreed.

Pieter said, 'I think you're right. It's a fiction. The performance is outrageous. No physical craft could behave that way.'

'Well, you're going to find out soon enough,' O'Farrell said. 'Tomorrow you can take them up. No Blue Lances on board for this first flight.'

'What's the forecast?' Pieter asked.

O'Farrell nodded. 'A small dust storm came through while you were on the sims last night but we were on the edge of it, so visibility should be okay. Just remember you're no longer in the simulator. If you crash tomorrow we'll be picking up the pieces.'

33

Dan accompanied Pieter and Rico to the changing-room, this time the one adjacent to the airlock. The close-fitting flight suits they'd worn in the simulators had been transferred to three lockers there. Handwritten self-adhesive labels on the doors read: Colonel Pieter Tyomkin, Colonel Carlos Henriques, Colonel Daniel Larssen. He opened his locker, took out the suit, and squeezed himself into it. They'd been told that the special helmets were already in the Morningstars, so he picked up the standard white helmet he found in the locker and put it on. There was no room in this outfit for a breathable-gas layer; the temporary air supply was designed to be carried in a small case. The helmet was fitted with a corrugated air hose and he plugged this into a socket on the case, turned a locking collar, then switched on the air supply. A green light on the case indicated that the helmet seal was good. The others had done the same, but they still checked each other over carefully for the integrity of the suits and the seating of the helmets. When they were satisfied Pieter nodded and, with his gloved hand, pushed the large red button that opened the airlock.

The inner door closed behind them and they waited in silence. Moments later the outer door slid back and they emerged into weak sunlight. In the east the sky was tinged with blue, the residual dust having an effect similar to that of Earth's atmosphere. It was sufficiently reminiscent to be almost comforting, an impression that dissipated the moment they took their first buoyant strides across the apron. This was Mars, and it was a hostile environment.

The Morningstars were out there on the apron, fuelled and waiting, three sleek black predatory birds poised ready to take to the air.

Dan stared incredulously. He walked towards the nearest one and around it, taking in the slender flattened shape of the fuselage, the silky black skin pierced with countless tiny vents, the tail pipes of the two huge engines. He was lost in admiration.

Lightweight construction, almost certainly: special alloys, graphene-reinforced plastics... And with engines like those...

For a brief moment he entertained the possibility that this craft might really have a performance to match the one in the simulator. Then he dismissed it. The sims had simply sharpened their reflexes for a flying experience that had no resemblance to the real thing.

He looked up and saw that the others had been carrying out their own inspections. They moved closer together.

'Sure is a beauty,' Rico said over the helmet coms.

'Amen to that,' Dan breathed.

'Let's see if it flies as good as it looks,' Pieter said.

Three ground crew were in attendance, and one of them came up now. Although Dan could barely make out the face behind the visor he saw that the name tag was

'DONALD' and the epaulettes on the yellow spacesuit said he was a Master Sergeant. They'd been introduced during the initial tour.

The man's voice sounded in their helmets. 'Colonel Tyomkin, you're in this one. Colonel Henriques, you're to take that one. Colonel Larssen, yours is the far one.'

As Dan approached the far machine another man in a yellow spacesuit was detaching a tow truck from a point high up on the nosewheel assembly. Then he moved the truck to the side of the craft and plugged in a power line and an air line. Dan couldn't see who it was, but he gave him a wave as he mounted the portable steps that had been placed there and climbed into the cockpit. After the sim sessions the interior was completely familiar. He flicked a switch and the canopy closed. Looking down through the side window he saw that the ground crewman had removed the steps but he was standing there, awaiting a signal. Dan gave him a thumbs up and the man bent to the tow truck and switched on the compressor to repressurize the cockpit. Once that was done the machine's own systems would take over environmental control. Dan watched the pressure rise on the environment display in the cockpit, then there was a rattle and a slight shudder as the crew man detached the air hose and unplugged the power line. Minutes later the man gave him a wave and drove the tow truck away. The other two trucks were also going back into the hangar.

Dan removed the white helmet, switched off the temporary air supply and placed it all in a box that was anchored to the floor to the left of his feet. Before closing and latching the lid he took out the special flight helmet and put it on carefully. He fastened his seat harness, checked the wireless connection to the comms channel was working, then began to go through the preflight sequence.

O'Farrell's voice came over the channel. 'Ground crew's blown off the runway, boys, so you can roll whenever you're ready. There's nothing else up there.'

That made sense. There was very little that could fly in this atmosphere. Skimmers would travel at low level, making use of ground effect alone. The only air traffic would be shuttles taking off and landing at Tharsis terminal, and that was several hundred miles away.

A few minutes later Pieter's voice came over the channel, calm and authoritative. 'Are we go for take-off? Rico?'

Rico answered, 'Affirmative.'

'Dan?'

'Affirmative.'

'Okay. Start engines.'

Dan checked around him to make sure the staff and the tow trucks were clear of the searing exhaust from the engines, which would incinerate anything in their path. They'd obviously been warned: the trucks were in the hangar and the staff were standing safely away to one side. He pressed the starter button and the engines whined up. Moments later all three craft were moving out onto the runway, Pieter first, then Rico, then Dan.

A thin haze obscured the end of the runway. If the simulators were to be believed, he wouldn't need anything like a full take-off run anyway. Which again raised the question: were the simulators to be believed?

Pieter and Rico took off and climbed away steeply enough to raise his eyebrows. He opened up the engines, accelerated down the runway, and a few seconds later he was airborne. The push he got in the back was something the simulator could not possibly reproduce. The craft fairly rocketed into the sky and he had to remember to stay very calm and think his way through manoeuvres, just as he'd done on the simulator. Lieutenant-Colonel Cameron had been right. The Morningstar was unlike anything he'd flown before and it would have been pure disaster to let him loose on it without all those hours on the simulators.

He stuck to the flight plan: no heroics, just gentle manoeuvres, turns, height and speed adjustments. Below him, Mars surface looked pale and strangely featureless compared to when they'd arrived, a consequence of light being scattered by the residue of suspended dust left behind by the storm. Despite this the haze was thin enough not to obscure the ground as he approached at the end of the morning for a landing that used the length of the runway. After he'd taxied off, Rico landed. Pieter came in last.

He applied the brakes and powered down the engines. Then he unlatched the lid of the box on the floor, changed helmets, and switched on the air supply from the case. The green light came on, confirming the helmet seal. It was now safe to depressurize the cockpit. A member of the ground crew had pushed up the portable steps, so he opened the canopy and climbed out. The three of them crossed back to the base carrying their small cases.

Once inside the changing-room they took off the white helmets.

Rico ran his fingers through his curly hair. His dark eyes were shining and there was a broad grin on his face. 'Jesus,' he said, 'does that thing go!'

Pieter wagged his head. 'I was wrong about the simulators. That's an amazing power plant. It's like sitting astride a missile.'

Dan said nothing. He remembered too well that particular feeling from his test flight of the Trojan shuttle. He preferred to have more positive thoughts when it came to the Morningstar.

Pieter turned to him. 'I was watching you come in, Dan. You landed pretty fast.'

He nodded, grimacing. 'I know, I took the whole runway. I was forgetting the ground effect from the vectoring.'

Pieter clapped him on the shoulder. 'We'll get used to it. Let's have some lunch. Then we'll go up again.'

*

O'Farrell's instructions for the afternoon's flying were to progress to some bolder manoeuvres. 'But don't go bloody mad, now; take it one step at a time.'

Dan began with turns to port and starboard. He dropped to a lower altitude and lifted back again. He began to manoeuvre with more assurance, tightening the turns, steepening the dives and climbs. He pulled a 360-degree turn, then copied it in the opposite direction. He swooped down to five hundred feet and screamed up to twenty-thousand, cut the throttles, turned the Morningstar within its own length, and swooped down again. A feeling of exhilaration swept through him. Never had he felt so totally integrated with a craft. It was as if his hands and feet had ceased to play any part in the chain of command; whatever he willed the craft to do, it obeyed instantly; wherever he wanted to go, it went. He was like a dancer with a new-found partner, pirouetting across a celestial stage, executing moves that neither one could have contemplated without the other. He banked and rolled, dived and soared. He slalomed through the sky, banking vertically to the left, holding the turn, then banking vertically to the right, holding it again, and repeating it six, seven, eight times. He hurled upwards into a loop and rolled out at the top to travel in the opposite direction. When O'Farrell came over the comms channel, telling them it was time to return to base, it was like a voice reaching out to him from another world.

34

After he'd taxied in, applied the brakes, and shut down the engines he sat there for a few minutes, absorbing what he had just done. If he survived this mission he'd never have the chance to fly a Morningstar again. Even so, something would remain with him, a sense of completeness he'd never known before. It was a deeply personal, almost spiritual feeling and although he knew Pieter and Rico had experienced it too, he also knew that they would never be able to discuss it between them – or wish to. He took a deep breath and prepared to disembark.

He changed helmets, switched on the air supply, decompressed the cockpit, and opened the canopy. The ground crew were already placing portable steps alongside each aircraft. The canopies opened on the other two craft as well, and the three pilots climbed out. Dan saw both Pieter and Rico put a hand on the aircraft to steady themselves. He frowned, wondering what the problem was. An instant later he nearly tumbled down the steps. As his boots touched the apron his knees buckled and he, too, had to reach for support. He'd been exhilarated by the staggering performance of the Morningstar but he was totally unprepared for the toll it would take on his body. In spite of the special flight suit, which was designed to withstand the g-forces, it felt like every muscle, every tendon and every ligament had been stretched to breaking point. His joints felt loose, unstable. In a curious reversal of his experience as a test pilot, it was his own human envelope that had been pushed this time around, not that of the craft. Evidently the others had enjoyed the same thrilling flight experience, with the same consequences.

They walked unsteadily back to the base building, entered the airlock, and leaned against the outer door while the pressure equalized. The inner door opened and they staggered into the changing-room. All the exhilaration Dan had felt had gone now, replaced by an overwhelming fatigue. He closed down and unplugged his air supply, removed his helmet, and sat on a bench to work the suit off. Then he leaned back, head against the wall, unable to move. Out of the corner of his eye he could see that the others had done the same. Several minutes passed before Pieter somehow struggled to his feet and reluctantly Dan and Rico dragged themselves up and followed him through to the briefing room. All three flopped into the chairs.

O'Farrell was waiting for them. 'Well, how did it go?'

They nodded wearily.

Rico winced, stretching out his legs. 'It was wonderful, but I am not sure what it has done to me.'

'Nor me,' Pieter agreed, making a circular movement of his head as if to relieve the tension in his neck.

Dan uttered a sigh. 'All I want to do is collapse into a hot tub.'

O'Farrell smiled. 'Sorry, no time for that. We'll have something to eat, then you're back on the simulators.

You've got to learn to fly the terrain to the target. It's been loaded into the server, ready for you.'

Rico groaned.

O'Farrell raised his eyebrows. 'Sorry to crack the whip, but it's my job to keep you on schedule. And it's better than having you go out unprepared and spreading yourself thinly over the side of one of those canyons.'

*

Dan tried to ignore the aches in his muscles and joints as he accompanied the others to the hangar with the simulators. He climbed in, glad for once to be doing it in one-third gravity, and settled himself into the cockpit for the new simulation. Although he was weary he was interested to see how accurately the simulator could reproduce the experience he'd had earlier in the day.

He took off, climbed steeply away, then levelled off and set course for the entry point into the Noctis Labyrinthus system.

The flight started over smooth, level terrain but soon the intersecting valleys came up ahead. The plan for each of them was the same. First they'd fly the route slowly, at altitude. Then they'd increase speed. Finally they'd descend below the lip of the canyon and try to fly the route at speed. To help with navigation the head-up display could be split to display a plan view of the canyons on the left and the instruments on the right. He scarcely had to refer to it; the time he'd spent during the flight from Earth to Mars had given him a detailed mental map of the canyon system.

The entry point passed below him. Still at height, he made the first turn, banked sharply into the second, and at the third he didn't react fast enough and overflew it. He'd have smashed into the valley wall if he'd been flying at lower altitude.

Come on, you'll have to do better than that.

He went back and repeated the exercise, correctly this time. Then he increased speed and did the same again. After one more run he decided to take the plunge and see what it would look like to do it below the lip.

He throttled back as much as he dared and came around in a wide arc, then dipped down into the entry canyon. The sky lifted and disappeared. Almost before he could think, the first turn was coming up, then the next, then the next. The twists and turns were being hurled at him faster than he could think. He soared out at the end of the target canyon and gasped. He realized he'd been holding his breath for the entire route.

The simulator was close to the real thing, all right. If he hadn't actually piloted a Morningstar that day he wouldn't have thought it possible that anything could fly at speed through this maze, in which every turn took you screaming round sheer cliff walls with only feet to spare. He went around to do it again, a little faster this time – and crashed at the second turn. The size of the challenge in front of them was only too clear.

He shut down the simulator, took he helmet off, and buried his face in his gloved hands, shaking his head from side to side.

This is no good, I'm just too damned tired.

By the time he crept into his bunk he was totally drained, physically and mentally.

*

They spent day four the same way. When the ground crew prepared the Morningstars this time they'd opened the rotating weapons bay of each craft and winched up a Blue

Lance missile fitted with a dummy warhead. At the end of the day's flying the three pilots compared notes on how the missile had influenced the handling.

'I can't say I noticed much difference,' Dan said. 'Maybe a little less quick on take-off and climb.'

Pieter nodded. 'Could be the extra weight. But I agree: once you're in the air it handles much the same.'

'The telonite warheads may be heavier,' Rico said.

'No,' Pieter replied. 'O'Farrell assured me the dummy warheads match the real thing in every way, including weight.'

Dan reached a hand behind his neck and stretched his head back. 'God, I don't know how much more of this I can take.'

Rico smiled. 'Too right. I ache in places I didn't know I had.'

Pieter said, 'I guess we just have to hang in there a few more days.'

When they'd finished dinner they went on the simulators again. By now Dan was really exhausted and he was having trouble maintaining his concentration. All the same he knew that total familiarity with flying the target system could make the difference, not just between success and failure but between life and death, so he pushed himself further than he'd imagined possible.

The challenge of flying a machine that was so incredibly responsive and agile, coupled with the strain of following the valley system on the simulators, had one good effect: the shared experience had created a strong bond between them. Rico and Pieter were like brothers to him now. He felt they could achieve anything together, even this.

On day five they went up in the Morningstars and

practised flying in the attack formation. Pieter was tacitly accepted as the natural leader, and it was immediately agreed that he would be out in front. To avoid any turbulence created by those powerful propulsion units Rico would fly above him, behind and to the left; Dan would be higher still, behind and to the right of Rico. They took up these positions, then maintained them as they dived, turned, and climbed together in the way they expected to do in the canyon system, doing it all at a respectable altitude. Just as Dan had established a rapport with the machine he now felt an instinctive connection with Pieter and Rico. Again he felt the joy that came with complete freedom of the sky, coupled now with the thrill of flying formation with the best pilots in the world. The three moved as one and as they soared upwards together at the end of the sequence Dan couldn't hold back an exultant shout. Over the comms he heard Pieter chuckle, and Rico saying, 'Way to go!'

After they'd landed, O'Farrell told them that he'd had the simulators loaded with Zone X, the practice area, which was slightly different to the target terrain. That evening they'd all have to learn it thoroughly in preparation for flying the system the following day. Dan had an hour to lie down on his bunk and rest his aching limbs. Even through his fatigue he felt a buzz of excitement at the prospect of doing something close to flying the real mission on the following day. The excitement was, however, mingled with apprehension. To fly a real canyon system would require maximum alertness and quick reflexes and in his current mental and physical state he had neither. They'd been in the air and on the simulators almost without pause ever since they arrived at the base. O'Farrell was pushing them too far. He'd have to put it to the man tonight, perhaps over dinner.

When he went along to the mess O'Farrell was already there. It seemed like a good moment to bring up the subject but he held back. The General's expression told him something was wrong.

'Just spoke to Mars Weather Centre – thought I'd better check, and it's just as well. A squadron of dust devils was spotted about two hundred miles from here. When that happens it's usually the prelude to a dust storm.'

'How bad?' Pieter asked.

'On current indications, pretty bad. A lot will depend on the route it takes.'

'How long's it likely to last?' Dan asked.

'Hard to say at the moment. Of course they can go on for months. If we're lucky it'll be a local affair, over in a couple of days.'

'This is not good news,' Rico said. 'The more time passes, the more likely the syndicate will find out what has happened. Things could change a whole lot.'

O'Farrell nodded. 'Let's not get ahead of ourselves. We'll see what the conditions are like tomorrow morning.'

35

The three pilots stood disconsolately at the window of the briefing room. They should have been looking at a rust-coloured, rock-strewn landscape, but all they could see right now was a moving, almost featureless blur. Dan had half expected the dust storm to be brown, but it was white – quite dazzlingly white – because the smoke-fine particles scattered all the available light. Visibility was not more than fifty metres. Just the day before, the nearby boulders had stood out in sharp relief, casting well defined black shadows. Now they appeared and disappeared, dust curling around and over them and spiralling upwards in vortices which rose and fell with every change in wind speed. From time to time a patch of dust would gather on the window, then peel away again from one edge. It was strangely quiet, just the occasional pattering of the larger particles of sand against the glass.

O'Farrell came in and joined them at the window.

'Any idea what the wind speed is, sir?' Dan asked.

'They say it's forty miles per hour, gusting to fifty. Not really enough to pick up sand on its own, but more than enough when it's fed by those damned dust devils.'

'Will it become global?'

'No, they're pretty sure this one will stay regional.'

'Did they say how long it'll last?'

O'Farrell shrugged. 'It might have passed through by tomorrow but that doesn't mean it's all over. The atmosphere's so thin the heavy stuff will settle out fast, but the fine stuff will linger. You could probably fly the Morningstars all right, but it'd be suicidal to let you go down the canyons in reduced visibility. We just have to hope it bypasses the Noctis system.' He bit his lip. 'Look, maybe this isn't all bad. I've been driving you people pretty hard lately. Use the time to get some rest. Go on the simulators if you like. We'll see how this storm shapes up.'

Dan met the man's eyes. Had O'Farrell guessed what he'd been on the point of saying the previous night? Well, now they had their chance to rest. The question was: for how long?

*

The dust storm raged all day and was still going strong as night fell. When the sun came up in the morning the weather at the base was only hazy; the storm must have passed through during the night. By midday things had improved considerably. His limbs still felt rubbery but his mind was clear and he found himself itching to get airborne again. He suspected the others felt the same way. Visibility was good enough to take off; what they didn't know was how conditions would be in the canyons. They had a snack lunch and O'Farrell went to the Comms Room to talk to Mars Weather Centre.

He returned, still looking troubled. 'The good news,' he said, 'is that it passed to the north of the Noctis Labyrinthus, so visibility in the target area should be unaffected. The bad news is it passed close to Zone X. It'd be unsafe to fly it today.'

They sighed. Then Pieter said, 'General, there's a limit to how much we can learn on the simulators. This stuff in the air is settling out. I suggest we fly that practice terrain from above. At least we can get used to the turns that way.'

O'Farrell frowned, then said. 'All right. I'll inform the ground crew. Give them half an hour to get things set up.' As they turned to leave he said, 'Just be careful. We've come too far now to louse things up by taking chances.'

Half an hour later they hurried to the changing-room, suited up, passed through the base airlock, and walked over to the apron.

*

Zone X lay to the east of the target zone and it looked every bit as hard as the simulators had suggested it would be. They started by forming up as before and flying the route as accurately as they could, high above the canyon. They flew at five hundred knots at first, then repeated it twice, faster each time, with a pull-up at the end to simulate the near-vertical climb out of the canyon. Dan was being tested to the limit, but he was enjoying the challenge of staying with the other two. Pieter led them in a steep banking turn to take them to the beginning of the system again. His voice came through on their secure channel.

'Rico, Dan, what does it look like down there to you?'

Rico said, 'What, in the canyons, you mean? Fuzzy. I can't see the bottom.'

'But the sides are pretty clear. What do you say we try a run below the lip?'

Rico responded, 'Sure, why not?'

Dan felt a stab of anxiety. 'Pieter, O'Farrell said we

shouldn't push it.'

'It's no big deal, Dan. We won't go deep, just below the surrounding ground level. Visibility looks all right to me. But if you'd rather not…'

Dan gritted his teeth. 'No, let's go for it.'

They formed up at five hundred knots and shed altitude towards the starting point, a vertical cleft in the landscape. Moments later Pieter's Morningstar disappeared from sight as it dropped into the canyon. Rico dived in close pursuit and Dan followed Rico. Abruptly the sunlight was all but eclipsed. There was a narrow slot of pale sky above, a gently undulating veil of dust below, and on either side the dark, rocky walls of the canyon flashed past, so near they seemed to be converging on him. Fear clutched at his heart. He'd done this on the simulator but now it was for real. One tiny mistake, one slight error of judgement, and death would be instantaneous. He fought to shut the potential dangers out of his mind, focusing his entire attention on the others, watching first Pieter, then Rico, banking then levelling off, gauging the brief delay before he did the same, fighting desperately not to drift too close to the valley walls while maintaining speed and formation. On every turn the g-forces dragged on his limbs, pressed him into his seat, and forced him hard against his harness. At the end of the pass they climbed back into the sky and he sucked in a deep breath of relief. His heart was banging and rivulets of sweat were running through his hair and down his neck. He knew the only way he'd come through that run was by following every move of the two ahead of him.

A feeling of despair settled heavily on him. What the hell am I doing here? Why was I chosen to go on this mission? I'm not remotely in the same league as these guys.

He followed them in a long banking turn and registered with a jolt of alarm that they were going back to the starting point.

And that was when he realized that something was the matter with the aircraft.

It was inconsistent, a slight sluggishness in response. He wouldn't have noticed it if he hadn't fine-tuned his every sense to the machine's behaviour.

Rico's voice came over the comms channel. 'That run wasn't so good: these birds are too sluggish at five hundred knots.'

Pieter replied, 'You're right. Let's pick up some speed and try it again, see if we can make those turns crisper.'

Dan said, 'Hang on a moment, slight problem here.'

Pieter said, 'What is it, Dan?'

He didn't answer for the moment. He was assessing the effect of minute movements of the controls. Everything seemed to be working, but some responses were slower than others. Then it dawned on him. His scalp was so damp with sweat that it was short-circuiting the helmet electrodes.

'I think it's my flight helmet,' Dan said. 'Can we go around?'

'You want to return to base, Dan?' There was concern in Pieter's voice.

Dan thought quickly.

It'd be better to return to base but then the Morningstars will have to be refuelled. We won't get out again today and we've lost valuable time already. Pieter and Rico won't be pleased. They may even think I invented the problem so I could chicken out of making another run.

He said, 'Let's see if I can sort it.'

They went into a wide flat turn and Dan reached down

to unlatch the lid of the box on the floor. He remembered seeing a small pack of desiccating tissues in there. The lid opened and he fumbled around inside, at the same time trying to keep his right hand steady. He couldn't find it. Perhaps the case with the temporary air supply was sitting on it.

He tried to prise the case up with his fingertips but it was too heavy. Then he felt the wrapper of the tissues protruding from one edge. He tugged gently and the pack suddenly came free. The aircraft lurched but he corrected it quickly. He removed a tissue, unfastened the helmet, and wiped underneath it, starting with his hair. Then, with a fresh tissue, he wiped the inside of the helmet. He repeated it on both sides, the Morningstar rocking around with the disturbances. It was the best he could do. He refastened the helmet, put the damp tissues in the box, and closed and latched the lid.

He tried out the controls again, banking right, then left, lifting up, dropping down. It seemed to be responding normally now. He took a deep breath.

'Okay,' he said.

Pieter's voice. 'You're sure?'

'Pretty sure. Lead on.'

They completed the turn, formed up, and he steeled himself for another nerve-wracking run. Pieter and Rico levelled out and accelerated, and Dan followed them down into the canyon.

They streaked along the valleys so fast the turns were coming almost more quickly than he could react. One... two... three... four... nothing existed for him but the two craft in front. He saw them bank vertically for the final turn, first Pieter, then Rico, and he followed, still travelling insanely fast. He heard a shout of 'Abort!' and at the same time Pieter's Morningstar rose almost vertically, followed instantly by Rico's. There wasn't time to think; his hand had already hauled back on the stick and he was soaring into the sky. The others banked steeply to the left and as he followed them around he perceived the problem: the end of the canyon was completely obliterated by a rising wall of dust that was now billowing out and spreading over the ground. With his attention fixed entirely on the others he'd failed to see what lay just ahead of them.

'Where in the hell did that come from?' Rico demanded.

'I don't know,' Pieter said. 'A rock fall? Another one of those dust devils?'

Dan moistened dry lips and swallowed. 'We did it ourselves,' he said heavily. 'We stirred it up on the previous run.'

'Yeah…' Pieter's voice. 'Yeah, I guess you're right. I should have thought of—'

O'Farrell's voice interrupted.

'Tyomkin, Henriques, Larssen. Return to base immediately and report to the briefing room. Repeat, return immediately. Do you copy?'

They heard Pieter sigh as he replied, 'We copy, General. Returning to base.'

They formed up and set course for base.

O'Farrell must have been listening to their coms. He'd heard Pieter's call to abort and he was furious because they hadn't followed orders.

*

They walked slowly across the apron to the base, passed through the airlock, and took the white helmets off. Then they sat down heavily on the benches. For several minutes they rested, unable to move. Then, reluctantly, they gathered themselves up and took the suits off.

'Pity about that,' Pieter said. He closed his locker door and leaned on it. 'Still, we were beginning to sharpen up the turns.'

'Yeah,' Rico said. 'The handling's a lot better at that speed.'

Dan said nothing. He may have been the youngest of the trio, but he was fast beginning to feel like the old man.

They made their way to the briefing room, where they dropped into chairs. Even in this reduced gravity Dan's limbs could scarcely support his own weight. Once again the extreme manoeuvres had taxed their bodies to the limit. The adrenaline had subsided, replaced by utter weariness.

Pieter managed to raise his head. 'Is there a problem, sir?'

The Major General looked grim. 'I don't know. Something's up. I was told to get you here and stand by for a transmission. I let them know you were on your way. It shouldn't be long.'

Dan blinked. *Not what I thought it was.*

O'Farrell went out and returned a few minutes later. 'Transmission's complete. Adrian's putting it through the decoder now. It should be with us in a moment.'

They waited quietly. The wall screen sputtered into life. They recognized the lean, handsome features of Captain Lauren Marks.

'Gentlemen, I've been asked to speak to you directly. Please just listen to what I have to say, because with transmission and encoding delays we can't make this a two-way conversation. There's been a new development. An infrared camera on one of our satellites has picked up a significant increase in traffic in and out of the target installation. It's possible the syndicate is suspicious about what happened to their driver and his cargo, but suspicions alone wouldn't be enough to make them evacuate a fully operational factory. We have to proceed on the basis that the organization's been tipped off.'

Dan, Pieter and Rico were sitting bolt upright now. She continued:

'We've mobilized all available units but for the moment we're lying low. If they haven't been tipped off we don't want to alert them, so we'll wait till you've hit the installation. The worry is that we won't get the principals behind this operation. If they know something's up they'll be transferring goods and personnel and maybe trying to salvage some of the equipment, and they'll be doing it right now. We can still catch them on the hop but the bottom line is this. Time's of the essence now. If this operation is to have any chance of success you have to go in tomorrow. That's all, gentlemen. Good luck.'

The screen went blank. There was a moment of stunned silence, then all three pilots started talking at once. O'Farrell held up his hand.

'Pieter?'

'Tomorrow morning? That's crazy! We're not ready! We're pretty good with the Morningstars now but that dust storm already lost us a day – more than a day. It's hairy flying down those valleys. If we don't know exactly what's coming next we'll just overshoot and end up decorating the valley wall opposite.'

'You've flown the actual terrain on the simulators, though, haven't you?'

Rico answered. 'We have, but I thought we had more time for that – and more time in the practice terrain.'

'Well according to Captain Marks you haven't.'

Rico said: 'She could be wrong. Maybe it's just a fluctuation in traffic.'

Pieter sighed. 'No, I don't think so. I'd trust her judgement. If she's gone to this much trouble, and persuaded Norton and Leighton as well, there's probably something in it.'

'I agree,' Dan said. 'Leighton and Kennedy will throw everything at it now. There'll be road blocks on Highway 4 and they'll pounce on the hangars and all the freightliners currently in Mars orbit and any that arrive in Earth orbit in the next month. Everyone's probably in place already but they'll be on standby. They can't make their move until the installation's been hit.'

They fell silent again. O'Farrell looked from one to another, ending up at Dan.

'So, Dan, what's your feeling about this?'

'Well, we came here to destroy that drug factory, and I'd hate like hell to be too late. But really it's up to Pieter and Rico. I've got a fair mental map of that terrain but when it comes down to it, I'll be following their tails.' His mouth tightened. 'If they go, I'll go.'

'Rico?'

Rico bit his lip. 'I don't feel one hundred per cent ready, but then I probably wouldn't feel one hundred per cent ready with the original schedule either.'

'Pieter?'

Pieter looked thoughtfully at Rico and then Dan. Then he turned back to the General. 'Okay, we'll do it. The three of us can discuss any remaining details over dinner. Then we can put in a couple of hours flying to the target on the simulators.' He sighed. 'And after that we'll need to get some rest. Looks like we're going in at dawn.'

All three pilots winced as they got to their feet,

stretched their backs, then left the briefing room and dispersed to their quarters.

Dan laid flat on his bunk bed, trying to relieve the aches in his muscles and joints. Even through the fatigue one thought kept gnawing at him.

We've been out here less than a week. How the hell did the syndicate find out about it so quickly?

36

On the fourteenth floor of the Customs building in Armstrong's Central District, Deputy Assistant Commissioner Henry Leighton stood with his back to his desk, looking out of the window. The sky today was an uninterrupted blue, the air so clear that in the small gap between the high-rise buildings opposite he could have viewed the mountains of the Sierra Nevada if his thoughts hadn't been elsewhere. He glanced at his wrist communicator. It was time to make the scheduled call to General Norton.

He sat down at his desk, paused to let the room camera find him, and entered the number of the secure videocomms channel into the panel at his right hand. Moments later the pastoral scene on the wall of his office dissolved, to be replaced by the bulk of Hugh Norton's head and shoulders. When Leighton had broken the news to him the day before, the Air Force General had been apoplectic. Looking at the man's face now, Leighton decided it was less puce – but not by a substantial margin.

'By Heaven,' the General was growling, 'heads are

going to roll for this, Henry. Tell me where we're up to.'

The Deputy Assistant Commissioner replied in his usual measured tones. 'Captain Marks has passed the message to the pilots.'

'So they'll go in a day early?'

'I don't know. She gave them the news. She didn't invite discussion. I think they'll do it.'

Norton sucked his breath in between his teeth. 'I just hope to God they're ready. They've only had five days, and they were on an accelerated schedule as it was. The Morningstar must be the very devil of a craft to fly and I expect it's taking a lot out of them. They ought to have had some rest, some more time to train.'

'There was no choice. You know that.'

'I know, I know. What about the freight traffic coming out of that installation? You still monitoring it?'

'Yes, of course. I'm afraid the trend's been maintained. If anything, we're even more certain of it now. Someone tipped off the syndicate all right.'

'Who the hell is it, Henry? It's not at my end, I can tell you that. The only people who knew about it here were Stansfield and Cameron – and O'Farrell on site, of course. I'd trust all three with my life. It's got to be at your end.'

Leighton grimaced. 'It's not us, Hugh, I'm quite sure of that. We handled the whole operation with a small team. Lauren Marks is coordinating things. Alec Kennedy is looking after Intelligence, and Martyn Strijker is our Communications Support Officer. That's it. Tight as a drum. It's not from the team.'

'What about the rest of the staff? They could get access couldn't they?'

'Not at this level. Even if they could, the answer would be the same. No one's even considered for this Division unless they have an unblemished service record, and every one of them's vetted thoroughly and at regular intervals. That goes for the staff in this building and the people on assignment out there on Mars. These people are handpicked, Hugh. They believe in what they're doing. And nothing like this has ever happened before.'

'Well maybe you've been bugged.'

'The offices are swept regularly but I ordered another sweep right away, just in case. It's very unlikely though. We don't have many visitors and none of them would be left unsupervised long enough to plant a device.'

'What about access from a higher level?'

'We're almost at the top level of security here – unless you're talking about the White House.'

Norton grunted. 'All right, let's talk about the White House.'

'Are you serious? The President of the United States of America has criminal—?'

'It doesn't have to be the Oval Office. There are dozens of others in the Administration with that level of clearance. Could be any one of them.'

Leighton was growing impatient. 'Come on now, Hugh, let's be sensible. Do you have any idea how much ordure would hit the fan if we told the President there was a mole in the White House? And how much of it would settle on us if it turned out not to be true?'

'Dammit, we've sent three brave men to fly their guts out for a mission that you and I know is nigh on impossible, and somewhere around there's a weaselly little bastard who may have compromised the entire show. Our guys are even more at risk now than they were to start with. So am I prepared to stick my neck out for them? You bet your goddamned ass I am!'

Leighton cut in. 'All right, Hugh, look, calm down. I don't disagree, but there's no need to jump in at the deep end. This Division runs dozens of operations. The White House has a right to know what we're doing but those people are seldom that interested and we're not obliged to tell them. In any case they'd ask the Commissioner for information and he'd pass the request to me. And that hasn't happened.'

'So where does that leave us?'

'We have to take it one step at a time. Clearly someone has been accessing our network. The first step is to find out who it is.'

'Can you do that?'

'Strijker's onto it. He's got some special software for sniffing out unusual patterns of activity. He's running it now on all the network traffic logged since the operation began. In fact in about ten minutes he'll be reporting back to me with Marks and Kennedy.'

'Okay, Hugh.' General Norton sighed. 'It sounds like you've got it pretty well covered. Let me know if you come up with anything, will you?'

'Of course.'

Leighton disconnected the call and substituted a clock for the mural that normally adorned the wall. He was in no mood for pastoral scenes. He paused, head bowed.

Hugh's reaction was understandable. He'd gone through the same process himself, mulling over everything he knew about each member of Hugh Norton's team and then each member of his own. It had quickly led him to dismiss the idea that any one of them would have leaked the information. Even so, the mere fact that he'd considered the possibility left a faint shadow, a taint, behind. The operatives in both teams probably felt the same way.

They'd worked hard on this mission and now they'd been badly let down. They would have had the same thoughts, suspecting one another while aware at the same time that they could be under suspicion themselves. It was a poison in their midst.

The digits on the projected wall clock flashed red for his next appointment, and almost simultaneously there was a knock on his office door.

'Come in.'

The door opened and Lauren Marks strode in, followed by Alec Kennedy and Martyn Strijker. Leighton remained behind his desk and gestured to the chairs opposite. He looked expectantly from one to the other.

'Before we start, any fresh ideas?'

After a pause Kennedy coughed lightly. 'It's just a thought, sir…'

'Yes?'

'Well, information on the mission is posted on a very high-security network. The only ones with access to it are ourselves and people at levels above. Er, I was thinking about the Commissioner, sir.'

'The Commissioner?'

Kennedy swallowed. 'He has access, sir, and he has to talk to politicians, defend our budget, and so on…'

Leighton held up a hand. All three were watching him now, waiting for the explosion. Instead he spoke in measured tones.

'Kennedy, you've almost answered this yourself. I handle operations. The Commissioner works at an entirely different level, the political level. He certainly knew we were planning an operation because I told him we were, but that was it. He could have accessed the network but I've never known him to do it and I'm not even sure he knows how to. If he wants an update he calls me in; that way he can be sure of getting the very latest intelligence. In this case he hasn't.'

'I'm sorry, sir, I just thought…'

'Don't be sorry. Look, I'm absolutely convinced the leak did not come from within this building, and General Norton is equally sure it wasn't one of his team. I want you all to banish the notion, even the mere suggestion, from your minds. This threat has come from outside.'

There was a slight slackening of tension. Kennedy and Marks shifted in their chairs.

Strijker was frowning. 'No one can hack into our servers, sir. We have firewalls twenty feet thick and the traffic is monitored continuously by packet sniffers. If anyone tried, all the alarm bells would go off at once. And this particular network is even more secure. You could steal the right passwords and it still wouldn't work. It can only be accessed from terminals with quantum encryption that matches the quantum decryption in our own system.'

'I know all that. I'm not talking about illegal access, I'm talking about someone logging on legally. Whoever it is may not have criminal connections, but it could be they're not as security conscious as we are. That's why I asked you to look for unusual activity. Did you find anything?'

'Nothing unusual, sir. Only one access from outside the building: high level, duration eight minutes. I traced it to Admiral Stott's office.'

Marks and Kennedy looked at Leighton. He pursed his lips briefly.

'The Fleet-Admiral was very helpful to us in getting the Blue Lance missiles transferred. It's reasonable for him to want to know how we're getting on. In any case his reputation's unimpeachable. He's on the Chiefs of Staff and he's an advisor to the President.'

'We're back to square one, then.' Strijker sounded disconsolate.

Kennedy sighed. 'Even if we do get the person responsible, isn't it closing the stable door after the horse has bolted? If information's been lifted from the network and found its way to the syndicate, that's it, isn't it? The damage has been done.'

Lauren Marks shook her head. 'Not necessarily,' she said. 'What they could get from the network at the moment would be very sketchy. They'd know only that an operation is planned. They wouldn't know who's involved, or how it's being done, or when. Standard practice is to post details like that at a later stage.'

Leighton's eyes narrowed. 'You weren't planning to do that, were you?'

She gave a short laugh. 'I wouldn't dream of it! I wasn't going to anyway, but after this – well...' She held up her hands.

'But,' Leighton continued slowly, 'whoever accessed the network doesn't know that, do they?'

Strijker looked at him. 'Then they could be back, to find out...'

'Precisely,' Leighton said. 'It's worth keeping an eye out, in case they do, 'How often do you run that software?'

'We generally run it at weekends.'

'Okay. I want you to start running it once an hour.'

Strijker's eyes widened. 'That's not possible, sir!'

They all jumped as Leighton struck the desk with the flat of his hand. 'We're directly responsible for the lives of three men, not to mention the consequences if that damned drug continues to reach our streets, and you're telling me it's not possible?'

Strijker licked his lips. 'Sir, with the best will in the world... Parts of the check close the servers down to new activity for minutes at a time. If we did what you say it would compromise the operational efficiency of every division in this building.'

Leighton's hand remained on the desk. 'Goddammit, is that the best we can do?'

The silence lasted for several seconds. Then Lauren Marks said, 'Martyn, if the servers go down, don't you have a backup?'

'Sure. There's a parallel server bank we can cut in.'

'Well, there you are. Alternate between the two. You can be checking the servers that are off-line while the others are carrying the regular traffic.'

'Yeah...' he nodded slowly, then smiled. 'Yeah, that ought to work. Takes a little time to do the switching though. I reckon we could manage checks at about two-hour intervals.'

Leighton nodded. 'All right, I'll settle for that. Get it going right away.'

'How long for, sir?'

'Until the operation's over.'

'You mean until they hit the target?'

'No, I said until the operation's over. The operation doesn't end until the pilots are safely back on Earth.'

37

An hour before dawn the ground crew went out to the camouflaged hangar to prepare the Morningstars. They lowered the Blue Lance missiles, removed the dummy warheads, and fitted the Telonite warheads with the hardened tips. Then they winched the missiles up again and closed the weapons bays. Finally they fuelled the three craft up and towed them out. Everything was ready.

O'Farrell came to the changing-room to see the pilots off. He shook hands with each in turn, adding a pat on the shoulder.

'Best of luck, all of you. Hit the buggers where it hurts!'

He was smiling, but the creases around his eyes betrayed his concern.

The rising sun cast their shadows long over the apron as the three suited figures walked to the waiting Morningstars. The ground crew were standing by.

Dan completed the preflight procedure, then looked up towards the end of the runway and beyond to the horizon. Conditions were excellent: the haze left behind by the dust storm had all but cleared, and they could expect visibility as good or better than this in the target area.

Pieter's voice came through on the comms. 'I'm go. Rico?'

'Affirmative.'

'Dan?'

'Affirmative.'

'All right. Start engines.'

Pieter and Rico taxied out to the runway and Dan followed. He felt a mixture of tension and relief. Tension, because whatever took place in the next hour or so would determine whether or not he ever touched down on this runway again. Relief, because at last this was it, the moment they'd been preparing so hard for. They were committed, and the success or otherwise of the mission was now in their hands.

His Morningstar trembled as first Pieter then Rico opened up their engines and surged down the runway. Then his own hand was advancing the throttles, the craft responding with a savage thrust in the back that seemed never-ending as they accelerated to flying speed. Two diamond-shaped silhouettes rose ahead of him and seconds later the ground fell away and he was following them into the lightening sky.

They formed up and banked in a sweeping turn that placed them on a southerly heading, a route they had chosen to avoid overflying Highway 4. Dan settled himself down for the flight, pulling lightly at his suit and harness to make sure he had full freedom of movement. They flew at two thousand feet in total silence. Their specially encoded communications channel would not be used now until the last moment in case the radio emissions signalled their presence.

On the south-west horizon the volcanic mountains of

Tharsis came into view, shimmering pink in the hazy sunshine. Below them the lowland plain was coated with a layer of pale dust, deposited there by the recent storm. It was smooth enough to give them the eerie sensation that they were barely moving. Then a sharp-edged crater would materialize in the distance, grow, race towards them and whisk away under the craft, reminding them of their speed.

They left behind the path of the dust storm. The plain now assumed a darker shade and became more rugged. Although the oblique sunlight was much weaker than on Earth it threw every feature into sharp relief, and the ground was striped with shadows cast by fields of rust-coloured boulders.

They changed heading to the south-west. Gradually the terrain became more grooved and fractured. Then, on the horizon, a chaotic tangle of chasms appeared and grew rapidly, spreading to either side of them. Somewhere in that system was the target. It looked unassailable, but there was a way in and they knew where to find it.

They formed up as they'd done during the practice sessions: Pieter in the lead; Rico above, behind and to the left of him; Dan above, behind and to the right of Rico. The entrance valley appeared ahead, rushing towards them, and first Pieter then Rico dived into it. Dan followed, feeling again the surge of adrenaline as the sky all but disappeared above him. He levelled out six hundred feet above the rock-strewn floor, keeping station with the others. They were travelling fast and everything was so close that it seemed ten times faster. He forced himself to stay calm; it would take only a second's panic to lose his line of flight – and his life. They threaded from one valley to the next, banking almost vertically this way and that between the steep rocky slopes. He seemed to be flying at some subconscious level, the Morningstar interpreting his every move, while he focused on Pieter and Rico and let their crisp manoeuvres prompt his own. Ahead of them the target valley opened up and in a final turn they banked into it.

Pieter broke the silence. 'Weapon bays open. Increase separation. I'm going in.'

They hurtled down the valley like three winged bullets. On the left, Rico was flying in shadow; on the right, Pieter and Dan were in sunlight. Pieter had moved further ahead of them, increasing speed and dropping to a height of fifty feet for the attack run. In the distance, but coming up fast, was that high curtain wall of rock, and somewhere in front of it, nestling at the foot of the valley, lay the target.

At that moment the Hostiles Indicator in Dan's cockpit went berserk, flashing both 'INCOMING' and 'COLLISION' in red letters. His pulse raced and every muscle in his body was poised to take evasive action – but from what? The Morningstar was invisible to radar. Had they crossed a laser beam or had the onboard systems picked up the infrared signature of a missile? The answer came almost immediately: something rose from the floor of the valley in front of them. For a brief moment he couldn't interpret what he was seeing, then it dawned on him with a shock.

Rocket net!

A chain mesh propelled by a line of small rockets was going up across the valley from one side to the other.

Rico shouted 'Break!'

Dan peeled right and soared upwards. Still climbing, he banked and looked over his shoulder to see where the others were. He could see Pieter's craft climbing and turning but he was too close – much too close. Dan's stomach clenched.

Please, not Pieter…

A ball of white flame expanded and continued to grow and grow. Its brilliance illuminated the valley from side to side, then it faded through yellows and reds to nothing. Dan felt sick. At that speed it must have been like hitting a brick wall. He looked for Rico and found him. Rico had been further back than Pieter. His craft was still rising – but so was the net. Dan swallowed hard.

He might still make it.

A ragged wave, set up by the impact of Pieter's Morningstar, travelled along the net. It buckled and began to fall away and Rico cleared it with feet to spare. As he did so a series of bright explosions followed him, and Dan glimpsed a stream of fireballs coming out of the wall of rock behind the target. Angrily he recalled his exchange with Colonel Stansfield.

'What about countermeasures?'

'So far as I know there aren't any.'

There are, Stansfield! There frigging well are!

The rocket net could have been automatic. What about the shell thrower? In spite of everything that was going on, including the fearsome explosion of Pieter's Morningstar, it had switched away from Pieter and tracked Rico well enough to get in a burst just as he climbed clear. Autotargetting systems weren't that sophisticated. It was more likely a human operator.

Damn them to hell!

As Rico and Dan came out of the valley each of them turned and levelled off, Rico to the left, Dan to the right, so as to stay outside the engagement envelope of the shell-thrower. Then they flew back towards the open northern end of the valley. Rico's voice over the comms channel was tight.

'Where did those air-bursts come from?' he demanded.

'Behind the target, extreme right, about five hundred feet up.'

'Okay. Stand by, I'm going in again.'

'You do and you'll be a sitting duck for that shell-thrower. Let me go in first and take it out.'

'They said we weren't to explode these babies on the surface. Remember?'

'Yeah, they also said there weren't any countermeasures. Remember?'

'You're right. Okay. Use our entry point and go in hard down the right side. It may not sight you immediately.'

Dan thought quickly. That would never work. He'd be in the line of fire far too long and they'd range him easily. To have any chance he'd need to enter about half-way down. There was a narrow valley branching off on the right. They'd dubbed it Mickey.

'Negative,' he said. 'I'll turn in from Mickey.'

'Dan, we haven't practised on that one!'

'Just watch me.'

Rico climbed away. Dan needed the missile to detonate on impact so he flicked the switch controlling the Blue Lance warhead fuse to 'DELAY OFF'.

The hours they'd spent together with the maps and the flight simulators, studying and memorizing this terrain, were paying off. He banked in a long turn to the left, then tightened the turn and dropped into a chasm below, picking up speed. He levelled out at five hundred feet, so as to be at roughly the same level as that shell-thrower when he went in, and with the map unreeling in his head he started the sequence of turns. There was no one to follow now, no Pieter, no Rico, but it hardly registered in his mind. At his centre there was a core of ice-cold anger, and all other feelings and emotions had been shut out. He, the Morningstar, and the missile in the aircraft's belly, had fused to form a single devastating weapon and he was going to ride it right to the target.

The last chasm was running out and ahead of him the target valley began to open up, the opposite wall deep in shadow. He switched on the head-up weapon sight, with its range markers and cross-wires, and banked vertically in a right turn that held him within feet of the mountainside. Beyond his right shoulder the sheer walls passed in a blizzard of brown rock. They curved away and the curtain wall at the end of the valley spread out in front of him. Almost immediately white fireballs materialized at the right-hand end. They seemed to drift lazily out at first, then ever faster as they shot towards him. He jinked the Morningstar to the left and back to the right, still perilously close to the steep side of the valley, trying to throw off their targeting system while maintaining his line towards its source. The fireballs seemed to be coming nearer; they were beginning to get his range. A shell exploded close to the canopy, and in spite of the gold metallization on his visor he was temporarily blinded. He looked at the weapon sight and a white after-image floated around in the centre of it. He blinked wildly but he could no longer see his target.

He was still travelling fast. The entrance to the factory must have gone by; he was leaving this terribly late. He banked towards the right and straightened up, his thumb crooked over the missile launch button, eyes half-closed, straining to see something, anything. If he stayed blind a moment longer he'd have to pull up. Another stream of fireballs came out of the rock face, just bright enough to show through the fading after-image in the centre of his weapon sight. That was all he needed. He made an instant correction, closed his thumb on the firing button and felt the Morningstar lift as it shed the weight of the big Blue Lance missile. With his left hand he pushed the throttles through the detent to full boost while with his right hand he hauled the stick back and to the left, streaking over the face of the jagged mountainous barrier that closed the valley off. The rocks sped under him in a continuous blur. A groan escaped his lips as the extreme g squeezed the breath out of him. He was pinned in his seat, his limbs so heavy he could barely move. The cockpit went dark as he flew into the shadow of the peaks and he tensed himself for the grinding impact of metal on rock. Then suddenly the cockpit lit up and there was sky everywhere.

He took a deep breath and levelled the Morningstar, flying back down the opposite side of the valley. Glancing over to his left he could see a huge mushroom of smoke and dust rising from the corner of the valley where the missile had struck. Below it a billowing skirt was descending into the valley, a landslide dislodged by the force of the explosion. Then he saw with dismay that it was spreading out over the valley floor, a tidal wave of dust and bounding rocks that would soon overtake the target and obscure it completely. Where the hell was Rico? If he was coming in along the valleys again he'd miss his chance.

Something prompted him to look up. It was Rico's Morningstar, diving vertically out of the sky. Dan's guts turned to jelly. What was it Stansfield had said?

'The valley's not that long. To dive in, sight the target, deliver the weapon, and climb out is probably too much, even for a Morningstar.'

Rico had the last remaining Blue Lance and he was coming down into the valley, steep and fast.

He watched, not daring to breath, expecting at any

moment to see the dreadful explosion as he cratered the floor of the valley. Then, incredibly, he flattened out of the dive, feet above the valley floor. He was less than half a mile from the entrance to the installation and behind the entrance a wall of dust fifty feet high was racing forward. There was a stab of white flame from the Blue Lance as Rico loosed it before he pulled the Morningstar up in a screaming climb. The flame from the Blue Lance disappeared. Had it gone into the entrance or into the dust cloud from the landslide? He banked gently to the left to keep the target in view. Out of the corner of his eye he could see the black diamond of Rico's Morningstar breaking clear of the mountains and rising into the open sky. Then the whole floor of the valley seemed to lift. The landslide continued to roll into a blurry ocean of dust that had risen from wall to wall of the valley.

Rico's voice came over the comms link.

'Job done. Come on, Dan. Let's go home.'

As they turned back towards base a plume of dust hundreds of feet high was rising over what had once been the Rostov syndicate's drug factory.

38

They taxied the two Morningstars up to the hangar. Dan closed down the engines and flopped back in his seat. After a few minutes he took a deep breath, gathered himself up, detached his harness, changed helmets, and opened the valve on the temporary air supply. This done, he decompressed the cockpit and raised the canopy. Master-Sergeant Donald was there, pushing the portable steps up to the aircraft. He looked up, his face, just visible through the visor, asking a question. Dan shook his head sadly. The man's shoulders slumped and he turned and waved back one of the three tow trucks which were standing in readiness.

Dan descended the steps carefully, carrying the small case with his portable life support in his right hand, his left hand on the aircraft for support. The moment his feet touched the ground his legs began to give way, but the Master-Sergeant was there and stepped forward quickly to take his arm. Now Rico came over, walking unsteadily with the help of another member of the ground crew. The four crossed slowly from the apron over to the main building.

The two pilots staggered from the airlock into the changing-room, slumped onto a bench and sat side by side for what seemed like many minutes. Eventually they stirred and took off the helmets. The rage that had sustained Dan during the last part of the mission had bottled up any other feelings, but now the sense of grief and loss welled up inside him and overflowed. He turned to Rico and they fell together in an awkward embrace.

They pulled back.

Rico's voice was a broken whisper. 'I can't believe it.'

Dan looked away to avoid seeing the tears in the other man's eyes. 'Neither can I.'

*

They'd just peeled off their flight suits when Major General O'Farrell hurried into the changing-room.

'I got your signal,' he said. 'Well done, very well done. I passed the codeword to Leighton right away. His people are probably going in at this moment—' He looked quickly from one to the other. 'Where's Pieter?'

Rico closed his eyes and shook his head.

O'Farrell blinked several times, then moistened his lips. His voice was a hoarse whisper. 'What happened?'

Rico told him about the rocket net and the shell thrower. The General clenched his fists.

'We should have known they had defences.' Then he shook his head. 'Such a fine man. What a waste. What a terrible, terrible waste.'

Dan and Rico followed O'Farrell to the briefing room and dropped into chairs. O'Farrell was anxious to have a more complete account of the mission, and as Rico was the senior pilot Dan let him do the talking. When he'd finished, Rico said:

'One more thing, General. I'd be lying in bits in that valley, too, if it hadn't been for Dan. He nearly flew up the barrel of that goddamned shell-thrower to take it out. I never in my life saw flying like it.'

Dan grunted. 'That's rich, coming from a guy who dived into the valley, launched his missile from about fifty feet up, and still managed to pull out in time.'

Rico turned and met Dan's eyes. He shook his head ruefully. 'I tell you, Dan, I was so fucking mad by then I didn't know what in hell I was doing.'

Dan closed his eyes and nodded. 'Same here.'

O'Farrell looked from Rico to Dan and back again. 'I think we can leave that bit out of the report, don't you?' He glanced at his watch. 'We'd better get over to the comms room.'

They sat down together and composed two short coded messages to a pre-arranged secure address on Earth. One was a bare account of the mission. It would suffice for the moment; there would be a full debriefing after they got back. The other was a quick message of reassurance to be passed on to Rico's partner and to Neraya. Sadly no such reassurance could be given to Pieter's family. Leighton or Norton or one of their staff would have to deal with that. They rose grimly and painfully to their feet.

It seemed to Dan that his legs would not support him for a moment longer. The violent manoeuvres of the mission had taxed him even more than the training flights. He'd been mercifully unaware of what was happening to his body during the heat of the action, but now it was really making itself felt. He went to his quarters, collapsed onto his bunk, and didn't move for a very long time.

39

To maintain the low profile of the operation the two pilots were taken to Tharsis City separately. Dan remembered little of the journey. He was checked into The Springs, one of the most luxurious hotels in the colony. Every facility had been made available to him for just as long as he needed it.

He'd expected to spend a day or two there at the most. The plan was that he would then fly himself back to Earth, where he would dock and make his transfer at some distance from the more frequented ports. That plan now went out of the window. It was a full month since he'd left his home planet, a month in which he'd had a three-week journey in zero gravity and a week on Mars in one-third gravity. The cumulative effect of all that, combined with stresses many times normal during the mission, had had a devastating effect on him. He felt as if every joint had been pulled apart and then put back, but not all the way back. Every muscle ached and his limbs were feeble and loose.

When he stood or tried to walk there was a constant risk that his legs would fold under him. The physical discomfort and disability fogged his mind and he had problems thinking clearly.

He slept a lot. His waking hours were spent mainly in the Fitness Centre, submitting his aching body to the attentions of the masseuse and the resident physiotherapist, doing gentle exercise and lying in warm mineral baths. He found it hard to believe now that he'd even managed to walk from the Morningstar to the base, although he supposed the adrenaline was still flowing in the immediate aftermath of the mission. At one point he wondered if Rico had fared any better than he had. Perhaps he had. It would have been nice to see him, speak to him – even just be with him – to share what they'd been through, but the security risk was too great.

The pain and mental exhaustion ebbed and flowed. At better moments his mind would become active. The operation had been more dangerous than he could possibly have imagined. Just reminding himself that he'd come through it alive gave him a flash of exultation. Then he'd be overwhelmed by feelings of guilt, of undue privilege, that he'd been spared and Pieter Tyomkin had not. With little else to think of, it preyed on his mind. Rico would be going to see Pieter's family, which he'd told Dan was as close to him as his own, and Dan didn't envy him. But his own life had also hung by a thread. Had things worked out differently, Pieter and Rico would be going home to their families, and Neraya would be the one left to grieve.

He desperately wanted to see her. This whole business had been very hard on her right from the start and even now she'd been told little more than that he'd completed the assignment. And the baby would be due quite soon – that was certainly something he couldn't afford to miss. But to fly himself back in his present condition was out of the question. What was the alternative? He could go to the commercial spaceport, where he'd board a scheduled service, arrive at a busy orbiting dock, and ride a packed shuttle down to Earth. But for a well-known pilot, in obviously poor shape, to be travelling in full view just days after a devastating aerial attack on the syndicate's most important installation would be sheer lunacy; it would place not only him at serious risk but Neraya, too. Could they get someone else to fly him? That was feasible, but still far from ideal. No one had any doubts about the reach of this syndicate, and the fewer people who knew he was returning from Mars at this juncture the better. Really the only secure way was the one he'd agreed to at the outset: wait till he was fit and fly back on his own. He did his best to contain his impatience.

*

One week after the transfer to Tharsis City he was lying on a narrow bunk, having knots massaged out of his neck and shoulder muscles, when a hotel clerk came over to him.

'Mr Larssen?'

'Yes,' he grunted. So far as the hotel knew, he was a civilian.

'Excuse the interruption, sir. There's a gentleman to see you.'

'Did he give a name?'

'It's a Mr O'Farrell, sir. He's waiting for you in one of our private conference rooms. Would you like me to take you up there?'

'Yeah. Let me get some clothes on.' He swung his legs round and sat up, then nodded to the masseuse. 'Thanks,

Linda.'

Mr O'Farrell, eh? I wonder what the Major General wants.

*

Major General O'Farrell was pacing the room wearing a blue, chalk-striped suit that may have been fashionable twenty years earlier. He turned as Dan came in and his careworn features lightened. They shook hands, and O'Farrell pointed to a couple of armchairs. Dan lowered himself carefully into one, aware of the scrutiny from O'Farrell, who'd settled in the other.

'Good of you to come over,' Dan said.

'It seemed the sensible thing to do. The comms line from the base to the hotel isn't secure. I could have sent a skimmer for you but then you'd have had to suit up to get into the base. I wasn't sure whether you could manage that.'

Dan winced at the mere thought. He said, 'I never actually asked. Is this hotel secure?'

'Oh yes, we checked it out thoroughly. It's part of a well-known chain, and there's not the slightest hint of syndicate involvement. Rest assured: top-level meetings are held here and privacy is guaranteed. How are you feeling?'

'Frankly, like I've gone fifteen rounds with a champion wrestler.' He added quietly, 'But I'm not complaining. At least I'm alive.'

O'Farrell looked at him. For a moment the pain flickered through his face and neither said anything.

'So,' Dan said. 'What's been happening?'

'Nothing much. Deputy Commissioner Leighton and General Norton both sent warm congratulations. And commiserations, of course.'

'Of course. But that's not why you came, is it?'

'No. I wanted to talk to you because we had a departure slot for you.'

'What do you mean "had"?'

'Have you been watching the Space Weather Forecasts?'

'No, I... to be honest, I've been pretty much out of it the past week.'

'Well take a look now.'

He dipped into an inside pocket and handed Dan a sheet of smart paper, headed:

INTERNATIONAL SPACE WEATHER BUREAU: SEVERE WEATHER WARNING

He scanned it quickly.

'**...activity is likely to persist for at least four weeks. The solar flares during this period will be powerful X-class events. There will be rapid fluctuations well over ten times the speed and density of the normal solar wind, and resultant disturbances to the magnetosphere, ionosphere, and thermosphere, including major geomagnetic storms. Moderate to severe disruption of all communications is to be expected.**

WARNING: Solar shields must be in place at all times on craft already in transit. Other flights should be rescheduled if at all possible.

Further bulletins will be issued on a daily basis.'

Dan looked up at O'Farrell. 'Sunspots?'

'Yes. A big cluster. And coronal mass ejections to match.'

'Must be unusual. It's the first time I've seen a warning like this.'

'It's unusual, but not unprecedented. As I say, it's a departure slot but in view of the space weather I thought you might want to pass.'

Pass? He thought about what the journey would involve, running the moves quickly through his mind. Mentally he felt sharp – there were no problems in that direction, not any more. Physically? Well, there was nothing too demanding. He should be able to cope.

'No, I can't stay up here another four weeks, I need to get back, I want to see my wife.' He glanced down again at the sheet and tapped it with the backs of his fingers. 'Even if these sunspots do generate some interference there should be a few gaps. They're probably exaggerating to cover themselves. I'll take the slot.'

'I thought you'd say that. All right, the liner's waiting in orbit: a Silverfish. Are you sure you'll be up to piloting it back yourself?'

'Yes, I don't think it'll be a problem.' The Major General was looking anxiously at him so he tried to give him a reassuring smile. 'After a Morningstar everything else will seem like a rest cure. How's Rico?'

'He said every part of him ached. But he left two days ago.'

'He must be tough as old boots. I don't think I could have done it two days ago.'

'He was very anxious to be home. By the way, he wished you well and he said he'll look you up some time.'

'That would be great.'

O'Farrell stood. Dan rose more slowly, using his hands on the armchair.

'Arrangements,' O'Farrell said. 'I'll send a skimmer to pick you up tomorrow morning at oh-two-hundred. I'll have a full flight plan drawn up and they can hand it to you then. The Earth Orbiting Dock we've booked you into is pretty remote, so it doesn't see a lot of use. It's a Tri-Dock, the coordinates will be in the flight plan. When you get there, head for Dock 2. If you do have trouble communicating with them don't worry about the usual procedures – dock anyway, they're expecting you. You'll find Dock 1 will be occupied by the crew's shuttle. Dock 3's been reserved for the shuttle that'll take you down. It's a Customs shuttle, unmarked – we wanted to keep it all very low key. A skimmer will be waiting to escort you from the Terminal.'

'Sounds good. You people have gone to a lot of trouble.'

'You delivered your part of the bargain. The least we can do is make sure you get home safely.' He sighed. 'I only wish it could have been all three of you.'

Dan's mouth set and he nodded without saying anything.

'Leave it with me, then.' He gripped Dan's hand firmly. 'God speed, Dan.'

Dan wondered where he'd heard that phrase before. It must have been a very, very long time ago.

*

In the Customs building Strijker had set up network surveillance. No outside access was recorded for several days. Then the software picked up a high level connection, duration seven minutes. As it was an isolated access it didn't register as being unusual.

40

The lights of the hotel lobby threw moving reflections back from the blue skimmer as it drew up in the service lane. The driver got out and saluted him smartly.

Dan glanced at the uniform and said, 'Let me see your ID, Airman.'

He examined the card carefully and had a close look at the man who'd held it out to him. He hadn't seen him before, but the base was probably back to strength now that the mission was over and there would be new personnel there. He was very young, probably still in his teens. This was probably his first off-Earth posting. He looked petrified.

'Where are we going?'

'Major General O'Farrell's orders were to take you to the shuttle terminal at oh-two-hundred hours, Colonel, sir.'

Dan nodded. It had been worth checking. 'All right, then, son. You'd better take me there.'

As they turned to the skimmer the front passenger door opened and a heavily built man got out and came towards him. The light fell on an Air Force uniform. He saluted and introduced himself as Sergeant Merrick. He held out a memory tile.

'Your flight plan is on this, Colonel.' He added laconically, 'I'm tagging along for the ride.'

Dan took the memory tile, noting at the same time the leather pouch slung over the Sergeant's shoulder. He didn't have to ask what was in it – or what else he was carrying. The driver opened the rear door for him, Sergeant Merrick took the front passenger seat again, and they moved off.

They cleared the City airlock, then accelerated to a fast cruise along the diffusely lit extension of Highway 4. There was little traffic at this early hour.

The passenger terminal was deserted. They boarded the waiting shuttle and took off almost immediately, the cabin occupied only by the sergeant and himself. Dan was entertained by the thought that the last time he'd gone up to Mars orbit with a strong-arm escort like this the situation had been a lot less congenial.

The pilot docked the shuttle and opened the airlock into the small Silverfish spaceliner that Dan would be piloting back to Earth. Dan walked through, turned and lifted a hand in farewell. The sergeant returned the gesture, the airlock doors slid shut, and the shuttle disengaged. Dan was on his own once more.

He settled into the cockpit, plugged in the memory tile to access the flight plan, and commenced the flight checks and departure procedures. As he did so, the physical and mental stress of recent weeks receded. It simply felt good to be back on a flight deck, going through the familiar routines. He set the coordinates for the Orbiting Dock and waited. Minutes later, Flight Control cleared him for departure. There was a three-week journey ahead of him but he had no intention of cryosleeping through it. He wanted to feel good when he arrived.

*

Lauren Marks knocked on the door of the Deputy Assistant Commissioner's office and heard 'Come!' She entered, together with Alec Kennedy and Martyn Strijker. Leighton gestured them to chairs.

Strijker was speaking even before he'd sat down. 'We've picked something up, sir. High level. First access was three weeks ago, but there've been two more since, one within the last hour and a half. Just a few minutes each time.'

'From…?'

'It's Admiral Stott's office again, sir.'

For a moment, Leighton was motionless. Then he pressed a button on his desk communicator.

'Josie? Get me Fleet-Admiral Stott, would you? Immediately.' He turned back to the others. Although they said nothing there was a new respect in the way they were looking at him. 'I want to know why those calls were made,' he said. 'It's three weeks since Rostov's factory was destroyed. Why's the Fleet-Admiral so interested at this late stage?'

The communicator buzzed. 'Sir, Fleet-Admiral Stott is on an extended trip abroad. He'll be back in three days' time.'

'Josie, did they say how long he'd been away?'

'They said he'd been gone for about a month, sir.'

'Well done, Josie. Thank you.' Leighton took a deep breath and let it out through his teeth. 'Now we know. Someone in Admiral Stott's office is accessing our network. They only log on briefly so they must be familiar with the system. I wonder who…'

'Sir!' Kennedy burst out. 'I bet it's Karl Stott – the Admiral's son! His father's office is a legitimate source. He must know the system and presumably he knows the passwords as well.'

'But why's he accessing the network? What's his interest?'

'Larssen faced a court martial last year – I read all about it before I went to see him. Karl Stott was discredited for tampering with the evidence.'

'He went to prison?' Lauren Marks asked.

'No, he got off,' Kennedy answered. 'But it was still pretty disastrous for him; he was a Director of SpaceFreight and he had to resign. He must have been sore as hell. I bet he's looking for some way to get even.'

'He couldn't know Larssen was involved, though,' Strijker said. 'The names of the pilots weren't posted on the network.'

'He probably put two and two together,' Kennedy said. 'And he'd only have to ask for him at the Test Establishment. They'd say Major Larssen couldn't be contacted at the moment and that would clinch it.'

Marks frowned. 'But why wait for something like this? He could have gone after Larssen at any time.'

'Maybe he's making it easier on himself,' Kennedy said. 'Larssen's spent weeks in microgravity. He'll be no match for Stott in that condition.'

'Great heavens!' Leighton exclaimed. All three looked at him in surprise. He spoke slowly, staring at each of them in turn. 'We arranged for Larssen to be protected all the way. On the way out he was taken up to Mars orbit with an armed Air Force escort. On the way back our people will go out in a shuttle to meet him at the Orbiting Dock and then they'll bring him down and whisk him away in a skimmer. But right now Larssen is flying himself to the Orbiting Dock. And when he arrives he'll be completely on his own.'

Kennedy asked, 'When's he due in?'

Lauren Marks looked at the wall clock. 'In less than an hour. My God…'

Leighton punched the desk communicator again. 'Josie, get me the Armstrong Shuttle Terminal. I want to speak to the Controller.'

They waited, watching him. He held a brief conversation, then terminated the call. When he looked up at them his expression was grim.

'Fleet-Admiral Jurgen Stott has a private shuttle,' he said. 'It left the terminal about half an hour ago. Piloted by Mr Karl Stott.'

*

Dan got a visual on the Orbiting Dock soon after commencing the deceleration phase. At this distance all he could make out was a gleaming, vaguely triangular shape.

The navcom frequency was already set. He flicked the switch to send.

'Africa One, Bravo-six-two-six-Sierra, Silverfish, inbound. Request clearance to approach.'

He flicked the navcom switch back but all he could hear was static. He wasn't surprised: it had been like this most of the way. The space weather warning hadn't been exaggerated after all. He maintained course.

*

They were on their feet at once.

'Sir, what's the situation on a V.I.P. shuttle like the one Karl Stott's taken?' Lauren Marks asked. 'Aren't there any disembarkation procedures, security checks…?'

'No, not normally. But because of the solar storm one of the security guards tried to stop him from boarding. It's legal to travel under these storm conditions, but it's foolhardy. When he tried to explain it, Stott went crazy. He shouted "Get out of my way, imbecile! Your job's on the line! Don't you know who I am?" – that kind of thing. So the guard let him through.'

Kennedy said, 'We've got to go after him.'

'We can't, there isn't time. But the escort shuttle should be ready,' Leighton said. 'We can get them to launch right away.'

Lauren Marks said, 'Can I use your desk comm?'

'Go ahead.'

Moments later they were listening to an exchange with a very relaxed shuttle pilot.

'I guess we're-all pretty much launch-ready, Captain. Our orders were to wait till he'd requested permission to dock, and then the crew up there would give us the go-ahead. Thing is, reception is shot to hell with this sunspot activity, so right now there's nothing but static. We-all were just talkin' 'bout asking you—'

'Okay, listen up. Here are your new orders. Launch immediately. I repeat, immediately. And when you get there, don't go to the reception area. There's a gallery connecting the three docks. You go direct to Dock 2. Got that?'

'Dock 2, yes. What's the—?'

'When he arrives, stick to him like glue. If you find someone else waiting there, arrest him.'

'Someone else…?'

'Do you have weapons?'

'Regulation Customs issue—'

'Take them with you. This person could be armed.'

'Jesus H. Christ, Captain! I thought this was a routine escort!'

'So did we.'

She clicked off the desk communicator and looked up at the wall clock again, chewing her lip.

'It's too late. They're not going to get there in time.'

Kennedy said, 'Are there any other manned docks close by?'

Leighton shook his head. 'We deliberately chose one that was isolated.'

'Then we've got to contact the crew of the Orbiting Dock. Tell them what's going on.'

'We can't do it from here,' Strijker said. 'We'll have to go to the Operations Room.' He was already at the door.

They hit the corridor at a run.

41

As the Orbiting Dock grew in size Dan realized the type was familiar. He ran through the layout in his head. There was no attempt to simulate gravity on these Tri-Docks so it didn't rotate. In the centre there was a smallish living quarters for the resident crew and any visitors. A circular gallery connected this area with the three access tubes, which projected out to their respective docking points like the spokes of a wheel. For safety reasons the access tubes didn't end directly at the docks. At the end of each access tube there was an expansion, an unfurnished chamber which could be sealed off quickly in the event of an emergency such as a sudden loss of pressurization. The chamber was entered from the docking side via an airlock.

It was all perfectly straightforward. Docking would be easy because there was no rotation. He'd pass through the airlock and cross the chamber on the other side, and at the top of the access tube he would take the gallery and go straight to the reception area. There he would report in and wait until they were ready to take him down in the shuttle. At long last the end of the journey, and of the mission, was in sight.

Two craft were already docked. One was a standard Space Fleet shuttle, beginning to show its age. The other was much sleeker, its gleaming all-black finish relieved by a thin gold stripe edged with red.

Smart rig. I haven't seen that livery before. Customs must have come early for me. O'Farrell said they'd be using something inconspicuous. Never mind, so long as they're here.

Dock 2 floated slowly towards him.

*

Strijker was turning dials and flicking switches but the screen looked like a snowstorm and the only noise from the panel loudspeakers was a fluctuating hiss. He slapped the desk in frustration.

'What's the matter?' Leighton demanded.

'It's the sunspot activity – it's blanketing everything! I'm sorry, I'll keep trying in case there's a break in the interference but right now they might as well be on the other side of the Moon. I just can't get through to them.'

Lauren Marks put her fists to her head and turned to the wall.

*

The Silverfish docked sweetly and he closed all systems down. A quick check established that pressure in the airlock was the same as that in the craft. He opened the outer airlock door and, wearing his simple flight suit, went in. Moments later he emerged into the chamber and the inner airlock door slid shut behind him. He turned, and froze. On the other side of the chamber someone was standing with their back to the access tube, and it was sealed shut.

It took him a moment to recognize Karl Stott. His eyes were strange, the pupils so minute that only a pair of grey irises stared out of the bloated, pallid face. What really got Dan's attention, however, was the electrolaser pistol he was holding in his right hand. Electrolasers fired millions of volts along a path ionized an instant earlier by a laser pulse. Even at the lowest setting a hit would paralyze him, putting his muscles into spasm for days. The indicator light was pulsing green, the signal for a full charge.

'Get away from the airlock, Larssen,' Stott snarled, waving the pistol.

'What the hell are you doing here, Stott?' Dan said, moving slightly into the area, but staying close to the wall. His eyes narrowed. 'How did you know I was coming in?'

Stott smiled his crooked little smile. 'If anyone was going to be involved in a caper like this I guessed it'd be you – in fact I was counting on it. Just to be sure I checked with the Test Establishment and they said you were "on leave".' The smile turned into a sneer. 'You see, Larssen, unlike you I have contacts, and I know how to use them.'

Dan frowned. Then, with a quick intake of breath, he said, 'It was you who tipped off the syndicate about the mission! You used your father's sky-high security clearance – you could get access to anything you wanted with that. You piece of shit!' He controlled his anger with difficulty, and exhaled softly. 'You've done some lousy things in your time, Stott, but I never thought...' The full implications dawned on him. 'You were in with these animals from the start! The Saturn run – Rostov's reception committee out beyond Mars! That was your doing too! You told the bastards I was coming!'

Stott laughed. 'It took you long enough, didn't it? Never

mind, it won't do you any good now.' His face set. 'You're going to suffer, Larssen. You made it your business to ruin me and you're about to pay for it.'

'What are you talking about?'

'Oh, I know how you set me up. With your backup memories and your smart lawyer friend. Very clever, weren't you? You put me in prison.'

'They released you. You didn't have to do time.'

'Ah, but I lost everything – my Directorship, my reputation—'

'That was your own doing—'

'Oh, that's right, blame it on me. Try to pretend you haven't been turning people against me, ever since Space Fleet Academy, trying to get me thrown out, trying to destroy my career…'

'Stott, this is ridiculous. You're ill. Let me get you to a doctor—'

'Oh, no. Not a doctor. Not for me. You, you're the one who's going to need the doctor, Larssen. I'm going to make sure you can't get at me again. All your clever plotting behind my back won't help you this time. Eight weeks you've been away. All that time I've been on Earth, in full gravity, but you haven't, have you? How are the muscles – weak, are they? How are the bones – brittle by now? Well, we'll soon see. Because I'm going to snap you in two, Larssen. I'm going to crush your spine, vertebra by vertebra. I won't kill you – that would be too easy. But you'll end up in a basket with someone feeding you through a tube for the rest of your miserable life. Let's see how much your scheming will help you then.'

He aimed the electrolaser at Dan's legs.

Dan thought fast. In his normal state of fitness he wouldn't have had much trouble handling a cumbersome baggage like Stott, but not in his present condition. The idiot was right; he could injure him really badly, especially if he caught him with that electrolaser pistol.

He knew he'd be a sitting target if he floated free, so he kept close to the wall, where he could interact with hooks and pipes and cabinets to keep himself on the move. The ceiling was low, too. He glanced up to judge the distance, then dropped into a slight crouch, focusing on the pistol but letting his awareness extend to the whole of Stott's body. Abruptly he shouted, kicked off the floor, turning at the same time so that his feet touched the ceiling and kicked off again. The sudden noise and movement were enough: Stott fired. Dan heard the crack as the charge sailed out behind him and forked streaks of miniature lightning arced all over the wall. He grabbed a cabinet to steady himself, trying to regain his balance. Stott brought the weapon around quickly but Dan could see that the indicator was pulsing red – in his anxiety to inflict serious damage Stott had turned the setting to maximum and now he couldn't fire again without recharging. He hadn't even noticed. He smiled and pulled the trigger. Nothing happened. His face fell, then he scowled and kicked away from the wall towards Dan. Dan waited as long as he dared and then pushed off sideways. Stott hit the wall but turned and came after him again, arms flailing. Again Dan ducked and dodged out of the way.

Stott was breathing heavily now, beside himself with rage. He looked wildly about him. There was a glass-fronted fire cabinet on the wall to his right. Inside it was a coil of hose and some emergency tools. With a snort of triumph he kicked over to it and used the butt of the pistol twice to smash the glass front. Instantly a siren started to shriek. Stott paid no attention. He plunged his hands into the cabinet and came out with a crowbar. Then he launched himself after Dan, swinging the crowbar at him in a frenzy, trying to catch him with the sharp wedge at its curved end. Dan dodged the blows, always keeping close to the wall, and with every miss the momentum behind the crowbar carried it into walls or cabinets, ringing and clanging in every direction. It looked like he would breach the wall at any moment and depressurize the whole area, yet he seemed oblivious to the danger. He came after Dan again, swinging the crowbar furiously, and a cloud of steam hissed out as it punctured a heating pipe. Another swing and another hiss, this time compressed air jetting from one of the feeds to the airlock. Without hesitation he lunged to the other side. Dan just managed to evade the blow but only by darting in front of the jet of compressed air, which pushed him away from the wall. As he floated helplessly towards the opposite wall Stott kicked off, holding the crowbar in front of him with both hands. He jammed it against Dan's throat, carrying both of them into the wall. Then he hooked his fingers behind the cables running down the wall and squeezed hard. His face was alight with vicious pleasure, his pale eyes with the pinpoint pupils inches from Dan's. Dan struggled, trying to push Stott up and away from him but the strength wasn't in him. Stott squeezed harder, jerking the steel shaft even more tightly into Dan's throat, his mouth widening in elation. Dark curtains began to move into Dan's vision. He felt the pulsing of his blood in his brain, each pulse moving the curtains further across. Everything started to spin slowly and tiny points of light sparked in the darkness. Then there was only darkness.

The siren continued to shriek, but for Dan the silence was complete.

42

The siren blasted a two-tone wail and Neraya felt her weight shift as the ambulance banked around a corner. The paramedic, a young African-American woman, leaned over and mopped the sweat off her forehead with a damp paper towel.

'Now don't you worry, hon'. This is a reserved skimmer lane. We be there real soon.'

Another contraction came. Neraya's eyes widened, her mouth opened, and she screamed.

When the wave of pain had subsided to an ache she lay panting. She was trying to recall what they said about this in the antenatal course. She'd followed it so carefully on virtual reality but now everything had fled her mind. Everything but the pain.

The paramedic gave her a reassuring smile. 'Try to relax,' the paramedic said. 'Who's your obstetrician?'

Neraya replied through tight lips. 'Dr Satie. Dr Louis Satie.'

'Okay, we going to send a message ahead and we going to get you straight in.'

'Please, you must contact my husband... Dan Larssen.'

'At the hospital, honey. They deal with all that stuff there.'

She lay there, tense, expecting another contraction at any moment.

The motion stopped and the engines whined down.

'Here we go,' the paramedic announced.

She was jolted from side to side as the gurney was taken from the skimmer, then pushed down a corridor. A succession of bright glow panels in the ceiling whisked past her eyes, there were voices, footsteps, people sweeping by close enough for her to feel the disturbance in the air. Then they were entering an elevator, coming out, and finally the noise subsided. She was in a single room. She felt a loosening as the restraints came off.

'Can you get into bed yourself?' a nurse asked.

'I'll manage.'

All the same the nurse helped her into the bed. She was breathing fast.

A junior nurse came in armed with a tablet computer and started on a battery of questions. It was too much.

'Do I have to go through this all over again? It'll be in my notes.'

The girl looked non-plussed but before she could respond Dr Satie appeared with an obstetric nurse and the girl withdrew. He was a rotund man with a cheery, buoyant disposition.

'Well, well,' he said. 'Let's have a look at you, shall we?'

He examined her, making approving noises all the while.

'Yes, things are progressing nicely. How long since you started contractions?'

'I suppose it was yesterday. I had a few twinges then but it was so mild I didn't think anything of it. I got a big one a couple of hours ago, and I waited in case it was a false alarm. When the next one came I contacted the hospital. I called my husband, too, but he wasn't answering his communicator. Could you get him for me? It's Dan Larssen – oh, here we go again…'

Her face creased with pain and she couldn't hold back the cry.

When she opened her eyes again he was applying a pressure injector to her arm.

'That should take the edge off it.'

She was still panting. 'I knew it would hurt, but this…?'

'You wanted your baby to have a natural birth. You're a young, healthy woman and I saw no reason to dissuade you. What you're experiencing is quite normal.'

'You're sure nothing's wrong? Is the baby really coming?'

He smiled. 'Yes, the baby's really coming.' He pulled a chair close to the bed, sat down, and took her hand in his. 'Shall I tell you something, Neraya? I have the best job in the world. Ninety-nine per cent of the time I see new life come into the world. I see babies drawing the first of the hundreds of millions of breaths they'll take throughout their lives. I see the smiles on the faces of the mothers when their babies are placed in their arms. It's a privilege, what I do. But with privilege comes responsibility. Once in a while, maybe one time in a thousand, something goes wrong. Even though it's rare I have to be on my toes in case it happens. Right now everything is going to plan. And in the very unlikely event that the situation changes, you can be very sure I'll do all that's necessary.'

'Sorry, Louis. It's just that I want this baby so much.'

She gave him a rueful smile. 'I used to have bouts of severe colic when I was a little girl. I thought that was bad.'

'I can give you more painkillers, but it's a delicate balance. They could depress fetal respiration.'

She rose on one elbow. 'No, no, definitely not! Listen, Louis, whatever happens, however much I scream and shout, you mustn't do anything that could harm the baby.' She fell back, breathing hard.

He patted her hand and stood up. 'Of course not.' He turned to the nurse. 'Set up external fetal monitoring, would you, nurse? We'll keep a close eye on things.'

Another contraction gripped her, the pain spreading through her abdomen into her back and down her legs. She was gasping when it subsided.

Satie studied her for a moment. 'I could give you an epidural.'

'No, I'll be all right.' Tears suddenly welled in her eyes and wet her eyelashes. 'I want my husband. I want Danny.'

He took out a communicator and tapped at it. 'I have all your details here. I'll try to reach him. There's an obstetric nurse at the station outside. Use the buzzer if you need her. Okay? I'll be back.'

She nodded, the movement detaching a tear which rolled down her cheek. She brushed it away with the back of her hand, then sank back, waiting for the next contraction. She hadn't expected to be so exhausted at this stage. Would she have the energy to push when the time came?

He returned a few minutes later. 'I tried the number but he's not answering. Where is he?'

She hesitated. The message from General O'Farrell had arrived three weeks ago. Ever since then she'd been counting the days. But she had to be careful what she said, even to Louie. 'He was on an assignment but he was due back yesterday or today. He said nothing would stop him from being with me for the birth.'

He shrugged. 'Well, I can't reach him at the moment. I'll try again later.' He placed the buzzer within her reach. 'Use that if you need the nurse. I'll be back in a short while.'

He went off.

Why isn't Danny answering? It's so unlike him, especially at a time like this.

43

Mr Dwyer and Mr Bayley had been the Stott family's lawyers for years. They had handled the Admiral's divorce, including the tricky negotiations whereby his wife had accepted a modest financial settlement in return for *not* taking custody of the eight-year-old Karl. After the divorce the two lawyers continued to handle matters for Jurgen Stott and his son alone, including the release of Karl from prison following the collapse of Dan Larssen's court martial. Although Dwyer, the older of the two, was now silver-haired, and his colleague Bayley no more youthful, their judgement was held in great esteem within the company.

The room spoke heavily of their senior status: the thick pile carpet, the draped windows, which nevertheless afforded a panoramic view of Armstrong city, and the walls lined, as was now the custom, with unfrequented leather-covered law books.

They rose as their PA showed Fleet-Admiral Stott into the room, and Bayley ushered him into a comfortably upholstered chair next to the massive oak desk. Dwyer sat down again behind the desk, with Bayley to one side.

Stott dispensed with preliminaries. 'Where is Karl now?' he demanded.

Mr Dwyer allowed himself a long look at the familiar face of the man sitting on the other side of the desk. Age had slackened the skin, which now hung in bags under the eyes and from the once square jaw. The grey eyes had changed little; they had the same flat deadness, belying the calculations that were always going on behind them. Dwyer took a breath. 'He's in a secure unit in the Malton Hospital.' He added quietly, 'The registered name is the Malton Hospital for the Criminally Insane.'

For a moment the face sagged even more, then it recomposed itself. 'That's outrageous. My son's neither criminal nor insane.'

'Admiral, I've known Karl since he was so high. It therefore grieves me to say this, but it's quite possible he's both.'

'What? Ridiculous! What's he doing committed to a place like that. There's been no trial. Why not?'

'Because he's judged incapable.'

'Incapable? Of what?'

'He's incapable of understanding what he's done or the charges against him.'

'Well I don't understand that, either. What's he been charged with?'

Dwyer looked at his colleague, who slid a piece of paper towards him. 'It's a long list. Attempted murder, assault with a deadly weapon, wilful criminal damage to an Orbiting Dock—' He looked up. 'I believe he took a crowbar to it, fracturing pipes and setting off a fire alarm; that's what brought the Dock crew in.' He returned to the sheet. 'Attacking the crew with the crowbar, resisting arrest

– they said he was screaming and struggling so violently they had to restrain him by tying his hands and feet with lengths of webbing.' He pushed the paper away and opened his hands. 'And so on. Of course it will be more serious still if the man he attacked dies.'

'Who was it?'

'A Space Fleet employee, name of Dan Larssen. Anyone you know?'

The Admiral gave a tired nod. 'I know of him. He's a bad lot, a very bad lot. Is he going to die?'

'We don't know. In fact we don't even know where he's been taken. But the police took a statement from one of the crew members on the Dock. He thought it was touch and go.' He shrugged. 'That's almost irrelevant now because Karl isn't fit to stand trial anyway.'

'Who says he isn't?'

'There was a deposition by two psychiatrists appointed by the State. You were still away, of course, but as soon as we heard about it we requested permission to have him examined again by two psychiatrists of our own choice. I have their report here. "Patient had been sedated but still showed violent tendencies... florid psychosis... severe paranoid delusions—"'

'Attacking that man doesn't make him paranoid! Larssen made an enemy of himself right from the time they met at the Academy. Karl had every reason to hate him!'

Bayley sighed. 'Apparently the violence and the delusions go much further than that. At any rate the conclusion reached by our own psychiatrists accords in every respect with the verdict of the State's. Paranoid schizophrenia exacerbated by severe addiction to Dramatoin.'

This time the Admiral's face went totally slack. The

dead eyes blinked once, twice.

Bayley raised his eyebrows. 'You didn't know?'

There was a long silence. The Admiral continued to blink. Then his voice came, unusually thin and weak. 'I thought he looked unwell, that's all. He...' His lips tightened. 'It must have been Larssen's court martial. You saw what happened in that court room. After that Karl lost his Directorship. The strain on the boy was immense.'

'The court martial was about nine months ago. According to this report,' he pointed at the pages, 'an addiction as severe as that would have started at least two years earlier.'

The Admiral lowered his head, raised his fingers to his temples and rubbed the stubble of grey hair. The lawyers exchanged glances but said nothing.

'Why?' the man said finally. 'Why would he do that? I gave him everything...'

Dwyer said softly, 'Sometimes even everything isn't enough, Admiral.'

Stott straightened up. 'He shouldn't be in that place. He should be receiving expert treatment.'

Bayley said, 'Dramatoin addiction is irreversible. The best he could have hoped for was a psychiatric hospital. That's not open to him now, they won't take anyone with behaviour as violent as his. He'll get the same treatment and regular reviews at the Malton, but he'll be held there under much tighter security. Besides, the judge wouldn't have countenanced anything less because of the criminal charges.'

'I need to see him.'

'The judge?'

'No, my son.'

Dwyer nodded. 'When—?'

'Now. Immediately. I don't want him in that place a minute longer than he has to be.'

Again the lawyers met each other's eyes. Dwyer said, 'If you'll wait a moment I'll have a word with the Director.'

Dwyer went out of the room and the other two waited in silence until he returned. He said:

'The Director's agreed. The Moreton is about twenty miles out of town. We can use my skimmer.'

*

The lawyers paused inside the entrance of the Malton Hospital. Dwyer pointed to the security check and then to the furnished waiting area to their right.

'Go ahead, Admiral. We'll wait for you over there.'

Stott walked confidently forward and was immediately stopped by the Security Guard.

'That's far enough, sir,' the man said, placing a plastic box on the counter. 'Empty your pockets in here.'

Stott looked at him in astonishment, then drew himself up. 'Young man, do you know who I am?'

'I don't care who you are, sir,' came the reply. 'You have to go through security.'

'That's preposterous. I—'

'Sir, are you going in or staying out?'

The Admiral took a deep breath and emptied his pockets.

The guard said, 'Legs apart, arms out.'

Stott submitted to a careful hand search with a muttered, 'You haven't heard the last of this.'

The man pointed to an arch and he passed through, eliciting a green light. On the other side another guard said, 'Are you expected here?'

'Yes,' he said through his teeth. 'The Director is expecting me.'

'We'll let him know.' He was conducted to a windowless room furnished only with a plastic table and four injection-moulded chairs. The walls were unadorned and the floor was tiled. The guard said 'Wait here' and left.

He tried to draw back the chair but it was bolted to the floor. He heaved an exasperated sigh, sat down and waited, drumming his fingers on the table. It was a full ten minutes before the Director appeared. He was with another man.

'Admiral Stott?' he said, extending a hand. 'I'm the Director.'

Stott ignored the hand. 'I wish to object in the strongest possible terms to being subjected to the indignity of—'

The Director said, 'Let me stop you right there, sir. If you're expecting an apology for our security precautions you won't get it. There are a lot of violent people in this establishment and a lot of violent people on the outside who'd like to help them escape. You haven't been singled out, one way or another. Everyone is treated the same.'

It was so unusual for the Admiral to find himself interrupted that he was speechless for the moment. This allowed the Director to continue:

'Now I've agreed to let you see your son on compassionate grounds. I strongly recommend that you use our virtual reality meeting room—'

'Virtual reality?'

'Yes. It'll be just like an actual visit for both of you, but much safer.'

'Director, he's my son, not my virtual son. I'll see him in person.'

The Director grimaced, then turned to the uniformed man with him. 'Henderson, what's the patient's current status?'

'He's had the usual sedatives this morning, sir. Seems to be stable at the moment, but he's hard to predict.'

The Director heaved a breath. 'All right, you can see him, but I will insist that you have Mr Henderson with you. He isn't just a prison officer, he's a qualified psychiatric nurse and Mr Karl Stott is in his charge.'

Stott's eyes flicked to the man and registered the electric baton at his belt. The Director noticed.

'It's the very last resort,' he explained. 'We do try not to use them but, as I said before, there are a lot of violent people in this establishment. Now when you go in, I want you to be very calm. Don't raise your voice or make sudden movements, you understand?'

Stott's lips set tightly. 'Can we get on with it?'

The Director sighed. 'Very well, I'll leave you with Henderson.' He stood up. 'Before I go, could I ask you if you know who Papillon is?'

'Papillon?'

'Yes, your son keeps asking for Papillon. The police are interested to know who he or she is. They think it could be his dealer.'

'I haven't the faintest idea.'

The Director nodded then gestured to the guard, who said 'This way, sir.'

They walked along corridors and through a succession of floor-to-ceiling gates. Henderson paused at each one to operate a locking mechanism while the Admiral looked around him, his nose pricking with air that was sharp with the smell of soap and disinfectant. Eventually they went down a long passageway with a succession of doors on the left. The echo of their footsteps on the hard tiles was counterpointed with vague human noises. One erupted into a scream, which subsided into an insistent gibbering that was taken up by a chorus of others. Stott shivered but set his jaw and matched the pace of the guard. They came to a halt outside a door. Henderson slid back a small cover to check inside, then turned to the man he was escorting.

'Virtual reality's good. Sure you don't want to change your mind?'

The Admiral bristled. 'If you knew anything at all about me, young man, you'd know that I am not in the habit of changing my mind.'

He shrugged. 'Okay, okay, it's your call.'

He held his communicator to a panel and punched in a number. The door opened and Admiral Stott stepped into the room. Glancing behind him he saw Henderson discreetly take a position next to the door. He'd left the door slightly ajar.

The room was a single module, formed out of a textured plastic with no sharp corners. It incorporated a bed, a chair, and a table. A partition screened an area that was presumably plumbed for toilet and washing facilities. The walls were a soothing blue-green, fading to a lighter hue near the high ceiling. There were no windows other than the small aperture in the door, but light came from glow panels fitted across the ceiling.

Karl, dressed in a loose grey overshirt and trousers, was pacing back and forth, rubbing his upper arm. He looked up and the Admiral got his first shock. The eyes were wild, the pupils so tiny as to be almost non-existent, so that he appeared to be wearing grey contact lenses. It was like facing something newly risen from the dead.

'Karl...'

'You've come to get me out, right? Okay, let's go.'

The Admiral held up a hand. 'It's going to be difficult

this time, Karl. You're accused of—'

Karl's face soured into a sneer. 'Oh, I see, you're going to leave me here. You've just come to gloat.' He spat the words. 'Just like all the others.'

The Admiral's voice hardened into his most commanding tone. 'Karl, listen to me. I'm your father—'

'Yeah, yeah. You'll just leave me here to rot, won't you? Suit you fine. You never wanted me.'

The Admiral's mouth had gone dry. 'Karl, I brought you up, I did everything possible for you...'

'You got something for me? Stuff?'

'What? What do you want?'

He gave a short laugh. 'You pretend you don't know?' He turned away, rubbed his arm again and began to whine. 'Papillon knows. She's the only one. She understands what I need. Why won't they let me go to her?'

'Karl, will you be quiet and listen to me!' He swept his arm towards the door. 'You can't just walk out of here!'

Don't raise your voice or make sudden movements.

Too late. His son turned on him, the eyes even more wild. 'Get out! The whole lot of you, get out!'

Stott looked around him, frowning. 'What are you talking about, Karl? There's only me here with Mr Henderson.'

He jabbed a finger towards Henderson. 'Hah, that's what *he's* always saying! But what about the others, eh? I know they're here, I can hear them talking about me all the time, plotting, waiting their chance.' He advanced. 'You're one of them, aren't you?' He raised his voice. 'Aren't you?'

The shove in the chest was hard and unexpected. It threw the Admiral against the wall, knocking the breath out of him. His head swam, and before he could recover, there was a fearsome shouting in his ears and heavy blows raining on him. He began to sink down the wall, crossing his forearms over face and head, trying to protect himself...

The blows stopped and he heard other voices, also raised. He opened his eyes cautiously.

There were two officers in the cell now, Henderson and one he hadn't seen before. Henderson was restraining Karl, who was bucking and heaving against him, crying with animal rage. Then there was a glimpse of a pressure injector and moments later Karl went slack, dropping to his knees and sobbing 'It's no good. I can't, I can't... It's not fair... Too many of them...'

The Admiral suddenly felt very old. He barely noticed the hand hooked under his arm, but found himself hauled to his feet and led out of the cell. The door slammed behind them. He made an effort to compose himself under the impassive gaze of the guard.

Henderson gave a wave to the departing officer. 'Thanks, Tom.' He turned back to Stott. 'We did warn you, buddy.'

Stott steadied his breathing. Another time he'd have given a dressing down to anyone who had the effrontery to address him as 'buddy', but all that seemed unimportant now. He allowed Henderson to lead him back. His face was still smarting from two of the blows his son had landed.

His son.

An unfamiliar needling sensation started up behind his eyes, and for a moment his vision blurred. Quickly he blinked back the tears, stood erect and brushed down his tunic.

When they reached the entrance he accepted his belongings and replaced them without a word. Then he walked over to where the lawyers were standing, his back ramrod straight.

Bayley peered at him. 'Are you all right, Admiral?'

The voice was as firm as ever. 'Would you drive me home now, Bayley?'

44

Neraya rolled her head on the pillow to see who was in the room. Satie was there, talking to the obstetric nurse. He gave her a smile, then scanned the displays on the wall behind her.

'Fetal heart rate's normal, sats normal. There's a way to go yet, Neraya, but baby's doing fine.'

'That's good. Did you get hold of Danny?'

'I'm afraid he's been delayed.'

'Did you speak to him?'

'Er, no, but I left messages. Sorry, Neraya, it looks like you'll have to see this through without him.'

She set her lips tightly together and nodded.

After Satie had left she felt a small tug of apprehension. There was something about his manner...

Then a contraction came and every thought fled her mind.

*

It was another eight hours before the baby arrived. It began to wail lustily, and other hands took over. Neraya sank deeper into the pillows as her baby was weighed, sponged down, and swaddled. She'd never felt so exhausted in all her life. Presently a tight white parcel was placed in her arms.

'Two point nine kilos,' Satie announced, with a satisfied grunt. 'On the small side but respectable, very respectable. What a lot of dark hair! She's going to take after you, Neraya.'

Neraya gave him a tired smile and rested her cheek on the baby's forehead. It was soft and very warm. She turned her head to look at the little face and her heart swelled.

Did this, this perfect creature, really come from me?

She heaved a sigh. Then she frowned.

Where on earth is Danny? Why isn't he answering his communicator? He should have been here!

The flash of annoyance passed. It was so unlike him.

The nurse said, 'Does baby have a name yet, honey?'

'Yes. Aida. We said we'd call her Aida.'

*

She was aroused by voices, opened her eyes, and saw Dr Satie looking down at her. He smiled.

She passed the tip of her tongue over parched lips. 'How long have I been asleep?'

'Oh, just a couple of hours. It's not surprising. You were tired out.'

Her eyes widened with alarm and she half sat up, then winced at the pain low down in her abdomen. She fell back. 'The baby...'

'Don't worry, baby's fine. She's in the cot right next to you, fast asleep.'

'Can I hold her?'

'Sure.' He lifted the baby carefully and Neraya held out

her arms.

'She's tired as well,' Satie said. 'That was a good feed she took on board.'

Neraya smiled and held the baby close. Satie waited. He didn't seem to be in any hurry to leave. After a few minutes she looked up at him. 'Any news of Danny?'

'Neraya...'

She stiffened at his change in tone. 'Yes, what?'

'There's something I need to tell you. It was a nurse who answered Dan's communicator. He's in hospital. It seems he was attacked the other night on his way home. I believe he's all right, though.'

She spoke quickly. 'What do you mean "all right"? Why's he in hospital?'

'They're keeping him under observation.'

'Why didn't you tell me before?'

He grimaced. 'Neraya, sometimes a doctor has to make difficult decisions. Please try to understand: my first duty was to you and your unborn child. I didn't want to say anything that could put either of you at risk.'

'But... I must speak to him!'

'That... may be difficult. It would be better if you spoke to the duty doctor. His name's Desai, Dr Sanjay Desai.'

'Do you have the number?'

'You'd better let me take her.'

She placed Aida in his waiting hands and he returned the baby gently to the cot. Then he took out his communicator, entered the number, and handed it to her.

'It's ready to send.' He left the room, closing the door behind him.

She looked at it, her thoughts whirling.

How badly is he hurt? Will he ever see his daughter? Oh God! Oh God, let him be all right...

She reached for the send button with a trembling finger, managed to press it, and held the communicator to her ear.

It buzzed once, twice, three times…

'Hello?'

A woman's voice. Neraya swallowed. 'I'd like to speak to Dr Desai.'

'I'll see if I can transfer you.'

Moments later there was a longer buzz followed by a man's voice. *'Desai.'*

'Dr Desai, this is Mrs Larssen. I'm told my husband is in your care.'

'Ah yes, Mrs Larssen, Dr Satie said you would be calling—'

'Can I speak to him?'

'Ah, not just at the moment. He is under heavy sedation, you see. He is needing complete rest.'

'What happened?'

'Somebody assaulted him in an orbiting dock. One of the crew gave him first aid and stayed with him on the shuttle down. They got him here very quickly.'

Her mouth had gone dry and she could scarcely breathe. 'What's his status at the moment?'

'It is good. There is bruising to the throat but we have not found any other signs of trauma. He did lose consciousness, though, so we have to monitor him very carefully.'

Her breathing quickened. 'Because of the possibility of brain damage?'

'Yes, of course. But please not to worry, Mrs Larssen. All the indications are good so far.'

'How long are you going to keep him in?'

'Well, of course that will depend on his progress. But I am hoping to take him off sedation tomorrow.'

She moistened her lips. 'Dr Desai, when he wakes up do you think you could give him a message from me?' Her throat caught, and she struggled to control her voice. 'Tell him... he has a baby daughter.'

She could almost hear the smile in the doctor's voice. *'I will tell him. I am sure he will be most happy to hear this.'*

'And say I'm sorry I can't come to see him, but—'

'I'm sure he will understand. Now don't worry, Mrs Larssen, everything here is under control. We are taking very good care of him.'

'Thank you. I'll phone again soon. Thank you for what you're doing. Goodbye.'

'Goodbye.'

She clicked off the communicator and lowered it slowly to the bed.

Then she covered her face with her hands and her shoulders shook.

45

Deputy Assistant Commissioner Henry Leighton and General Hugh Norton had arranged to make their way separately, and in unmarked cars, to the Test Establishment. The Establishment was suitably secure and immune from conventional surveillance and Barry Curtis was happy to make the private conference lounge available to them again.

Leighton arrived first. Barry showed him up to the conference lounge and gestured to a chair, but Leighton evidently preferred to remain standing. Norton appeared at the door a few minutes later, and Leighton barely waited for him to cross the threshold.

'Hugh, what's the latest on Larssen?'

'Spoke to his doctor again this morning,' Norton replied. 'They kept him in an induced coma for a couple of days, just to be on the safe side. He's out of it now. You know, when the crew on that Orbital Dock intervened one of them clapped an oxygen mask on him right away. Probably saved his life.'

'He's all right, then?'

'Seems like it.'

The tension in Leighton's body ebbed away. 'Thank God.' He sank into a chair, and Norton took one next to him. For a few moments they sat in silence. Then Leighton asked, 'What about the mission, Hugh? Any repercussions from Mars?'

'It's been handled. That Blue Lance detonating on the surface actually helped: the landslide buried any evidence of what had been going on there and what we'd done to it. Of course they picked up the explosion on seismography and started to ask questions. We told them that unfortunately an unarmed craft had crashed when it didn't pull out of the valley in time. We were testing a new, highly volatile fuel and that accounted for the size of the bang and the extent of the damage. That was it, file closed. It fitted, of course: three craft went out; one, sadly, didn't come back.'

'Pieter Tyomkin,' Leighton sighed. 'The mission was hazardous enough without the factory being tipped off. I gather Karl Stott's been removed from civilized society.'

'Yes, for good. There's been some fallout for his father, too. When the White House learned about the security leak in his office they went ballistic. He must have seen the way the wind was blowing and opted for retirement. It was overdue anyway. So he's no longer on the Chiefs of Staff and I gather his security classification and his privileged access have been revoked. Effectively he's finished. Some may regret it. I don't.' Norton got up and crossed to the window. He looked out briefly, then turned around. 'Seen any impact on the drug trade yet?'

'Yes, Alec Kennedy's been monitoring it. You remember the two large consignments we intercepted during the run-up to the operation? We picked up another three after that – presumably they'd been tipped off by then and they were trying to shift the stock. Then the factory was wiped out. So no fresh supplies of Dramatoin to the market for well over a month. Big syndicates must have been affected badly enough, but the smaller distributors and dealers have gone crazy. Each one thinks it's being squeezed out by the other.'

'Is that what's behind these gang wars, then?' Norton asked. 'Tegucigalpa, Guatemala City, and now Los Angeles?'

'Almost certainly. We've dealt that evil industry a heavy blow.' He stood up. 'I owe you for this, Hugh.'

'Not as much as we owe those pilots. I spoke to Henriques, you know.'

'What did he say?'

'Well, when he'd finished telling me what a total ace Larssen was, I asked him about flying the Morningstar. He said it takes more than skill; it's a whole new world. Unfortunately it nearly tore them apart. He said we're going to have to develop a much better g-suit to match that performance. I've put it in hand.'

'Apart from the g-suit...?'

Norton smiled. 'He said it's the nearest a man ever came to sprouting wings and turning into a bird.'

46

'Neraya!'

Dan had been sitting in an armchair by his bed, fully dressed, reading a tablet. She took in at a glance the fleeting look of surprise, then delight, that crossed his face, how he used his hands on the armrests to get up, how thin he was. Then, without a word, they were in each other's arms. She held him tightly, needing to feel him close. Finally she relaxed, gave a sigh, patted him on the back, and they separated. She kissed him.

'Dr Desai said you could come home.'

'Yes, a full systems check and I seem to be airworthy. He's arranged for me to attend rehab as an outpatient.' He gazed at her. 'I didn't expect you to come. They were going to get me a taxi.'

'I decided to collect you. Aida's asleep and the nurse is with her.'

'She's okay?'

'Yes, she's doing really well.'

'And you, you're okay?'

She smiled patiently. 'Yes, I'm okay.'

His mouth tightened. 'I'm so, so sorry, I should have been with you.'

'I missed having you there, of course, but look, you're all right, that's the main thing.' She glanced around the room. 'Nothing else here. Are you ready to go?'

'Yes, yes. I want to see the baby.'

'Of course you do.'

*

Neraya opened the door of their apartment and turned to wait for him. 'Sorry, was I going too fast?'

He paused in the doorway and took a few breaths. 'It's okay.'

They went in and she opened the door to the nursery. A mature woman of Hispanic appearance got to her feet.

'This is Carmel. She's a qualified nurse. She'll be with us for a week or so, until I can cope on my own.'

Carmel smiled and nodded. She said, 'Baby's awake now. I'll go see to the washing.' She inclined her head to them and withdrew.

Dan stepped forward to the crib and gazed at his daughter, who looked back at him with large, dark eyes. He extended a finger to touch her hand, and her tiny fingers closed around it, each one a miniature marvel.

'Hello, Aida,' he said softly.

He turned to Neraya, his mouth open in wonder.

'She's beautiful!'

'Well, what did you expect?'

'I didn't know what to expect.'

He turned back to the baby. His heart was bursting.

Abruptly Aida waved stiff arms and the blankets around her legs humped up and down. Then she stopped, still regarding him, and made a small noise in her throat.

'God, I can't believe it! I'm so lucky.'

He reached out to Neraya, took her in his arms and whispered into her hair, 'Thank you.'

He said it over and over again.

*

He lowered himself carefully into an armchair and closed his eyes. 'Oh, it's so good to be back.'

She stood behind the chair, her hands resting on his shoulders. 'Do you need anything?'

'No, I'm fine.'

She walked round to sit on the sofa opposite him.

'General Norton phoned me. Said he'd never met a braver man or a finer pilot. He said he couldn't award any medals, but he arranged for your promotion to Full Colonel to be permanent.'

'That's nice. More than I expected, actually.'

'He also told me about Karl Stott. Thank God they've locked him away, and for good.'

'The police told me I wouldn't have to go to court. They said he wasn't fit to stand trial. I'm not surprised.'

The mere mention of his name had cast Stott's malign shadow across the room and they were quiet for a moment.

Then she said, 'Leighton phoned me, too.'

'Leighton? What did he want?'

'He told me your contribution was absolutely key to the success of the mission. He said it had been a privilege to work with you, and that I should be very proud.'

'That's a whole lot, coming from Leighton.'

'Well it's very nice to hear, Danny, but I don't actually know what it is you've done. They said they'd leave it to you to tell me about the mission.'

'All right.' He took a deep breath.

He gave her an account of the trip, the challenge of flying the incredible Morningstar, his elation when it all came together, and what happened during the mission. Her eyes brimmed with tears.

'I remember Pieter Tyomkin,' she said. 'He was a role model for every cadet in the Academy. What a tragedy!' She looked at him. 'Danny, it could so easily have been you.'

'Don't tell me.'

She leaned forward impulsively and covered his hand with hers. 'You mustn't take risks like that ever again.'

'I've been thinking about it. I'm going to throw in my job at the Test Establishment.'

Her eyes opened wide. 'Why? You love that job.'

'Yes, I do. But sooner or later I'd have to pull duty on Mars or the Moon – it wouldn't be fair to the rest of the team if I didn't. And I've had enough of cryosleep and microgravity. Look at this.' He clasped his hands around a wasted thigh. 'My body just can't take it any more.'

'What will you do?'

'Well, what I had in mind was the Space Fleet Flight Training Divisional HQ in London. I know they're short-staffed – we always seem to be lending them pilots to help out with off-Earth training. Mostly docking on the Hexagon.'

'The Hexagon' was the popular name for the huge International Spaceport. It referred to the shape: a hollow, hexagonal cylinder rotating about its axis. It was accessed via the Thames Shuttle Terminal.

She tilted her head to look at him. 'After being a Test Pilot? Wouldn't that be a bit tame for someone like you?'

'I don't think so. I did a stint there a few months ago, remember? It was only for a week but I really enjoyed it, trying to remember what my own problems were, seeing where each student was having difficulty, figuring out ways to make the exercises more interesting. It went really well. At the end the Director came along to thank me personally. She said if I ever felt like joining their permanent staff she'd be glad to see to it. I've thought about it ever since. Simulated gravity on all levels – except when you're actually flying – feet back in full gravity at the end of the day, I could live with that. I wouldn't do it unless you and Aida could come with me, though. Could you work for Strategic Planning in London?'

'I think so. It wouldn't make a whole lot of difference, not with secure networks and videocomms. There's a lot of contact with the London HQ at the moment actually, so it might even be useful to have me on the other side of the water. And I'd like to get to know London better. All those single-level airlanes following the old street system – so much more interesting than Armstrong.'

'It would only be for two or three years. If all goes well I should be able to get a transfer to the Flight Training Centre here.'

'Where we learned to fly when we were cadets?'

'That's right.'

She took a deep breath. 'Oh, Danny, what a long way you've come!'

He hadn't thought about it in that way before; he'd simply accepted that sooner or later he'd be transferred to Space Fleet Academy as a Senior Flight Instructor. But now he blinked, taking in what she'd just said, and his mind drifted back...

Back to that dirt-poor farm in West Virginia, watching with horror as his father ripped up the letter from Space Fleet Academy. 'Get used to one thing, m'boy,' his father was saying, 'you ain't taking up no goddam scholarship to space pilot school. No, sir.' And young Daniel Larssen had run across the fields, the wind tearing the tears from his eyes and drying them on his cheeks.

That wasn't going to happen to his daughter. Aida would have his support, whatever she chose to do, and it would take more than Stott and his ilk to stand in her way.

Neraya got up and kissed him on the head. 'Won't be a moment, just have to check my message board.'

'Sure.'

She returned less than a minute later and her expression was grim.

'Danny, I think you should see this. There's been a drive-by shooting in Los Angeles. Happened early this afternoon. Seems the target was Henry Leighton.'

Dan's mouth went dry. 'Oh my God! Can you put WorldNet on?'

She used her communicator and the wall screen flashed up. The item was getting top coverage.

'...was on his way back from an official visit to the Divisional HQ of the Drugs Enforcement Agency in Los Angeles. Emergency services were summoned but he was pronounced dead at the scene.'

The familiar, florid face of Miles Nicholson appeared on the screen, subtitled 'Commissioner of Customs, Miles Nicholson'.

'This heinous crime has robbed our organization and the country of a fine man and a devoted servant of the public. Henry Leighton dedicated his professional life to the eradication of drugs of addiction, the evil substances that blight the lives of so many of our countrymen and fill the fat coffers of crime syndicates. Only recently I had the occasion to commend him for the part he took in destroying

314

an orbiting drug factory. This cowardly murder was, I believe, carried out in retaliation for that action. Let those responsible know that the forces of law will pursue them with the utmost vigour, and that we will not lessen our determination to rid the world of them and their deadly trade.'

Dan drew a deep breath and said, 'Turn it off.'

For a few minutes they sat in silence. Then she turned to look at him.

'Do you think the murder was ordered by Raoul Hernandez?'

'Almost certainly. It was his drug factory. He must be hurting badly.'

'Do you think they'll get him for it?'

'Almost certainly not.'

Her voice became almost inaudible. 'Danny, I'm frightened.'

He looked at her eyes, wide and dark. He'd never known her to say such a thing.

'What are you frightened of?'

'That you'll be the next on their list. If they knew Leighton planned the mission how much more do they know?'

He thought about it carefully. It was no good brushing aside her fears, she was far too smart for that. How much did Karl Stott actually find out and how much did he pass on to the syndicate? He had more than himself to consider now: he had Neraya and Aida to think about.

He shook his head. 'Leighton's been an implacable enemy of their organization for years. They probably didn't know who was involved in the mission but they didn't need to ask. They'd have guessed he was behind it.'

'Well, I hope to God you're right.'

315

He sighed. 'I'm sorry they got to Leighton, I really am. He was a prickly customer and we started off on the wrong foot, but you couldn't fault his commitment. That syndicate really had something to worry about when he was around, but now...'

She glanced sharply at him. 'It's not your problem, Danny. Not any more.'

'I know.'

But even as he answered, Dan Larssen was thinking:

The syndicate's lost this factory, but sooner or later they'll set up another.

Will that be someone else's problem?

Or will it be mine?

Acknowledgements

Saturn Run was the first book in *The Planetary Trilogy*; *Mars Run* is the second.

As always I'm grateful to my wife Paula and our children, Graham, Daniel, and Debby, for their encouragement and feedback. Graham, in particular, gave me invaluable help on aviation matters. My thanks also go to fellow members of the Liverpool-based Rose Lane Writers' Group (now Wordsmiths), particularly Kate Jack, and John and Rachel Sayle, for their helpful comments on a much earlier version of the manuscript.

Printed in Poland
by Amazon Fulfillment
Poland Sp. z o.o., Wrocław